T0065423

THE BODINES

THE BODINES

Richard M Beloin MD

Rev. date: 11/11/2020

To order additional copies of this book, contact:
Xlibris
844-714-8691
www.Xlibris.com
Orders@Xlibris.com
822422

Contents

Dedication

This work of fiction is dedicated to the unsung heroes who protect the lives of their clients, while placing their own lives on the line—the bodyguards.

Preface

This western fiction is a sequel to The Bodine Agency. Although it can be an independent self-standing fiction, to assure this, the prologue covers the essential sequences leading to the current story.

If you wish to know the details of the interpersonal relationship that led to this sequel, I recommend that you take the time and read the original story as it was always intended to be presented. Either way, enjoy.

Prologue

'How We Got Here'

Palmer was living in an orphanage when the local sheriff adopted him at the age of twelve. He adjusted quickly to family life with the Bodines and by his mid-teens, he started working in a gun shop. There he learned the trade but also became proficient in fast draw and point & shoot with a pistol or shotgun. After high school he tried cow punching for a year and finally became a deputy sheriff while working for his dad. Palmer was not satisfied that he had found his destiny and decided to make a change. All thru these times, he continued practicing his shooting skills.

One day, after a cold and snowy winter in Amarillo, he admitted to his parents that he wanted to help people while becoming wealthy. That spring he announced that he was going on a trip. He was heading to New Mexico which had warmer weather and a strong mining community. Alone with his horse, Chester, he embarked on a cross country trip of +-400 miles—trying to avoid the well-traveled roads which would add 100 miles to his trip. He had planned to stop in towns along the way to replenish his vittles and other goods.

Once on the trail, he met some travelers in the middle of nowhere. Not working with a wealth of experience, he was almost waylaid by outlaws, but saved by his horse who did not allow Palmer to place his back on these innocent appearing travelers. After nearly being killed, recognizing the fact that his horse had more sense than he did, he realized that to stay alive he had to start thinking or gain experience the hard way. Throughout the many miles, Palmer met outlaws with nefarious intent who failed to waylay him and instead met their own end. It was an enlightening when he brought in some dead outlaws, was able to sell their horses and firearms, kept whatever money was in their pockets or saddle bags, and kept the bounties offered by their wanted posters.

In a short time, the income from waylaying outlaws was adding up. He then started helping local lawmen in hunting bank robbers and even arresting outlaws in town—again collecting the horses, firearms, cash, and bounty rewards. It was during his travels that he met a gunsmith who had modified a double barrel shotgun by shortening the barrel, adding a pistol grip, converting the double trigger to a single one, and adding self cocking and shell ejection. This firearm was a devastating tool with OO Buckshot.

After several gunfights with impossible odds, Palmer earned the moniker of "The Shotgun Kid." His entry in a new town was always a welcome from the local law who utilized his talents—as he earned more income from bounties and other assets.

As he approached his destination, he met a trail exhausted wagon-train of miners who were moving to New Mexico from Colorado. After thwarting an Indian attack and saving the wagon-train, he rode ahead and gave a local merchant nearly a thousand dollars to resupply the 18-family wagon train—anonymously as the first recipients of his Benefactor Fund.

Arriving in Las Cruces, he took the train to Deming. Deming was a railroad town, population 1000, where the South Pacific met the Atchison-Topeka-Santa Fe railroad and provided spurs to Silver City, Lordsburg, or Lake Valley. In Deming, all businesses were tied to the railroad. Palmer chose to move to Silver City, population 2000, whose economy and livelihood was tied to mining.

Once in town, Palmer decided to start a detective agency specializing in security and protection. He befriended the local sheriff, Branch Belknap, by doing him a favor. He brought a wife beating scoundrel to signing a well-deserved divorce for the victim. Next, he rented an office with an apartment in the back from the local merchant Elmer Craymore. His first paying job involved guarding a payroll for a mine in the Pino Altos area, reachable only by stagecoach. With a modified coach shotgun and steel plates to protect the jeju and himself, he was able to put down the road agents' attack. Returning back to Silver City by stagecoach, he needed to protect some important ore samples and be a bodyguard to the mine owner's niece. Of course, the stage was robbed of the ore samples and Palmer's charge, his future wife, was kidnapped. After rescuing her and a long ride back to town, Palmer fell in love with this beautiful and astute woman. After returning to Silver City, one fine day Myra appeared in his office and announced she would be Palmer's office staff, partner on assignments, and lover.

And so the capers started. Merchants being extorted for cash to guarantee their stores would not be torched, kidnappings of wealthy miners' wives such as the Longley kidnapping, claim jumpers, and business threats from competition. During these early capers, the Duo, found a Navaho Indian buried up to his neck by Apaches. Saving his life, Mistah Lightfoot became a trusted and reliable partner.

Now the Trio was undertaking more serious cases such as guarding a train's express car loaded with fortunes in gold from several miners—especially from Archibald Longley, again. The Trio then started a guarded wagon-train of freight wagons to deliver multiple mines' ore to the smelter in Silver City.

Things were going well for the Trio, when Myra was kidnapped again as an "intact woman" to be placed in the human trafficking network. After rescuing her again, he realized that he came close to losing her. He proposed and they were married. Myra's name was changed to Mia because Palmer could not make love to someone named Myra—which was the name of the old battleax that used to beat him as a kid in the orphanage.

Once married, the Duo realized that living by the gun would not be sustainable in a family structure. So they started looking for a gold/silver mine to purchase. The name of Archibald Longley came up for the third time—for he had a mine for sale within reasonable distance to Silver City. After long and nearly argumentative negotiations, the Bodines ended up paying all of $1 for the mine. This reflected an unpaid fee of $50,000 for the half million in gold bars saved by the Trio weeks ago.

Mistah Lightfoot worked as a guard on the ore wagon-trains, as the Duo delved into underground drift mining. Fortunately, for a very competent and dedicated mine manager, Harvey Elliot informed them on the day to day workings. After getting their feet wet, they started to work on making improvements. With Harvey, they decided to add a second air shaft, and a coal powered compressor to add power drilling and loading of ore in the mine. The "mucker" which loaded minecarts with ore proved to be a life-long reliable addition.

As any business, accessory buildings needed to be added or improved. The Weber construction company was busy building a new bunkhouse, barn, and a cook shack. The old barn was renovated, and lean-tos were added for storing wagons.

Once the "Silver Crash" occurred, where the US currency backing changed to gold, Harvey convinced the Duo it was time to hire a dynamite expert who could drill and blast closer to a gold vein and minimize the excess of valueless rock. A Dutch driller, Liam Johanson, was immigrated with his family. His value was quickly seen when he found a new gold vein to replace the closed tunnel to the silver deposit.

By the time the improvements were made as well as the additional buildings, Mia was getting disappointed in her need to be useful in the mining operations. It was then that the neighbor, Elmer Craymore's Mercantile, offered the Bodines the opportunity to open a "Mining Emporium" in the now empty old agency office. Elmer wanted to slow down and stop selling mining pants, shirts, gloves and all the mining tools used in the trade. Mia saw a challenge and accepted the offer, but instead of continuing to rent, the Duo bought the building outright.

Marc Weber arrived with his team and gutted the downstairs office and the two vacated apartments upstairs. The upstairs was left wide open for future use and the downstairs was converted to a retail store with a large front window displaying the words

"Bodine Mining Emporium." Shelves were added to display pieces of clothing to include denim pants and duck canvas pants/overalls as well as racks for mining tools.

The Emporium was a total success and before long Mia decided to utilize the upstairs as a manufacturing section. She bought several commercial sewing machines and hired local mining wives with sewing experience. Before long they were producing their own line of modified Bodine denim jeans with the "B in a circle" logo. The modifications included knee patches, a loop to hold the mining hammer, wide belt loops, and extra thigh room for bending down.

The manufacturing and retail floors had access to an inside stairwell as well as a manual elevator to bring supplies from the first floor receiving area. In a matter of a few months, with adding more stitchers and machines, Mia's team was supplying the 100 denim pants sold in their store, and started generating a surplus of 70 pants per week.

With a real surplus building up, entered Waldo Steiner, a clothing distributor. Waldo took the entire surplus to Colorado and sold out in a matter of days. Upon his return to town, he tried to convince Mia to build a factory and go commercial. Mia hesitated at jumping into such an endeavor. It was Palmer who suggested they expand the building into the rear parking area instead of building a separate factory. After hiring more seamstresses and machines, the workforce eventually increased production to 350 pants per week. This gave Waldo +-225 pieces a week to distribute to his garment stores in Colorado mining towns.

At the end of the year, an accounting of both businesses revealed that Mia had generated a profit of $20,000 while the two gold veins generated an outlandish profit of $60,000. In addition, Liam Johanson had also just found an area rich in copper—its value was yet to be determined. After some reflection, Mia expressed her sentiment, "In 1896 no one makes that kind of money or should be able to make that kind of money legally. But we did it legally with working long hours and spending money to make improvements." Palmer added, "and we can do it for another year, before we consider changes, heh?" "For sure!"

***

NOW THE STORY CONTINUES

CHAPTER 1

Life Continues

With that end of year meeting being held on a Sunday evening, after a replenishing breakfast, the Duo went back to work Monday morning as usual. Palmer saddled Chester and rode to the mine. Two miles down the road, Chester came to an abrupt stop and reared up. Palmer was caught off guard and slid off the saddle, landing on his butt. At the same time a rifle shot rang out and, with Chester still standing on his rear legs, the saddle horn exploded. Palmer quickly grabbed his 44-40 Win 73 from the scabbard, rump slapped Chester away from the line of fire, and jumped behind the nearest boulder.

Palmer knew there was a shooter somewhere who wanted to kill him. To find out where the shooter was hiding, Palmer grabbed a twig, cut it to the right length, put his hat on it, and stuck it in the ground just enough to show the hat over the boulder. A shot rang out and the hat went flying. Palmer sneaked over his boulder just in time to see the shooter scoot back behind his boulder.

Now Palmer played chicken. He shot a rock at least 10 feet from where the shooter was hiding and quickly levered another round in place. As expected, the shooter looked up over his hiding place, only to catch a 44-caliber bullet in the face.

Palmer eventually loaded the shooter on his mare and lead the cargo back to town. Sheriff Belknap did not recognize the corpse. Checking his pockets and saddlebags, they found almost $500 in greenbacks. Sheriff Belknap said, "I doubt he was trying to waylay you for more money, this looks like an execution. Looks like someone wants you dead." Deputy Sheriff Liam Burke came outside with a bunch of wanted posters and said, "I've seen that face, here it is. "Ike Hughes, professional assassin wanted in Colorado, Wyoming, and New Mexico. Dead or alive. $5,000. Proof of death required by lawman."

To everyone's surprise Mia was standing on the boardwalk and said, "what's this about an assassin and why does your hat have a hole in it?" "Oh, it was just a decoy!" "And since when is your brain a decoy?" "Now dear, how on earth did you know I was here?" "One of the workers happened to look out of the window when you rode by with that thing." "I see, well there is so much more to the story, why don't we meet at Bert's Diner for dinner and I'll explain everything, heh?" "For sure!"

With Mia gone, Sheriff Belknap asked, "what I don't understand is how Chester knew something was off enough to buck you out of the saddle?" "Pretty clear to me. Look at the assassin's mare's rear end. As you can see, she's in heat." "But Chester is a gelding!" "True, but likely he's a 'proud cut' since I've seen him mate with mares in the pasture." As Deputy Burke adds, "and that's why he's now standing at attention."

After making arrangements with the sheriff to dispose of the assets and wire proof of his death, the sheriff adds, "keep in mind, that whoever hired him, still holds a grudge and will send someone else to get you. It's a shame we'll never be able to find out who that man is." "I agree, it's worse than finding a needle in a haystack, since we don't know which haystack to search."

Arriving at Bert's Diner, Palmer had two cups of coffee before Mia showed up. Mia kissed Palmer, sat down, and said, "I'm scared husband, please settle me down!" Palmer went thru the entire event without leaving out many details." Mia pondered a bit and said, "so my husband was saved by a horny horse and we still have someone who wants us dead. At least, I hope Chester gets the mare out of all this." "Heck, as I was trying to load the shooter on his horse, Chester pushed me away and settled the mare 'real good.'" "Yeah, but he's sterile!" "Well the mare didn't know that, and I assure you she didn't care." Mia finally laughed and took Palmer's hand.

Mia finally said, "so what do we do." "We wait, it's going to take some time before the man with a grudge and money finds out his man failed. Then it's going to take more time to find a substitute. Just be very mindful and aware of your surroundings. Always wear your Bulldog on a belt holster—instead of relying that it's in your reticule somewhere, heh?" "Why?" "Because if they can't get me with a sniper, they'll try to kidnap you to get to me." "Oh great, I've already been kidnapped twice and this time, I'll be ready to shoot it out instead." "Ok, so tell mom that whenever someone enters the emporium wearing a side arm, to pull the cord and call you down from upstairs. Until those customers leave, keep your hand on your gun and be ready. Also, never walk home alone." "Ok, but we'll talk about this again tonight, heh?" "For sure."

*

Mia went back to work, and Palmer finally headed to the mine to meet with his mine manager. "Good afternoon Harvey, before we have a business meeting, let me tell you of this morning's event...............and so I mention this only for you to watch out for some strange men walking about talking with our workers. So what is new at the mine?" "Well I have had several ore samples analyzed for copper from the tunnel where we found the oxidized green rocks. The average yield is 1% and a few samples were even a bit higher. So, at 1%, for 2000 pounds of ore, you get 20 pounds of copper. At $3 a pound, that comes to $60 a ton of unprocessed ore. Hell, that is worse than mining for silver which we've abandoned. Do you know how many men, materials, and time is involved in pulling a ton of ore from our underground mine?"

"I'll guess the cost of labor and dynamite is more than the value of the copper." "Correct. The irony, at the same time, we pull out a ton of gold ore that amounts to a pound of gold worth $320. Now there is a way of making money mining for copper but not underground. I am researching this and will get back to you later." "So, there is no reason to build a third air shaft since the two gold veins are well aerated by our two air shafts?" "That is correct."

"Is there anything we can add to streamline our operation?" "Yes, but let me explain, you are making some big money with our two gold veins. Last month, I calculated that you made $7,000 of clear profit as things presently stand. So there is no real reason to change anything." "I look at it differently, making things easier and more efficient for the workers. and or make more money, is my goal—I can always give the money away. Actually, I want you to start designing a retirement plan for workers with a 20-year work history in this mine. I think that +-25% of their 20th year income is a place to start. In addition, add full medical coverage in this retirement package for the worker and his dependent family."

"Well, since you are spending so much money, I have an idea how you can make more money to finance this plan. Build a railroad spur to Longley's #3 mine's rail line, which is only a half mile away. This will allow our men to dump the minecarts full of gold ore directly in the open boxcars and even allow us to dump waste rock into separated cars for sale to the railroad as fill for trestle bases and ballast between cross-ties. As a side benefit, you won't need the freight wagons or their security guards. If you remember, last year the other freight wagon team earned $10,000 in hauling and security fees from other mines. Now this team can also hire out and earn income."

"Harvey, now I know why I pay you the big bucks. You're a financial genius." "As I said a few days ago, what I'm researching now will either bankrupt you or make you a millionaire." "Well, when you're ready, let me know. Truth be known, I'm a bit bored and look forward to a new challenge. For now, I'll work on adding that rail spur."

Riding home, Palmer realized that the mine did not need his day to day assistance, and what he really needed was a new endeavor. Finding himself wool gathering, he then wondered why Mia seemed to have a change of personality that would randomly wax and wane with periods of melancholy. Tonight, he would address this issue with her. For now, he was headed to the railroad office to order a rail spur to his mine.

When the agent realized that the Bodine spur would tap in the existing Longley #3 mine's rail he said, "before I can place this order, you need to have Archibald Longley sign this release giving you permission to install a switch onto his private line." Palmer's eyebrows lifted up in a question—this would either be easy or totally impossible. Being mid-afternoon, Longley would be in his office. Palmer decided to strike while the iron was hot or before he lost his drive to make this happen.

Stepping into Longley's office, the receptionist brought him directly to her boss. "Nice to see you Palmer, it's been a while. I hear you are doing well with your mine and many miners are happy to use your guarded freighting service. So what brings you here today?" "I need a favor from you," as he hands him the railroad release form. Longley looks at the form and says, "well, this looks like I'm going to make some money today." "True, money is always good, but you don't need it, and my owing you a favor, as long as it's legal, is priceless!"

Archibald was silent and obviously pensive. He asked, "as long as it's legal, you will not resist taking on my request even if it is dangerous?" "Again, including the danger factor, I promise my God." "Heck, this is better than money in the bank," as he pens his name to the release and has it notarized by his receptionist/legal secretary.

Returning to the railroad office, the agent sent the order in, with the release, and said to Palmer, "an engineer will be over to scout the land and measure the exact distance to the mine. It would include two rail switches, two side rails at the mine's loading area, and a fee of $16,000 per mile— excluding bridges, trestles and tunnels."

*

Palmer then walked over to the Emporium to pick up Mia and walk home. Mia was noticeably quiet and had red eyes from crying. As soon as they got home, Palmer sat next to Mia and said, "it is time for me to ask what is bothering you. It's obvious that when you have your monthly cycle that you start with crying spells. You have everything you need in life to make you happy, and it tears my heart to see you in the doldrums. So, speak to me, please."

Mia paused, blew her nose, and dried up her tears. Finally she spoke, "you're right, you deserve an explanation. You are wrong, I don't have everything. I am missing a child and my husband." "Whoa, let's take these two issues one at a time, heh?" "Ok, my monthlies are not monthly, they are anywhere between 3-6 weeks, and that's because I am not ovulating." "And what is the medical treatment for not ovulating?" "Doc Sims says it's getting pregnant and going thru pregnancy and delivery." "WHAT, that don't make any sense. So let's attack this problem from the cause. Why are you not ovulating?" "Because I am stressed and fatigued from working so hard. Heck, we both overwork and can't stay awake after supper."

As pragmatic as Palmer was, he added, "this is good, we can solve this fatigue and stress problem. Now what is this about missing 'my husband?'" "Palmer Bodine, we are down to having relations on Sunday night and not always weekly. I'm never going to get pregnant working 10 hours a day and having relations three times a month."

After some quiet reflective time, Palmer broke the silence. "Amazing isn't it, we did it to ourselves with our drive to succeed. Well we have succeeded with our businesses, but we have missed the target—maintaining the time when we were the happiest. When was that Mia?"

Palmer watched Mia and the transformation was obvious that she had an epiphany. She looked at

Palmer and said, "the day I walked into your office and announced that I would be your friend, partner and lover. I recall you kissing me and taking me in your arms as you said you would spend your life making me happy. For months thereafter, we worked together at the detective agency—the point is that we worked together, and it wasn't always safe dealing with violent people and guns, but we were happy."

Mia went silent as Palmer pondered the situation. Minutes passed as they joined hands. Palmer looked at Mia and added a smile as he said, "I agree, those were the best days of our lives. We can regain those life changing days!" "How, time has passed by and that bell has rung?" "If you recall what I told you about certain bells could be rung repeatedly." "Yes but that was about reaching our nirvana, this is different, it's about a time that has passed." "Why can't we bring it back?" "HOW?" "By leaving our businesses in the hands of our capable managers, I have Harvey and you have Alice and Agnes, and we REACTIVATE THE BODINE DETECTIVE AGENCY—SECURITY AND PROTECTION.

***

CHAPTER 2

Reactivating the Agency

A few days later, The Duo had a general meeting at their house, off Main St on Myers Avenue. Invitees were Harvey, Alice, Agnes, Ralph and Ella Bodine, Sheriff Belknap, Mistah and Missi Lightfoot, and Deputy Sheriff Liam Burke. The meeting moved smoothly along and within an hour everyone knew that the Duo was stepping out of the business world for an unknown period of time. There was no hesitation on the part of Harvey, Agnes and Alice. They would take the helm and would only involve the Duo in face of a major event that would threaten the survival of the mine or emporium.

Ralph and Ella would continue working at the emporium, but Ralph agreed to support the Duo if his old lawman skills were needed. The Lightfoots agreed to move from guarding the ore freight wagons to join the detective agency full time. Sheriff Belknap was super enthusiastic to resume a relationship with a private firm willing to help maintain law and order—especially over situations that were not part of the sheriff's duties. The next morning after a replenishing breakfast, the Duo went out looking for an office to rent. They wanted to find something on Main Street for easy access and taking advantage of indoor plumbing with city water and natural gas. After checking out the listings, a recent lawyer's retirement provided such a location next to the Waterman Gun Shop. It included 700 square feet of: a small waiting room, a fairly large main office, a separate receptionist area, and a private mini kitchen and water closet behind the private office. The building was owned by Waterman himself. A monthly rental fee of $70 included water/sewage, a gas heating stove, and gas lamps throughout. The office was fully furnished and even included a typewriter and several filing cabinets.

The Duo signed a one-year lease and then moved in. The first item out of boxes was the old Bodine Agency sign. Mia then went to Elmer's store and stocked up on paper goods, snacks, noon canned goods, and plenty of coffee. The Lightfoots would await assignments while helping their tribe in the craft manufacturing building two blocks away.

With the office ready, the Duo decided to dress the part of a modern agency. Palmer asked Mia to do the shopping as he requested, fine linen or wool light grey pants, white shirt with a Texas shoestring necktie to match his dress pants, and a tan summer vest to go along with his black hat and boots. Mia was left to her choices for dresswear—as he assumed she would return with a combination of a riding skirt and a frilly shirt.

Palmer locked the office, attached a notice to leave a message if the office was locked, and stepped next door into Waterman's Gun Shop. "Mister Waterman, my wife and I are restarting the agency. She is comfortable staying with her Smith & Wesson in 38 backed up with a coach shotgun. I'll stay with my Smith &Wesson in 44-40, but I think it's time to upgrade my shotgun and my rifle. What's new and available?"

"First, my name is Winn, Mister was my dad. We have a new shotgun and a new rifle. Let's start with the shotgun. This is the new full- size Winchester Model 1897 pump shotgun." "Nice, but I use my current double barrel as a pistol." "I know, that's why I have modified it." As he pulls a drastic version from under the counter, he says, "I have cut the barrel down to the sliding fore-end and did the same to the lower tube that holds three extra shells. I have also removed the stock and replaced it with a pistol grip. In actuality, it's the same size as your present double barrel. The difference is that it shoots four rounds like a handheld gatling gun. Let's go outback so I can demonstrate."

Winn loads three shells in the magazine tube and one in the chamber. Without warning he lets go--bang, bang, bang, bang. Palmer jumps up with a hip-slapper as a sign of approval. "How did you shoot so fast?" "It's called 'slam fire.' Every time you cycle the fore-end grip rearward the spent shell is ejected, but when you slide the fore-end forward, if you keep the trigger depressed, it will fire automatically. Along with an action job, this is a firearm that will cause havoc and devastation when needed."

"I'll take it along with the unique speed holster." "You may change your mind when you find out what the price is!" "No sir, there is no price I won't pay to guarantee our safety in a gun fight. Now, what is new in rifles." "Smokeless powder and jacketed bullets at high velocities." "Really tell me more."

This is a Winchester 1894 that shoots a 160-grain copper jacketed bullet at 2000 fps. Unlike the black powder guns that lob a heavy lead bullet at 1300 fps to its target, this projectile almost flies flat. For example, it the gun is sighted 2-inch high at 100 yards it will be 'on' at 150 yards, 5 inches low at 200 yards and 15 inches low at 250 yards. But don't forget that the velocity at 250 yards is still +-1500 fps—way enough to put down a deer or man!" "Wow, how is that possible?" "New stronger metal that can handle the high pressure of 30-35 grains of smokeless powder."

"Impressive, what's the downside?" "The magazine holds 5 extra longer rounds, not the 15 shorter rounds of present rifles." "My downside is the fact that beyond 100 yards, my vision is poor. I know I wouldn't be able to hit a 5-gallon pail at 250 yards with open steel sights." "I agree with you, but because this rifle ejects from the top, I have made a side mount to hold a new shortened Malcolm scope in 6 power. The side mount and scope are detachable, with wingnuts, as one piece and stored in a padded wooden box left in your saddlebags. This rifle is slim and sleek and made to fit in your standard scabbard. When a long-range shot is needed, you'll have the time to attach the scope."

"Great, how much for both of these guns with a crate of ammo for both guns?" "Well, seeing you're my tenant, $140 will take both, with one holster, one detachable scope, and 100 rounds of ammo for each gun." Palmer left the store and returned to the office. Mia arrived shortly and was explained the ins and outs of both new guns. Then Palmer tried on the new wardrobe. Once fully dressed, Mia said, "not bad, kinda brings out the winsome in you, husband!"

Mia was next to redress, she stripped nude and then snuck into tight denim pants. The shirt was no frilly blouse but a tight fit showing plenty of cleavage. Palmer was shell shocked and said, "by gosh and by golly, where did you get those britches?" "Alice came up with this new design. We removed the wide belt loops, the hammer loop, the extra knee patches, the wider thighs; and added more room in the rear end while removing the crotch potato sac to form a streamline ladies crotch area. Along with more hip room and tight leg pants, we have the new look called slimline ladies 'jeans.' Do you like em?"

"As your husband, I like em a lot. But to the public, you are showing way too much 'lower cleavage,' and what are those bumps on your hips?" "Those lumps are 'love handles,'" and as far as low cleavage, well that is your fault as well." It was then, that for the first time in a year, the Duo stripped and had loving spontaneous relations on the hard office floor—of course with the office door locked. After getting dressed, Palmer asked, "what will the gossip mongers and guards of societal niceties say about a gun toting woman with new style low cleavage britches, a round butt and prominent love handles. "I don't care, this is business, heh?"

*

Half an hour afterwards, their first customer arrived, Sheriff Belknap and a cattleman. The sheriff started, "this is Arnold Calhoun who has a ranch west of town on the road to Gila. He just lost 6 breeding bulls of that new crossbreeding line. He found the six bulls on his neighbor's land, despite both ranches having their land fenced in." Mia was dumbfounded and added, "why did he do that, it's obvious he's guilty of rustling." Arnold spoke up, "because he is charging me $500 a year for water rights—for the use of a river that has its origin far from here but goes thru my neighbor before it enters my land. The bulls are considered his pay since I refused to pay for water rights."

Palmer interjected, "wait a minute, this just doesn't make any sense, there has to be more to the story." Arnold hesitated but finally said, "all of Dean Delaney's neighbors are breeding their longhorns with the new stock of Herefords, Shorthorns, or Black Angus. Dean wants to stay with the traditional Longhorns, but the buyers won't buy his beeves. He is too proud to admit defeat and he's fought back the only way he knows how."

Sheriff Belknap then added, "now the long and short of things is that if I go see Dean and find Bar C brands on those bulls, I'll have to arrest one of my friends, and Dean will end up doing prison time. I can't do it Palmer, so please find us a solution." "Darn it sheriff, I don't have the wisdom of King Solomon, I just have common sense. I don't know if that is enough, but my team and I will ride over there tomorrow to see if we can find a solution benefitting everyone."

That evening after supper, Mia asked what they should be charging for their services. Palmer said, "we are wealthy and don't need the money. But this is a business, and we must charge otherwise the customer will feel there is no value to any company that doesn't charge for their services. So, let's bring back our old fee system--$50 a day plus expenses and $100 a day if there is gunplay involved." "Ok, now how do we pay Mistah and Missi?" "We keep them on their present daily salary of $7 a day as a couple, but we give them a 20% share of bounty rewards and sold assets."

The next day, the team took off for ranches to the west of town. After riding by five ranches with the new breed of bulls in the pastures, Palmer had an idea. He explained what he wanted and sent the Lightfoots off on a mission. The Duo continued to Delaney's ranch. Seeing the Calhoun bulls in the pasture, Palmer asked the ranch foreman what was going on, and he answered, "we ride for the brand and we follow Mister Delaney's orders. You need to talk to the boss who's in his office."

Stepping on the porch, the lady of the house answered the Duo's knock. Seeing the Duo, she smiled and said, "I know who you are and why you're here, please follow me." Dean Delaney was standing at the window looking out at the animals in the pasture. After introductions, Delany spontaneously said, "those new line of bulls are amazingly prolific. They are breeding cows like there is no tomorrow while the Longhorn bulls are idly standing by and showing no interest in servicing cattle in heat."

After some hesitation, Palmer spoke up. "Sir, it is against the law to commandeer a natural river as your property. You cannot charge your neighbors for water rights. It is also against the law to steal your neighbor's bulls as payment for water rights. Now Sir, I know you are not stupid, so how can we solve this situation?" Delaney sat down and simply stared at the top of his desk, as if drained of all motivational energy.

Palmer finally asked, "how much did you want for water rights?" "$500." Palmer stands, pulls out a wad of money and peels off five $100 bills. As he slides the money over, he suddenly pulls it back and says, "I will telegraph Emmett Powell in San Antonio and order you six bulls—two Herefords, two Shorthorns, and two Black Angus, and pay to have them delivered right here at your ranch."

Delaney was surprised and said, "you would do that for me with your money, heck you don't even know me." "Correct, but you're a friend of Sheriff Belknap and that's good enough for me." At the same time, some unusual mooing, bellowing and snorting was heard in the front yard. Everyone stepped to the window. There sat the Lightfoots with five neighboring ranchers each trailing a new breed bull. Delaney said, "what in blazes is going on?" Palmer looked at Mia and said, "your neighbors agreed with my helpers to let you borrow one of their new breed bulls till your own arrive from San Antonio. That way every ranch will be starting to convert their herds together—including you, Sir. Just get those Longhorn bulls out of the pasture asap, heh?"

*

The next morning, the sheriff met the Duo and the Lightfoots at Grady's diner, located equidistant between their office and the sheriff's office. "Well guys, looks like we could make this diner our secondary office, as he slaps a pile of paper currency on the table. "What is this for?" "$500 of your money back, and $500 for your fee." Mia took $100 out handed it to Missi as their 20% share. The remainder disappeared in her tight britches' back pocket.

After ordering coffee, Sheriff Belknap started explaining the origin of current crimes in town. "Since you started the original agency a couple years ago, things are different. We now have a large collection of 'no-goods' that live in tents outside of town and are likely the cause of a new wave of muggings and robberies. So, let's go back and I'll explain how this all came about. Just remember that there has always been two groups of people— those who work to earn money and those who take it from them. Well in this case, it's those who become rich from finding gold and those who failed, and now take it from the successful ones."

"For years, there has been an influx of men trying to find gold and make themselves rich. Men arrive with a stake and buy a claim, tent, camping equipment, food and gold-digging tools. After working their claim, and not finding gold, their funds dry up. So, they sell their mining tools and move their tent and necessities to the tent city."

Mia adds, "I follow you so far, but what's the point." "The point is that these men don't work, so how do they survive?" "I get it, by taking money from the working man." "Correct, these men seem to spend their days drinking beer in saloons, eating in diners, visiting prostitutes, and gambling. Consequently we now have a rash of home robberies where the robbers only look for hidden money. But worse we now have robberies by footpads that are called muggings. People walking the boardwalks alone at night simply don't get home with their wallets. Last night we had our first murder from what appears to be a mugging gone bad."

"We see the problem, so what have you done to stop the process. We try to find the culprits, but there are no witnesses and the victims never see their attackers face. The home robberies are done when there is no one home. We can have several robberies each night and all we can do is perform a wild goose chase. So, starting tonight, Liam and I are starting to patrol Main Street and we'll provide an escort to anyone who wants it."

Palmer added, "that may cause a lull in the footpad robberies, but not in the home robberies. We need to identify the potentially determined thief and stop him in the act. The big question is when does a potential thief decide it's time to replenish their dwindling funds?" "Heck, that's simple. When one cannot pay his bar bill, he is told that he cannot return without paying his old bar bill first."

"That's it, we need some spies to identify these miscreants and give them a means of notifying us as the footpad leaves the saloon. Mia was doubtful and said, "sounds good, but where are you going to find such individuals?" "Fear not my dear, I have a plan!"

After breakfast, Palmer said he was going to the mine to talk to his security guards on the freight wagons as well as the underground miners. He said, "I'm certain that I can find some single men that frequent the saloons in the evenings." Mia added, "please don't go alone. Bring Mistah along since, in the outlaw world, we still have a price on our heads. I need to finish writing contracts for new customers and Missi will now have time to see Ellsworth Myers at the bank and set up an account." "But dear, Missi is a Navaho Indian?" "I know, but don't you notice the facial difference between her and Mistah? She is a half breed and has a legal birth certificate with her Caucasian mother's name—which qualifies her, by law, to have her own bank account." "Yep, that's a true fact, heh?"

On their way to the mine, Mistah asked how he expected to be paid if they accepted this caper. "Most thieves have a history. At some point they robbed someone, got a warrant poster, or spent some time in prison. This all means, that their warrants will still stand. All we need is their correct full name, and there are ways to get that information." "Without a doubt, and I'll be first to volunteer."

Arriving safely at the mine, Palmer went to see Harvey. "How is that new venture research coming along?" "Very well, but I'm not ready yet to make a presentation. What brings you here, I thought you were on an 'other working sabbatical.'" "I am, I need four single men who frequent saloons regularly in the evenings." "Well, you're in luck, since today is the monthly noon get together with all our workers."

The dinner was beef stew with fresh bread. The meeting covered the final information on the new retirement package with medical benefits. Palmer had no idea Harvey would stick this issue in today's agenda, and he was convinced it was intentional. After all the applause and general appreciation, Harvey asked all single men to stay after the meeting. Ten men stayed in their seats. Palmer asked for drinking men that frequented the towns saloons—four more left. With six left, Palmer explained what he was looking for.

"I need four spies to sit about, drink beer and watch for men who run short of money gambling, or can't pay their bar bills, and suddenly decide to leave the premises. We need you to step outside as if you need some fresh air. We will then take over." "Is there a pay for this work?" "You make

$20 a night and don't have to get to work till the noon dinner the next day—with a full day's pay. For Friday and Saturday evenings, we pay $25 a night since closing is much later." Two men asked to be excused since they were not secure in doing this kind of work. The other four were happy to take the job and were told it could last up to two weeks or less.

On their way back to town, Mistah suddenly stopped his horse. "Boss, look at the tracks going off the trail towards those trees. Could it be someone's camp or an ambush?" "Good pickup, let's go see." They both got off their horse, tethered them to a mesquite tree, placed their moccasins on, and Palmer grabbed his Win 1894 with the saddlebag holding the scope and extra ammo. Mistah was an expert in meandering about without exposing himself. Palmer followed without any hesitation.

After walking what Palmer thought was an estimated 150 yards, Mistah suddenly collapsed to the ground—as did Palmer. "Boss, there is a man behind that huge oak, about 250 yards from here. He's scoping the main road with binoculars." "Well, I may be wrong, but I suspect he followed us from town and knew we were going to the mine. Now he's waiting for us." "But how do we know he means us harm?" "Remember that huge pine by the road. Well, walk back, wear my white hat, and ride your horse to that tree. After hiding behind it, stick my hat out and see if he shoots at it. If he does, I will take him out."

While Mistah was making his way back, Palmer installed the scope, found a good solid rest, spotted the man with the leather hooded scope and waited. Suddenly, the binoculars came off his face as he grabbed his scoped Win 76 and fired. Palmer knew the die was cast. He took aim at the man's face, knowing his shot would be 15 inches low, and squeezed the trigger. Keeping his eye in the scope, the shooter was pushed back and toppled backwards. Palmer slowly made his way to the downed shooter. The man had a bullet hole in mid chest and pieces of his spine in the exit hole. Palmer was impressed what this new rifle was capable of doing using copper jacketed bullets at high velocities.

Arriving in town, Sheriff Belknap checked out the shooter. Liam was looking at his assortment of wanted posters. The shooter had a thousand dollars in his saddlebags, a nice rifle, and a good horse. Sheriff Belknap then added, "well, I wonder what your nemesis will throw at you next, for this was likely a high-end assassin." "If you start thinking like any vengeful person, you won't send another assassin using a rifle. He will send a pair of experienced gunfighters—maybe even three for a face to face confrontation. Guess I'd better inform Mia and prepare her for the inevitable."

*

For the next week, the team concentrated on ridding the town of footpads. Each saloon had an assigned mine worker, as the Duo or Lightfoots were back up. It was Missi who had the most memorable save. She got the signal from her partner and followed the possible suspect. He made his way behind the buildings, where the privies were located, and walked up a dark alley and waited. Missi was hidden behind the building. Suddenly, the man drew his pistol and jumped behind a man on the boardwalk. Silently, she crept behind the footpad and dropped her war club on the thief's head. There was a thud that enticed the victim to turn around. As Missi was putting manacles on the thief's wrists and ankles, she picked up the victim's wallet and handed it to him. "But you're an Indian, aren't you going to keep the money and rob me like that piece of crap tried?" "No Sir, I work for the Bodine Security Agency." "But there is a lot of money in that wallet." "I don't care how much there is, I am well paid, and this is my job as this is your money." "No ma'am, it's now your tip—and I'll have you know there is a thousand dollars in there."

Missi was at a loss, "but Sir, I cannot accept this, my boss won't allow it!" "What won't I allow Missi?" As Palmer walked by, escorting another thief to jail. "This gentleman wants to give me a tip for capturing his attacker." "Why of course you can accept it." "But you don't understand, there is $1000 in this wallet." "Wow, that's enough to buy you a house." "Are you sure you want to do this, Sir?" "I assure you, I can afford it, and am proud to do it." "Great, and what is your name Sir?" "Just call me Henry for now, Ok!" *As Henry thought, saved for the second time.*

The rounding up of foot pads continued for ten days. Judge Hawkins and Prosecutor Craighead were busy holding court every day. When the victims refused to file charges for fear of retaliation, the footpads were given a train ticket out to Deming and told not to return or face a year in prison. The thieves who were prosecuted, with a victim's complaint, all got 9 months in the territorial prison in Santa Fe. The remaining tent residents knew they were being watched, so they finally started menial jobs. At least, it was enough to feed and support themselves.

Three days later, the team met with the sheriff at Grady's Diner. Boy, what a clean-up your team made. Thirty-two thieves out of circulation. Ironically, the 18 in prison are the ones that had bounties for misdemeanor robbery. The $200 bounties were automatically paid and here are telegram vouchers totaling $3,600. The city council and merchants' association decided to get together and they matched the telegram vouchers. And that's a total of $7,200 for a job well done." "Ok, here is how we break down this amount. My mine workers get at least $200 each for a total of $850. You get the usual 5% or +- $350 for you and your deputy, The Lightfoots get their 20% which is +-$1,400." Mistah objected and added, "we've already collected $1,000 so we'll only accept another $400." Mia also objected, "oh no you don't. A tip is not part of the distribution of bounties or fees—it's a private benefit."

Palmer then says, "and we get the balance, $4,600." In closing the business meeting, Mia asks, "and what was the gentleman's name who gave you this nice tip?" "He said his name was

Henry, is all!" "Hu'um Henry huh, I wonder if it could be—but I doubt it."

*

Finishing their hardy breakfast, the Duo went back to the office as the Lightfoots went to look for a house in town that would be a convenient access to the Bodines in town. Arriving at the office, a lady was sitting on a porch chair. Mia addressed her and said, "may we help you?" After some hesitation, the lady said, "yes, I need your help!"

Sitting in the office, the lady said, "my name is Corinna Brewster. My husband of ten years is Malcolm of 'Brewster Real-Estate.' The problem is that my husband stopped having relations with me six weeks ago and I want to know why."

Mia added, "in order to know what we are looking for, we need to know what your sex lives were like before the recent change." "I see, but I find it very difficult to describe my personal activities with my husband." Palmer spoke for the first time, "Ma'am, my wife and I have been married for almost two years and we have been very liberal, so I doubt you'll reveal anything we haven't already experienced."

"Very well, I'll try to be clear. For nine years we had a highly active sex life. Malcolm was an aggressive lover and always made me reach my peak. He was so prolific that he could copulate three times in an evening and spill seed every time. Eight weeks ago his needs clearly changed. First, he wanted to have oral sex. Still being satisfied, I didn't object. Then after a week, he surprised me and performed anal copulation without asking me. After a week of sodomizing me against my will, he started getting home late and never approached me again, and that's why I'm here. What happened and where do I go from here?"

That same day, the Duo informed the Lightfoots of Missus Brewster's situation. Their mission was to spot Malcolm at work, and then follow him as he left the office until they were satisfied where he went, before he returned home. Walking into the real-estate office, two men were seen talking, so they assumed one was Malcolm Brewster. Waiting for closing hours, the Lightfoots were well hidden, and saw the same two men exit. They followed them at a distance when suddenly both men slipped into an alley and disappeared in the woods behind the privies.

Mistah suspected what was going to happen, but he knew his innocent wife would be shocked, to say the least. Without time to warn her, they followed the two men deeper in the forest. When they stopped, the men started kissing and dropped their trousers. Missi was silently mortified, but when the men copulated, she collapsed to the ground on her knees and silently vomited. To make it worse, when the men exchanged their position, poor Missi again silently retched.

Reporting to the Duo, it was clear that Missi was still in some state of turmoil. Mistah explained what they found, and it was Mia who decided to address Missi's concerns. "I know this kind of behavior is not practiced in the Navajo Nation. This is a rare white man's abnormal behavior that no one accepts in 1897. It is immoral and likely an illegal form of fornication. Now put this all behind you and resume your marital life with your husband. Will you?" "Ok."

That evening, the Duo themselves were pensive. Finally, Mia said, "how do we inform Corinna of our findings?" "We are duty bound to report the facts as witnessed by our staff." "Well, let's not be too graphic, shall we?" "You're right, and that's why the report has to come from you, heh?" "Chicken!"

That night Mia tossed all night and by morning was totally disgusted at having to face Corinna. Without warning, Mia rushed to the water closet and lost part of last night's supper. Palmer, suspecting that he was placing too much emotional strain on his wife, he said, "I'll be giving Corinna the report. It may be a watered-down version, but it will be clearly explanatory."

Waiting for Malcolm to appear at work, the Duo went to see Corinna. After sharing a cup of coffee, Palmer started, "we already know what the answer is. It appears your husband suffers from a disease called paraphilia." "I didn't know he was sick, what actually is this illness?" "Your husband is a latent homosexual and is copulating with his male secretary." Corinna drop her cup of coffee and turned white as a sheet. It was Mia who, slowly and softly, explained what Malcolm was seen performing. After a silent pause that was probably only a minute, but seemed an eternity, Corinna finally spoke. "I'm a healthy 28-year old and this cannot be the end of my life. I want a sexual partner and I want children. I want a divorce and some monetary compensation. Can you help me?" "Yes, let's all go see a lawyer and we'll get it done today."

The lawyer prepared the standard divorce papers and added a financial compensation form. It basically stated that for a final one-time sum of $15,000, Corina would depart with her personal belongings and leave the house and its furniture to Malcolm. The alternative would be to leave the house to Corinna and add a monthly allowance of $100 till Corinna either remarried, cohabitated, or died.

With papers in hand, the Duo went straight to the real-estate office after dropping Corinna at their own office to await Malcolm's decision. Escorted by the Lightfoots, the Duo entered the real-estate office only to find that male secretary sitting on Malcolm's desk. Palmer grabbed the secretary, punched him in the mouth to get his attention, and walked him to the outside door, as he told him, "don't come back in the office till we leave." As he punched him again in the face, the man stepped backwards, fell off the boardwalk, and landed on his back in a pile of horse manure. The Lightfoots were there to prevent him from reentering the office.

Palmer started, "Two of my agents saw you fornicating with your male secretary last night. To cut to the chase, your wife wants a divorce and a quick settlement. She is charging you with paraphilia and other associated charges for ruining her marriage. Now you have two choices, sign the papers or get ready for a messy open trial where you're going to lose anyways. I suspect a trial will ruin your business, bankrupt you, and push you out of town. Malcolm looked at the papers and screamed out "this is highway robbery." "Yes, it is, but that's the price you pay when you put your pecker in your bank book or other unconventional places."

Malcolm kept reading and thinking. Eventually, he took out his bank book and wrote a bank draft for $15,000, signed the non-contesting divorce paper and the financial agreement. The Duo signed as witnesses to Malcolm's signature. "Tell her to get out of my house no later than 6PM today, or I'll have the sheriff serve her eviction papers." "Tell you what, if you get the sheriff involved or this bank draft is short of funds, you'll lose your front teeth and I'll have my Indian agent circumcise you with a dull knife. And that is not a threat, it's a promise."

The Bodines picked up Corinna, proceeded to the courthouse to file the papers, went to the bank to deposit the bank draft, went to help her pack her belongings and then helped her to find a ladies boarding house. Before leaving, Corinna asked how much she owed us. I answered, "on our first case a grateful rancher overpaid our fee. On the second case, a grateful city council and merchants overpaid our fee. So from now on, unlike two years ago, we don't have a fee schedule. Pay us what you think our service is worth but based on what you can afford." "In comparison, my ex-husband charged 5% for real-estate fees, but this is more important. So, I'm writing out this draft equal to a 10% finder's fee—for professional services, as I was never humiliated when talking and dealing with you two. Thank you for giving me a second life."

While walking home Mia said, "well, we've been at it about two weeks—one day with the rustler ($500), ten days with cleaning out the footpads ($4,600), and two days on this caper ($1,500). And, we put $6,600 in the bank or that's $500 a day. Oops, I forgot the $300 we owe the Lightfoots who suffered the most trauma on this case, for sure!" Palmer added, "and we did it without firing a single shot. Let's hope the trend continues."

Hand in hand, the Duo walked home to Myers Avenue, still mindful of watching their backs, rooftops, and alleys for hired gunfighters.

***

CHAPTER 3

Shades of the Past

The next day, the Duo was having a replenishing breakfast at Grady's. Mia wasn't her usual hungry self, but Palmer was busy shoveling it in when Deputy Liam Burke showed up in a huff. "Sheriff Belknap needs you in a hurry at the courthouse. It appears that someone has kidnapped Judge Hawkins' wife."

Stepping in the judge's chamber, the sheriff and the judge were almost yelling at each other. It was the sheriff who broke off and addressed the Bodines. "It looks like someone kidnapped Rosemary this morning after the judge left for work. A saddle bum just dropped off this note: *Find a way to release my boss Carmine Gray or you'll never see your wife again*. "Who is this Carmine?" "Last night, a card four-flusher that had been losing at cards, got mad at the winning flimflam and simply pulled a gun and shot the flimflam dead. The bartender held him at gun point till I got there, and this morning Prosecutor Craighead charged him with murder. There are many witnesses, and the flimflam did not have a gun. Now the judge wants to cancel the charges, release the man, and he will then resign the bench for malfeasance."

"How can we help, sheriff?" "We have no idea where the kidnappers took Rosemary, who they are, and we need a solution for our judge." Palmer looked at Judge Hawkins who had been silent. "Mister Bodine, I am not like you. You rescued your wife twice from kidnappers, but I don't have your skills. I have the right to release this man on a technicality, but I will lose my position. This is all I can do to free my loving wife of 50 years. I want those few years together before we leave this earth."

"No argument from us, but let me offer you my skills. You do realize once you release this outlaw, you'll never see your wife again and it will all have been for 'naught.'" The judge looked at Palmer and asked, "do you have a better plan?" Mia looked at the judge and said, "Judge Hawkins, my husband always has a plan, so get ready to be shocked."

Palmer smiled and said, "my plan is to follow your plan. I want you to release this Carmine, and Sheriff Belknap will have a very public 'dress down' fit, up and down the street. Being the sheriff's order, your releasing Carmine will now not be malfeasance. My team, especially my Indian team, will follow Carmine since the first place he'll go is to his gang's hideout. And if God permits us, we'll bring your wife back alive." Mia added, "why sheriff, that's a real sound plan you came up with, heh?"

That morning, the sheriff and judge appeared at the jail while shouting at each other. Play acting, the sheriff said, "I don't want to release this dude, he's a murderer." "You have to since you abused his rights by selling his horse, guns and personal items. I've told you before, you can't do that without my permission. So, let this be a lesson, and release him."

Once out of his cell, Carmine said, "I need my horse and guns!" "You 'idjit,' didn't you hear the judge tell you, I sold them. Get out of here and walk to wherever you need to go. I'm sure we'll be seeing you again, soon."

Carmine took off and headed for the woods north of town. The Lightfoots were on his heals but well hidden. After an hour of meandering thru trees, Carmine started walking in a well-traveled trail with wagon wheel marks. Mistah stopped and told Missi, "follow the trail south and get the Bodines. I know where this dude is heading—he's going to an old prospector's cabin owned by Rufus Whitlow. I will capture Carmine and tie him up till you come back with all of you on your horses." Missi took off running at full speed as Mistah sneaked up to Carmine. He got the war club on the head without ever knowing what hit him.

In a short time, the Duo arrived with Missi, Sheriff Belknap, Liam Burke, Mistah's horse and Judge Hawkins. Palmer looked at the judge and said, "Judge, this is not a courtroom scene and there may be some shooting as well as a possible bad outcome. Are sure you uh......you want to be here?" "Without a doubt, I can handle my shotgun and I insist on helping if possible. This is something I have to do." Without further resistance after Mia's nod, the team made their way to the cabin and hid away till dark. Around 3AM, the team was within 25 yards of the cabin.

Whispering, Palmer said, "this is 'shades of the past.' We've been here before. Like last time, there can be no shooting till Rufus and Rosemary have been rescued. Mia, show your face in the window, flash your badge and whisper the word 'pee' to Rosemary—if she's awake."

With luck Rosemary gave Mia the nod. Everyone heard her waken an outlaw with the request to go to the privy. A gruff voice said, "wait till morning." "I can't, I got to go poop and if you don't take me to the privy I'm going to 'she...et' all over your floor."

Rustling about meant they were on their way. As soon as Rosemary entered the privy, Mistah dropped his war club and the sleepy outlaw went to the ground with a loud thud. Rosemary opened the door only to find her husband waiting for her. The reunion was taken to the team's spot. Palmer then had Mistah load a slug in his coach shotgun and let fly 5 feet high thru the front door. The splinters went flying and the inhabitants were harshly awakened. Palmer then yells, "hey you pinheads, we have your hostage and your leader. We'll trade him for old Rufus and I'll give you my word that we'll then leave. The outlaw then yelled, "do it boys cause we're all going to hang."

Shortly afterwards, the front door opened with Rufus being led out with a gun to his head. Halfway, the outlaw was released as Rufus was simultaneously freed. Sheriff Belknap finally spoke, "that was some nice negotiations, and we saved both hostages, the only downside is that we have to let these pinheads go." "Now sheriff, I said we'd leave, but I didn't say we'd leave alone, heh?" Palmer looked at Rufus and asked, "do you want us to use dynamite down the stove pipe or just plug it up and smoke them out?" "As much as I'd like to see them get their due, I'd rather clean up the smoke than lose my home." "Fine with me, Ok boys, let's help Missi up on the roof to stuff this blanket down the stove pipe."

In a short time, people were coughing and trying to close up the leaking stove. One yelled out, "we've got to get out before we lose our eyes and can no longer fight our way out. Open the door and let's go." Four men crawled out and stopped once off the porch. "Stop right there. You haven't killed anyone yet, so if you don't go for your guns, you may get a prison sentence instead of hanging. If you choose this route, put your hands up." All four men seemed to be frozen in time when three of them put their hands up, saying they had nothing to do with the kidnapping. The leader, the kidnapper, was steadfast with his hand on his pistol grip. "I'm a wanted man and I'm not going to hang." The sheriff spoke up, "so, it's going to be suicide by lawman?" Palmer looked at Mistah who nodded a no, but pointed at the cabin's roof where Missi was standing on the edge. Palmer nodded a yes as Mistah lifted his war club toward the sky. With enough moonlight, Missi let her war club fly. Mia recalls three events, the first when the outlaw's hat went flying, when the thud of the club met the soft head, and when the outlaw crumped to the ground.

After the outlaws were secured to their horses, Judge Hawkins said to Rufus, "come to town with us and I'll treat you to a steak and eggs breakfast; and you can then bring back a cleaning service to clean up the smoke damage at my expense." "Wow, that's a deal, thank you judge."

After the kidnappers along with Carmine were in jail, Judge Hawkins asked, "may I have your bill for services?" "You owe us nothing, we'll collect whatever bounties are available plus we'll sell their horses and guns as full payment." "That is generous of you, and Rosemary and I will never forget what you all did for us. Thank you."

*

Walking back to the office, a woman was seen sitting on the porch. Mia was first to recognize her, "Missus Longley, what brings you to our office.

"My husband wishes to see you today if you are available." "Certainly, lead the way." "And please call me Agnes!"

"Thank you for coming, I need your services." "Oh, oh, is this the payback for allowing us to tap into your rail line?" "No, I happen to know that was a $60,000 savings for you, and this is not that guaranteed pay back. This is a personal matter. Agnes's sister, Marie Ashworth, has a son who is a drunk—yes, our nephew. He's 28 years old and has not been sober a day in the past 10 years. He is now actually dying a bit daily from liver damage and Doc Ross doesn't expect him to make the month. There is apparently only one sure cure. He has to stop drinking today and has to be treated for the DT's if he's going to survive." Mia interrupted, "what's the DT's?" "Delirium Tremens, the withdrawal malady from the body's acute withdrawal from alcohol." Palmer added, "how can we help?"

"The family has all signed an 'intervention order' approved by Judge Hawkins—possible because this young man is committing suicide. I want you to pick him up, lock him up and treat him according to Doc Ross's medicine schedule to manage the DT's. There is a possibility that he may not survive the DT's, but you are free of that liability as it's written in the intervention order. The major work is that he must 'never' be left alone and may need restraints to prevent self-mutilation or suicide. Before you pick him up, you need to see Doc Ross, get his advice and his medicine. If you are willing to do this favor for us, we will pay you $5,000 up front." Mia quickly said, "of course, we'll do it, but no money up front. We can talk about that later. For now, we need to talk to Sheriff Belknap to use a cell in the jail, then go see Doc Ross, and we'll have your nephew in jail today. See you later."

Sheriff Belknap was more than willing to use the jail and would also help watching him, but Palmer got the subtle message that there was a clear payback in the works. Sitting in Doc Ross's waiting room, the Duo individually thought how it would be nice to be here for a pregnancy test, but both were taken out of their reverie as Doc Ross greeted them. "Please come in, and how may I help you?" "We are going to serve the intervention order on Archibald Longley's nephew." "Ah yes, Brock Ashworth, a sad situation and you are here to learn how to treat the DT's." "Yes, and please assume we know nothing on the subject." "Very well, have a seat."

"Alcoholism is an addictive disease, where eventually every organ in the human body needs it to function on a daily basis. Ironically, these same organs are destroyed by alcohol, and the worse organ damage is to the liver which is usually the cause of death. Alcohol withdrawal is the only way to save the person's life, and this is where we are with Brock."

"The acute withdrawal of alcohol causes a violent response in the human body. Every organ goes thru cataclysmic changes. The heart has skips or abruptly stops, the kidneys fail, the lungs malfunction, the GI track rebels with vomiting and violent diarrhea, but worst of all, the brain goes 'berserk.' Thru out the stages of withdrawal, the patient will scream out that he will go crazy if he doesn't have a drink. The stages are: shakiness, anxiety, panic, hallucinations of insects crawling over his body, and ghosts trying to kill him. This last hallucinatory stage is your sign that treatment needs to be provided or convulsions will start, and sudden death is likely to occur. The treatment is a specific sedative called paraldehyde." Doc Ross passes the open bottle for the Duo to smell.

Mia says, "that is awful. It smells like vinegar and a dying animal, how can anyone drink this?"

"Because it fools the person to think this is a concentrated alcohol substitute. The dose is a teaspoon measured by this graduated jigger. The first dose may need to be repeated in one hour and thereafter it usually lasts +-4 hours, but keep in mind that every patient has individual needs. Just treat him before convulsions start. Otherwise, make sure he has plenty of fluids to drink, because the excessive sweating and diarrhea will lead to dehydration. Fortunately, paraldehyde will likely stop vomiting so the patient can hold down liquids. Don't feed him food till he asks for it."

Palmer asks, "I've heard that some men cannot stand the stress and turn to commit suicide!" "Yes, that is true. So only have a cot and a pot for waste in the cell. If he starts hurting himself, wrap him up in a sheet as a 'straight jacket,' but if you do so, keep him on his belly or standing up to avoid choking on his vomit. This is not an easy job, and someone has to be watching him 24 hours a day for +-7 days. As a last precaution for your benefit, give him a good bath before you throw him in his cell—and yes, I do recommend a jail cell. If you need me, feel free to contact me anytime, and good luck."

On their way to Brock's boarding house, the Duo stopped at the Navaho craft shop to pick up the Lightfoots. Looking about, they couldn't locate them. When asked if they were present, the lady simply pointed at the two individuals next to them. The Duo turned to look and just about fell to the floor. Mistah had short hair, dressed as a cowboy with chaps, vest, boots and a real cowboy hat. Missi had her hair short like Mia, some rouge on her face, a beautiful riding skirt with blouse to match, and her cowboy hat hanging on her back. Both were wearing a pistol at their side with their war club hidden in their backs. Palmer finally spoke, "what brought on this drastic change in appearance?" Mistah answered, "we now have a house in town, new cowboy horses, work for a white couple, and behave like white agents supporting white man's law—guess it was time to look the part, heh, as you say!"

Entering Brock's boarding house room, the smell of alcohol, vomitus, and body odor was overpowering. Brock was still dead drunk. Palmer and Mistah man handled him to stand and walk by himself as the team stayed a few feet away. Brock kept demanding that they leave him alone, but Palmer said, "we have an intervention order and we're going to dry you up." Stopping at a Chinese bath house, Brock was thrown in a hot tub and scrubbed with a long handle brush and lye soap. The gals went to Craymore's Mercantile, and bought three sets of clothes.

Arriving at the jail, Sheriff Belknap was pleased to see a clean tenant with new clothes. Palmer added, "within a few hours, you're going to see a very different person. As Brock's demeanor changed, Palmer explained the changes to the sheriff and the Lightfoots. When the spiders appeared, Brock went wild. When offered his first jigger of paraldehyde, Brock smelled it and stepped back. Palmer just stood there holding the jigger as Brock started running away from what appeared as ghosts chasing him. Brock finally begged Palmer for the medicine. The result was a miracle. Brock stopped running about, stopped scratching at the spider bites, finally sat on his cot, and amazingly laid down and went to sleep.

As expected, two hours later Brock was back to running in his cell while looking back at his attackers. This time, Brock pleaded for a dose of the medicine. And the next 24 hours was a repetition of Brock's antics on a regular schedule. At least the vomiting and diarrhea stopped, and Brock would take fluids. The next week, all five team members took their +- five-hour shifts. On the sixth day, Brock asked for some food and only required a morning and evening dose of medicine.

The team was finally free. Brock showed few disappearing signs of DT's. He was eating three meals a day, bathing regularly and started reading to pass the time. It was during these last four days that Sheriff Belknap approached Palmer with a problem. "For the past week there has been a murder on the streets without any evidence of robbery, witnesses, or any leads to follow." "Who are the victims?" "Married businessmen between the ages of 40 to 50." "Have there been autopsies performed?" "Yes by Doc Simms." "Fine, we'll start there."

The Duo went straight to the doctor's hospital. Doc Sims was more than pleased to meet with them, since he had been given permission to discuss the cases by Judge Hawkins. After pleasantries, Palmer started, "are there any findings that would link these five victims?" "Yes, they all had untreated 'clap' and had their wedding bands in their pockets." "Well that only means that they likely visited prostitutes and that's where they got the 'clap.'" "Correct, plus the fact that each victim was found on the boardwalk next to several houses of pleasure."

"Doc, isn't this an infectious problem?" "Yes." "But weren't their wives affected?" "Unfortunately, this court order does not cover the victims' wives." Mia persisted, "I beg to differ Doc, if the wives were affected, then they certainly had every right to commit murder—if not murder at least a motive." "I understand, but when we discuss the manner of death, you'll think otherwise." "Oh, sorry, please continue."

"Each victim was killed by getting his skull bashed into his brain from the violent thrust of a small instrument. I have kept a scalp sample from each victim as proof of cause of death. Take a look at them in these glass bottles with preservative." The Duo steps and there was instant recognition of a rectangular depression measuring 1X2 inches. Mia says, "what kind of instrument could cause that, I don't know of any blacksmith tool or general hardware implement that could cause that." Doc Sims answered, "how about a Christian crucifix." Palmer was stunned, "yes that would work but why would you think of that specific item?"

"Well, had you been at church last week, the pastor's sermon was about fornication out of wedlock. By the end of his sermon, the men looked pale and the wives wanted to kill. But there was one man who kept standing and repeating, "justice will be done, thanks to the Lord Almighty." Even the pastor looked a bit peeked and wondered if he had been too judgmental." Mia looked at the doctor and said, "Doc, it sounds like you found our first suspect, and possibly the murderer. What's his name, we'll look him up and question him." "Well, with a church-full, I am not divulging anything that is not public knowledge, his name is Darius Wagner, the undertaker's assistant, and likely a religious fanatic."

The Duo went straight to Crandall's Funeral Services. Darius was at the front desk and recognized the Bodines. Palmer said, "we'd like to ask you a few questions about the recent murders." Darius exploded with a litany of sanctimonious declarations. "Fornicators are doomed to hell where they belong, I shall never stop bringing them to eternal justice." Palmer simply stepped up and placed him in manacles and added, "this is really a case for Judge Hawkins. Mental insanity will put him away in an asylum for years, if not forever."

Getting back to the jail, the sheriff asked if Doc Sims had been helpful. Mia answered, "yes, just a bit!" Shortly, Palmer showed up with a manacled man dressed in black and ranting to high heavens. Sheriff Belknap was shocked and asked what was going on. "Just a murderer of five fornicators." "What, but I just asked you to look into it." "All in a day's work." Placing him in a cell next to Brock, the sheriff asked what he could do to shut up this motor mouth. Mia said, "well we have plenty of paraldehyde left over, just hold his mouth open and I'll pour a dose down his gullet." Brock added, "I'll second that!"

Three days later, Brock was eating and not needing paraldehyde. The Duo gave him all new clothes and boots and escorted a well shaven young man to Longley's office. Agnes asked, "and who is this young man with you?" "Aunt Agnes, it's me Brock." Archibald did the same thing but when reality set in, everyone including Mia was crying. Recognizing the need for family time, the Duo left renumeration to another day, as they left it to the Longleys to bring Brock to his mother.

The next morning, Archibald and Agnes Longley showed up at the Bodine Agency. "Time to pay my bill, is it still the $5,000 I offered you?" "Give us whatever you think it's worth, as long as it's within your means." Agnes starts laughing and says, "you are asking that of a wealthy scrooge, and the biggest cheapskate in town." Agnes starts writing a bank draft and hands it to Mia. "Is, that satisfactory?" "More than expected." As the Longleys were leaving, Archibald insisted on knowing the amount, but Agnes adds, "come along dear, you can swindle him another day." The next day, the Bodines gave the Lightfoots $2,000(20%), the sheriff $500(5%), and Liam $500(5%) for their share in watching over Brock.

*

The next week turned out to be some down time. Things seemed to quiet down in town till Horace White showed up one morning. "What brings you here this fine morning?" "We need help to stop a new round of business extortion. Last week a total of six gunfighting men, in teams of two, visited some 20 merchants in town, including my hardware store, and extorted at least $10 from each business—all under the guile of security to prevent sudden devastating fires. It appears that these are footpads that didn't get arrested when you cleaned them out, or are new in town, but they are clearly gunfighters."

Since then, we have had a merchant's meeting and followed Elmer Craymore's suggestion of fighting back immediately before the racket expands and the miscreants develop a network that is impenetrable. So, for this reason, the Merchant's Association would like to offer you $1,000 to stop these gunfighters and bring them to the law for prosecution."

"This may sound simple for you and the merchants, but let me explain what will happen. My team will collect them the next day they show up, they will be arrested, we and the merchants will have to testify at trial, they'll get 6 months in Santa Fe, and when they are released, they'll be back in town and burn some of your businesses to the ground." Horace was clearly shocked and confused, "well how do we prevent this from happening." "As it is now, you can't. When a man is humiliated with a prison sentence, he is going to get his revenge."

Horace added, "there has to be a way to put an end to it, short of killing them!" "There is and it involves scaring the ba-geezus out of them." "Good, then do it." "Ok, but the cost now has gone up to $2,000 for the roundup, and you'll never know what we did to scare them to death, or a condition worse than death. When are they expected to do their next collection?" "Tomorrow morning on opening." "We'll be there. Just give us a list of merchants and their opening times."

That afternoon, the Duo got another visitor, Ellsworth Myers, president of the Community Bank. Ellsworth started with a story of the times, "with all the home robberies we had, the parent bank forced us to install a new steel safety deposit rack. The depositors have the only key, and the only way in without a key is with an angry blacksmith. With the recent house break-ins, the rich people are abandoning their home safes, and using the easy access of safety deposit boxes." "Interesting story, but how does this affect our agency?"

"Because, there are 30 boxes rented by rich mine owners. I suspect there is about +-$30,000 per box or +- a million in all. Now we insure each box for $10,000 and......" Mia interjected, "but you said that without the key, it would take an angry blacksmith to open all of one box." "True, but the outlaws won't believe that we don't have a second key, and if they have a chisel and sledgehammer, they only need to open one box to steal $30,000— after they beat the crap out of me or my employees."

Palmer paused and finally added, "and how can we help you?" "By your team becoming our armed guards five days a week." "Never happen for two reasons. First, you can't afford us with our daily rate of $100 for the two of us, and $150 a day for the four man team—that will eat up your daily profits. Secondly, it is not fair to this town to not be available for emergency situations by being full time employees. What you need are full time employees that are good with a shotgun and post them inside and outside the bank when open. Four good men will cost you $50 a day."

The next morning Palmer and Missi were hiding in White's Hardware Store. Right on opening, two well healed gunfighters entered. "Well Horace, the fee today is $15, and it will be $20 next week—so fork up or we'll take four gallons of coal oil for another project." "That is ridiculous, I cannot stay in business with these rates and I might as well liquidate my inventory and close my doors. So. If that happens, the predators will starve to death, heh?" "That's it you puke, pay up or I'll break your arm."

Out of nowhere came flying a 2-inch rock with an attached handle. The rock hit the menacing outlaw in his right knee and shattered the kneecap. The man collapsed to the floor as his partner drew his pistol. Palmer then dropped his cutoff shotgun on the head of the pistol carrying gunman, just enough to stun him to his knees. With both restrained in manacles, they then gathered the other four extortionist and brought them to jail where they manacled them to the cell bars before throwing them inside the cells.

Palmer then started, "well boys, your days of collecting free money are over. You'll be heading to Santa Fe for a vacation in the penitentiary. Now, some of you are thinking of coming back to town someday, and provide retribution for your vacation in prison. So to deter you from ever coming back to town, I will promise you, that if you ever show your face in Silver City, I will send my Indian friend to circumcise you or geld you of one nut. To show you how this will happen, I need two volunteers. With no takers, Mia stepped up and started pointing, as she recited, "eaney-meaney-miney-mo, you're first. This one gets circumcised, Mistah. Continuing on, eaney-meaney-miney-mo, you're next. Mistah, this one gets a half geld." Mistah steps forward saying, "Yes ma'am!" As he approaches the first customer, after unbuttoning his fly, the poor man passed out as the other one scheduled for a half gelding, threw up.

Palmer then added, does any one of you pinheads doubt that we would not carry out our plan—as it's not a threat but a promise? At that point, the extortionists were more than happy to have the manacles released as they entered their cells. Suddenly a messenger busted thru the door and said, "the Community Bank has been robbed and President Myers is in bad shape. Sheriff Belknap is requesting your help."

*

The entire team made their way to the bank. Ellsworth was being loaded onto a wagon to go to the hospital. Palmer stopped them and asked what happened. Ellsworth said, "five masked men busted the front door with a steel bar and then proceeded to beat me to a pulp. They were ready with chisels and sledgehammers, as if they knew about the safety deposit boxes. They forced me to say who the richest man in town was, and when I said Archibald Longley, they put a gun to my head and said, "what box number or your brains are going all over the floor." "Any idea how much they got?" "Rolls of $100 bills, probably at least $30,000."

From a voice in the crowd, the team heard, "actually $50,000 to be exact"—from Archibald Longley himself. Ellsworth added, "that's a $10,000 loss for the bank because of our guarantee. We'll offer you a finder's fee of $5,000 for the money's return." Archibald added, "and I'll double that." Palmer added, guess we're going for a trail ride. "What direction did they head out?" Someone said, "northwest towards Gila."

The deputy then added, "by talking to bank employees, the leader had a bad limp, another was missing two fingers from his left hand, and one man had the overweight appearance of a recently fired employee. By those description, you are dealing with the Rinsler gang last seen in Shakespeare. The four-member gang is worth a bounty of $3,000, dead or alive. Be careful, they are wanted for murder and are labeled killers."

The team got geared up with two pack horses carrying tents, cooking utensils, jungle warfare tools and plenty of vittles and ammo. It was Mistah who analyzed the situation, "it's 55 miles to Mule Creek which is a mining town and the last town in NM before Arizona and the great north woods. We hope they stop in either Gila, Buckhorn, or Mule Creek to spend some of their heist. If not, they'll be hiding in the great north woods." Palmer added, "heck, once they realize how much money they stole, they'll be riding non-stop to the great north woods to hide till the law cools off their trail, then they'll head to parts unknown. Sounds like we'll catch up with them in the great north woods when they least expect it."

The first day on the trail was a bit tiring for Mia because of a low back ache. After two hours on the trail, they stopped to water the horses. Mia asked Palmer what they were going to do with all the money they had already earned and may add from this caper. Palmer said, "I've been thinking about this, and I cannot believe that we will continue this agency. I just have the feeling that we are destined for greater things, but I don't know what that would be. For now, we continue what we are doing until that big step becomes clear." Mia gave the appearance of being satisfied, but in the back of her mind, she knew that an idea was brewing.

Three hours later brought them to a brook, so they veered of the traveled road to a campsite 200 yards off the road and set up camp.

> Meanwhile, some 15 miles northwest, the Rinsler gang had stopped to rest their horses. Rinsler took the time to count the money and was shocked to find over $50,000 in his saddlebags.

"Boys, we've hit jackpot, with all this money. This means the law will stay on our trail till they find us. So, we can't stop in any town till we get to the great north woods. There we'll set up camp and load up with supplies from the nearby trading posts, and we'll stay hidden for a couple of months." "But boss, there was just an old sheriff in Silver City. Why stay hidden so long?" "Because of that Bodine Agency who will come after us for our bounties and the reward money."

With two good cooks, the team had a meal of canned potatoes, cheese, and four large beef steaks. With several pots of coffee and fresh bearpaw pastries for dessert, the team settled down for a good night's sleep in their tents. Both couples did not miss an opportunity for intimacy. In the morning, after ablutions and responding to nature, the team made a large breakfast of bacon, canned beans, oatmeal and coffee before hitting the trail.

The day was spent riding, resting and watering the horses, eating snacks during rest periods, and continuing to ride on the main road. Once they went thru Buckhorn, they stopped at a mercantile and replenished their vittles. With the threat of rain, they bought a third tent for their saddles, several tarps to make a temporary shelter for the horses, and four rain dusters.

Five miles out of town, Missi spotted tracks heading north into the great woods. With dusk around the corner, the team elected to set up camp before entering the great woods. After finding a small stream surrounded by a crop of cottonwoods, the three tents went up and a small cooking fire started. Their quick meal of canned beef stew and coffee was prepared, and the fire doused before darkness fell upon the camp. During their meal, Palmer pointed out that all further camps would have to be safe and cold camps until they located the outlaws.

The next morning, the team covered the last open five miles and entered the great north woods. They stayed on the only trail that appeared well traveled with freight wagons. Eventually, they arrived at the Winngate Trading Post. Standing at the service counter was a middle-aged couple. "I'm Charlie and this is Melanie, how may we help you?" Mia answered, "as you can see by our badges, we are the Bodine Agency, and we're after a bunch of bank robbers. Have you seen a man with a limp, one with half a hand missing, and one who is overweight?" The lady responded, "why yes, they were here yesterday, they were all hardcases and Charlie shot one."

Palmer reacted and said, "is he dead?" "No, but he has a belly full of rock salt and probably still howling. They were an arrogant and impolite bunch. After cleaning me out of tents, tarps, cooking equipment, and vittles, they paid their $52 bill with a $100 green back. It took all my small bills and coins to make their change. When fatso asked how much my wife cost for services, as he put his hand on her waist, that's when that fat turd's belly started melting under rock salt."

Mia added, "well I don't blame you, but these are murderers, and they may be back to burn you out or worse." "That's why we sleep our turn while the other watches with our shotgun loaded with buckshot." "Well, if luck holds out, we should be back with them in manacles. What trail did they take?" "Straight north." "Before we leave, we have plenty of small bills and we would exchange them for that $100 bill so we can return it to the bank in Silver City." With that information, Melanie suddenly pointed at Mia and added, "Bodine, of course. I know who you are, you're that woman who has an emporium that make and sell denim mining trousers. I recently saw a sample of your work—very nice I may say!" "Thank you, you're very kind."

The team traveled the trail which followed a small rivulet. Two hours later, Missi suddenly pulls up and says she can smell camp smoke. Mistah added, "I can't smell it, but she's younger, so let's believe her." All four came off their horses, after finding the rivulet's small pool, they watered them and then tethered them in some good grass. With moccasins on, Mistah prepared to go investigate when Missi insisted she was coming as well, and added, "I know you're good and will find their camp, but if you get in a shootout, you'll need my help. So 'git along' without an argument."

An hour later, the Lightfoots returned. Mistah explained what he saw and heard. "All five are drinking that fire water and are arguing with the one who limps. Their point is that they all have $10,000 in their pockets and no place to spend it." "Good, I know you are an excellent tracker, but after 50 miles, it's nice to know we have the right bunch—for what will fall on them could never befall an innocent group."

Mia asked, "so what is the plan?" "We have three choices when our target is in their own camp. First, an all-out frontal attack with blazing guns in daylight"—all three heads turned in the negative. Second choice, wait till they are all sleeping and hope they are in a drunken stupor before we sneak into camp." Mia hesitated, "with all that money, they'll have a guard hiding in the bushes—not safe. Third, and I agree this is the only safe way, we disable them to the point that they won't even know what hit them or where they are—if at all conscious." All heads nodded in the affirmative as Mistah pulls out three sticks of dynamite and his bow—short, medium, or full length?" "The 'Real McCoy,' Mistah, 'The Real McCoy!'"

"This is the plan, we all sneak up there, the three of us stay 100 yards from camp as Mistah sneaks up to 50 yards, hides behind a large boulder or tree, and lobs an arrow loaded with one full size stick of dynamite on a short fuse. We all stuff our ears with these spongy things that came with the dynamite, we lay down with our heads against a good size tree, and cover our ears with our hands. As soon as the concussion passes us, we get up and run to the camp with our pistols drawn."

The team went to work. With everyone in place, Mistah was standing behind a 3-foot oak, and used a cheroot to light the fuse. Once the fodder was in flight, he dove for the ground and covered his ears. From afar, Palmer saw the rocket's fuse burning brightly. As it implanted in the camp's ground, all he heard was "dynamite," and saw all five hard cases stand up only to become airborne as the explosion went KABOOM.

As planned, the team went running in and found two outlaws retching, one was unconscious, one was crawling about aimlessly, and the leader was on his knees, gyrating in a circle, while holding an imaginary post as if it was going to prevent him from falling on his face. The camp was a total mess. The cooking tools and utensils were gone, the tents were gone, cases of liquor were broken, and their vittles scattered about.

The team quickly went to work and had all five outlaws manacled with their hands behind their backs and anchored around their own tree. After dowsing the many fires, the outlaws' pockets were emptied of bundles of money as well as a large roll of $20 bills in one saddlebag. Mistah and Missi went off to find the outlaws' horses which had spooked and pulled out their tethers.

As Palmer went back to get their own horses and supplies, Mia counted the money and came up with $59,912. When Palmer and the Lightfoots returned, they separated $50,000 to return to Longley's safety deposit box, and each member got $2,478. Missi was about to object when Palmer held out a finger and said, "this is not your 20%, it's a bonus for a job well done. You two made this capture possible, and we appreciate that. Back home you'll get your 20% of the rewards as usual."

After preparing a fine supper of beans, bacon, fried potatoes and coffee, the team retired. During the night, the outlaws finally came out of their stupor and demanded water and assistance to go to the bushes. Palmer got up and addressed them, "Until we get back to Silver City, there will be no water or food for you, and if you have to relieve yourselves, then do it in your pants. You are nobody to us, and will get no benefits from us. Tomorrow, you'll be tied to your horses' saddles by a manacle to a stirrup, and if you fall off, you'll get trampled—a tough way to die. If you call again, you'll get a mouthful of firewood. Goodnight."

The ride to town was a two-day affair. The first day was smooth as the outlaws were able to ride independently. The second day without food or water was different. Most outlaws would fall onto their saddle horn and their horses had to be trailed on a rope to continue moving along. Despite the delays, the team arrived at the bank before closing. Palmer brought the $50,000 to President Myers, but without the $5,000 fee.

The team's next stop was the sheriff's office. Palmer said, "here is the Rinsler gang, they need a bath and are a bit dehydrated." "Wow, they are plum wore out, I bet they would welcome a hanging right now, heh?" Disregarding the sheriff's comments, Mia added, "we'll be back to write our statements and collect the bounties when available. Now we are going home for a bath and a home cooked meal." "Well, one of these days you'll have to explain to me how I could get the town's miscreants to look like these zombies."

That same night, after a supper of steak and baked potatoes, the Bodines heard a knock at the front door. Opening the door, there stood Archibald Longley—shades of the past. Mia out of fatigue said, "well Mister Longley, you're like a bad penny, you keep showing up, but do come in."

***

CHAPTER 4

Changing Times

"Thank you for seeing me this late. I have two reasons for being here. First, is to give you this bank draft for $10,000 as I promised you. I was certain that I would never see a penny of that money, and even in my hands, losing $50,000 would have been a business hardship. So thank you for your service—excellent as always." "And as always, it was a pleasure doing business with you, now could the second reason for your visit have anything to do with our IOU."

"Correct, in case you don't know, since you went on the hunt, your access rail line was completed, tapped into my line, and you have already sent three railcars to the smelter. To remind you, your cost of $7,500 was almost a $60,000 savings. But enough, let me explain what issue is at hand that demands your services."

"Several of the larger mine owners have accumulated 400 pounds of pure gold bars worth +- $128,000 and 100 pounds of pure silver bars worth another $1,600. We need to get this shipment to Deming where they will then be on their way to multiple mints by the AT & SF rail system." Mia interrupted, "we follow you so far, but why don't you send it by our local rail line from Silver City to Deming?" "Because they refuse to take more than $10,000 worth of bouillon per trip and won't insure the value of the metal." "Why?" Because they say any value greater than $10,000 is a powerful incentive for rail agents to derail the train, cost many lives and insurmountable expenses for the line." "Where is it now?" "In the smelter vault, but their insurance carrier wants it out." "So, what are you proposing?"

"We want you to take it to Deming." Mia hesitated and said, "so you want our team to take five packhorses, each carrying two large saddlebags loaded with 50 pounds each, travel 50 miles over mountain terrain, spend one night in camp, and risk an ambush at every corner! Seems suicidal to me, heh?" Archibald simply shrugged his shoulder.

Palmer was quiet and thinking. He broke the silence and said, "could it be that the bulk of this shipment is your gold?" Longley smiled and nodded in the affirmative. "Then, if we do this, will this pay off our IOU?" "Absolutely, 100 %." "So, you don't care how we transport the shipment, as long as it all gets to Deming." "Correct and you don't have to provide a guarantee, I will trust that you will do your best to protect my gold." "Is there a possibility of there being other such shipments in the near future?" "Yes." "Then the fee will be 10% of the shipment's value as long as its value is $100,000 or greater, agreed?" "Agree, and I'll put it in writing." "Then we have a deal, we have things to get ready, and we'll get back to you after we get all our ducks in a row."

After Longley left, Mia looked at Palmer and asked what he had in mind. "This is a blessing in disguise, with our rail line hauling our ore to the smelter, those guarded ore wagon-trains will now be furloughed. We have one wagon-train being rented out, but I don't think there is enough work out there for two guarded wagon-trains. So this is what I propose, we take one of these freight wagons that is surrounded with steel plates, add the gold, six good men with coach shotguns and rifles, and trail a replacement team and two riding horses. Now we have an armored and guarded war wagon—so let them try to rob us."

Mia thought, "that war wagon would certainly protect us from a direct attack of outlaws on horseback, but what about dealing with ambushes?" "Remember those three Navaho Indians we had trained? Well we can send them ahead as scouts to locate such strongholds and warn us." "Sounds like a fairly safe plan. I'm all in." "Ok, well we had said that we would periodically go check up on the emporium and the mine. Why don't you show up at the shop and store, and I'll go see Harvey at the mine to find the help we need."

*

Mia walked in the emporium unannounced and Ella gave her a firm hug. "How are things going mom?" "Everything is perfect. I have three gals that do all the work and all I have to do is wrap sales, collect the money and keep my inventory up to date so I can place my weekly orders and not run out of goods." "Do you see areas that need improvement or changes?" "To be honest, you have designed a perfect system for operating a retail store, and we shouldn't change a thing. The only issue, that I know is in the gal's mind, is salaries and benefits." "Trust me, like the mine, I will be adding work benefits, and retirement options in the near future, but keep it 'shush' for now, heh?"

Walking upstairs, Mia simply watched for a long while. Agnes was working a station as likely someone was missing from work. Alice finished an issue with one of the gals, and finally came to see Mia. "Well I am just happy to see you, I know you have been busy, so what brings you here today?" "Just checking if you have any major problems, what your weekly output is, and I'm curious as to what happened with that new line of slim ladies' jeans."

"There are absolutely no internal problems, Agnes and I have 16 gals working for us, and we put out 400 finished pants weekly—of which Ella gets 100 pieces a week and the rest goes to Waldo. Recently, we had a slim well-built stitcher model a pair of slim jeans to Waldo. He went crazy, jumping around like a silly clown, and wanting all his allotment split 50-50 between ladies' slim jeans and miner's pants. Actually, every time he shows up here, he acts like a newborn chick out of the egg— squawking with its beak wide open, wanting more food from mama. The other day, he offered you a $10,000 gift to build a factory and go big out west."

Mia went pensive and Alice noticed the change, so kept quiet. Mia eventually said, "Alice, just for giggles, why don't you and Agnes prepare in secret a list of changes were we to build a factory—just in theory, mind you. My sixth sense is telling me that changing times may be coming." Alice winked and said, "will do and we'll keep it in our reticule in case you show up and want to discuss it, heh?" "For sure."

Upon leaving Mia turned around and added, "and tell Waldo to keep that $10,000 liquid and not to spend it. I haven't said no, yet."

Meanwhile, Palmer and the Lightfoots arrived at the mine. "Well, Palmer this is a surprise, what brings you here today." "Couple of issues, how is that gold vein coming along." "Incredible, it is now an inch wide and dwindles out at 4 inches of height. The ore is high grade, and many rock pieces are as much as 30% in gold. I don't know how long it will last; heck it may even get richer. For now, you are silently getting rich, but that's Ok, for you'll get a chance to spend it on your next project." "Which is?" "Not yet ready to discuss it—later."

"Ok, then assuming you don't need anything from me, I need something from you. Now that the rail cars are moving the gold ore to the smelter, what has happened to the security guards?" "Some of the men have found other jobs, some have retired, but I still have a bunch that will need to go on furlough." "Then in that case, I need an armored freight wagon, a driver, two team of draft horses, three gunmen armed with shotguns and rifles, and three Navajo Indians to serve as advance scouts. This is for a one-time job but has the potential of growing. The pay is $50 a day and there is likely going to be some shooting involved." "Fine, when do you want them." "Three days from now at sunup at the smelter."

That evening, the Duo discussed their day. Mia started, "the store is doing well under Ella's control. The shop is up to 16 stitchers, two pattern cutters, one man in receiving and shipping (your dad), three ladies making accessories that also serve as backup, one floor expediter, and two working managers. With all that, Waldo wants more products, despite the fact that he now gets 300 pieces per week to Ella's 100 units. With the addition of slim ladies' jeans, he wants more products to expand his distribution from New Mexico and Colorado to Nevada and Arizona. For now, he has to stay in New Mexico and Colorado."

"Hu um, does that mean you're thinking of expanding your business and build a factory to meet your needs?" "I admit I'm warming up to the idea. If an expansion is considered, after watching the operation in full swing, the 4,500 square feet above the emporium is presently utilized at maximum occupancy. Time will tell, and it all depends on the direction the agency takes." "Well, until we are ready, let's go talk to the sheriff to find out who could muster an attack on our war wagon."

"Ok you two, when you invite me to my favorite diner for dinner, that means you want something from me, so out with it!" Mia explained what they were planning to do, down to the value of the shipment. The sheriff pondered the issue and finally said, "there is only one organization that can fund a dozen outlaws to attack you guys, and that's the 'mob' from Albuquerque. I hear from the lawmen on the wire, that this group is growing in numbers and strength and specialize in prostitution, extortion, robbery, and human trafficking. Now, let's talk about human trafficking. It was your agency who put Courtright and Donahue out of business when you busted their ring in town. The wire is suggesting that the mob wants to reopen their access to Mexico, and that takes a major investment. What a better way to quickly make a hundred grand to fund their new corridor. Yes, I expect you had better get ready for a massive onslaught of outlaws that want you all dead."

As they were walking to the office after dinner, Mia asked, "do you think we have enough fire power to handle a dozen attackers?" "We do if they attack us on horseback. With our coach shotguns we can devastate them and stay safe. Now an ambush is different matter since they'll be using rifles out of range of our shotguns. We'll be sitting ducks for them." Arriving at the office he added, "we need more firepower. Ah.....hah, I got it, let's go see Winn in his gun shop."

"Winn, we have a special shipment that requires more firepower to fight off a dozen bushwhackers." "Hell, I've got something that will fight off a small army. Step into the back storeroom." The Duo followed Winn to a tarp covering something. As Winn pulled the tarp off, Palmer exclaimed, "A GATLING GUN?" "Yes, this was ordered by the army for Fort Grims. It has recently arrived, but I have not yet notified the fort. You can borrow it. It is the newer mini model that can be fitted in a wagon by a blacksmith. It is fired by a manual crank, can move 360 degrees on a peg, fires a 30-caliber bullet thru six 10-inch rotating barrels. And it fires 200 rounds a minute." "How much to rent it for one day. "How about $25 to help pay the freighter's fee to bring it from the railroad yard to the shop, and you pay for the ammo. A reel of 1,000 rounds, that will last 5 minutes, will cost you $100 or 10 cents a round." "Cheap enough."

"Do you think you might need a 2,000-round reel for $200?" "I can't imagine needing more than 5-minutes of devastation to bring this gang to their knees, if anyone is lucky to survive? But just to be on the safe side, we'll take the 2,000-round reel, heh?" "That's wise, just remember that you need three people to shoot this thing, one to crank the handle, one to aim it, and one to feed the ammo reel. The rate of fire is controlled by how fast you turn the handle, you can slow the turning and it will fire less than 200 rounds a minute, but you can't go above the maximum rate as there is a limit on how fast you can turn that handle. On the shipping day, I suggest you set yourself up in the wagon, and fire off a few rounds just so you understand this firearm's needs and capabilities. Oh, I almost forgot, if you were to lose this thing, you and I would need a good lawyer and about $10,000 in replacement costs."

*

The Duo went to the mine the day before the event. After the blacksmith built an adapter to hold the gatling gun, a trial run was planned. Expecting some loud repercussions, the Duo and Mistah placed those spongy things in their ears. After setting all up, Mistah was told to rotate as fast as the machine allowed and for a half minute. Mia was ready with the first round in barrel #1 as Mistah slowly rotated the arm to fill the five other barrels. Then Palmer let off the firing lever and nodded to Mistah. The target was a small pile of a half dozen firewood pieces at 50 yards. The noise was impressive, and the target started blowing apart. After the half minute and 100 rounds down range, Mistah stop cranking. The Trio walked down range and viewed the results. The firewood was turned to splinters and chips.

The next day, the wagon arrived at the smelter along with Pappy as the driver, three men known to be good with a gun, and the three well trained Indians on horseback. In the middle of the armored wagon was the gatling gun, well-hidden under a tarp, and trailing it was the relief pair of Belgian draft horses. After the wagon was loaded with the smelter's shipment and the cooking utensils/vittles for the trip's meals, the war wagon took off with at least two riding horses trailing the draft horses— for emergency situations.

Meanwhile, in Deming, Lionel Courtright was meeting with a dozen gunfighters/riflemen sent to him for a special purpose. "This shipment took off this morning at the smelter. In the wagon was an old driver, three armed miners, the Bodines, and their two Indian friends. That should make for easy target practice. Do not leave any survivors. Hide the bodies in the bushes and drive the wagon to the rendezvous location just north of town. Remember, this is not a gunfighting game, set yourselves behind trees and ambush this bunch with your rifles—I want them all dead."

The first day on the road was quiet. The horses were watered and rested every two hours as the men stood guard with their shotguns. The wagon was actually comfortable with temporary seats added for the men's and ladies' comfort. Mia found the rocking of the wagon to be irritating her bladder and she had to go to the bushes as soon at they stopped for the horses—yet not peeing in large amounts.

That first night at camp, special precautions were taken. Two men were left rotating on guard duty and several bear traps laid out all around the camp as a precaution against an attack. Yet, nothing happened. In the morning, after a large breakfast to feed 11 people, Palmer had a talk with the three Navaho Indians. "We expect being ambushed halfway to Deming. Ride ahead and find the spot so we can get ready for them. They will likely be 50 yards off the road, but their horses will be as much as 100 yards behind them. Find the horses, and you have hit the jackpot. Make your way to the main road so you can give us some landmarks before the ambush site, then double back to us with the info."

Traveling was a bit slower to guarantee not getting ahead of the Indian scouts. The team was ready at the gatling gun and Pappy was holding his reins from the bottom of the wagon as a precaution. When hoof beats were heard, the war wagon came to a stop. "The ambush is a mile ahead. There is a massive 3-foot oak by the road, and they are hiding some 50 yards beyond the oak. You can't miss them. Do you want us to stay with you?" "No, go back to their horses and stay in that area in case some outlays escape. Once the shooting stops gather their horses and bring them to the road."

The war wagon proceeded at a good clip till the massive oak was seen from afar. With everyone in place, Pappy moved ahead. As they passed the oak, suddenly gun fire exploded from the woods. All the men had their heads below the steel armor and hundreds of pings were heard on the side of the armor. On Palmer's signal, all the men started firing back as he started cranking the handle. Outlaws were flung back, trees were falling, and rocks were exploding. The gatling gun had no mercy. Everything in its path was turned to rubble. When Mia hit the reel's halfway mark, she was supposed to tap Palmer's shoulder as a warning. In the heat of the moment, she plum forgot, and the roar continued. There was so much smoke that all the Duo's men stopped shooting since targets were no longer visible. Palmer, not getting that tap on the shoulder, kept mowing the forest down till surprised by that 'click.'

Hearing the click he said, "are we out of ammo, I never got the shoulder tap." "I was so busy feeding that reel that I just forgot. This was insane." "Hell no, it was the only safe way to deal with this lopsided situation. Boy, I want one of these toy guns!" "Yeah right, at $10,000!"

Once the smoke cleared, reconnaissance revealed that every outlaw was dead, and many rifles were ruined by direct hits. The grim task of loading the dead outlaws in the wagon was possible after the gold/silver bars and the gatling gun were moved ahead. The Indian scouts arrived with the twelve horses. After the outlaw pockets and saddlebags were checked, some +- $1,650 and several pistols/rifles were recovered.

They made Deming by late afternoon. Their first visit was the local sheriff, Wayne Stickney. "I suspect most of these hombres are wanted. I'll check our wanted posters." "If you do that for us, I'll give you 5% of the bounty rewards for your time. Here is $40 to get them buried. If there are bounties, send our share to the Bodines, c/o the Bodine Emporium in Silver City. Before we leave, we'll sell their horses, but we'll bring the guns to our gun shop at home."

Their last stop was the railroad headquarters who took possession of the bouillon. After a nice supper at a local diner, the entire team went to liveries to sell the horses. In a short time they sold all twelve outlaw horses with saddles for +-$85 each. The $1,000 was evenly divided amongst the miners and Indians as their pay. After loading the war wagon on a flat car, with the horses in the stock car, the gatling gun was locked up in the guarded express car. And the team made it back home in style.

*

A week later several gunfighters arrived in Deming at the Crazy Eight Saloon and Gambling Hall. The owner, Lionel Courtright, met with them in the saloon before opening time. "Well gents, I am told that you are all experienced gunfighters. The headquarters sent you here to get rid of a security agency that has been a hindrance in reopening the trail to Mexico. With this team alive, they won't try to reopen it. So far, two attempts at bushwhacking Bodine himself failed, an attempt at ambushing the entire team failed—and all these men were killed.

You eight men are our last straw. We want you to goad them in a face to face gunfight, and you eight should be able to take care of a white and an Indian couple."

"Any idea how we can goad them into facing us off?" "Just find the sheriff as he makes his evening rounds and rough him up enough to put him in the hospital, and the Bodine Agency will be looking you up bright and early in the morning. Now take the train and head out to Silver City."

The past ten days had been a bit slow, but the Duo did not mind the down time. One telegram was a real surprise. Sheriff Stickney sent a note saying that he had collected $8,000 in bounty rewards and was sending a telegram voucher for $7,600 after paying himself $400 for services rendered. After paying the Lightfoots their share, the Duo placed the balance in their bank account. That evening a second telegram arrived. The address was unknown but the telegraph 'sign off' was Albuquerque.

Palmer read it out loud:

You have caused us enough grief and money STOP

Your nemesis is already in town STOP

Your ticket on earth has been punched STOP

Make your will today, tomorrow is too late STOP

"Well Mia, it looks like we may finally find out who wants us dead. Personally, I think this is a blessing in disguise. For now, since this could be our last night, let's celebrate the best way we know how." "Oh boy, that will mean a replenishing breakfast in the morning, I'd best check the larder and plan the menu. Ok, it's flapjacks, syrup, eggs and home fries."

The next morning, sleeping late out of necessity, a loud knock woke the Duo up. Palmer put his union suit on and went to the door. There stood a clearly upset Deputy Burke. "What's the problem Liam?" "Last night, during his evening rounds, some miscreants jumped the sheriff, beat him senseless, broke his left arm and several ribs. He's been in the hospital all night and this morning, he says he's leaving, against medical advice. Doc Ross asked if you would come to the hospital and try to talk some sense in that old fool who wants to go arrest these bullies—with a shotgun." "Oh great, it's going to take a jail cell to keep him under control, but we'll be over and give it a try."

Making their way to the hospital, the Duo could hear Sheriff Belknap two blocks away. Walking in his room, Doc Ross was applying a cast to the sheriff's left arm. "Palmer, will you tell the Doc that I have to arrest my attackers before he puts me in a cast!" "Well Doc, keep going since it looks like you're almost done anyways. If I may suggest, add a lump of plaster about there, to keep his shotgun from sliding off, heh?" "Great, I'm beginning to think that you're just as bad as he is. But if it's going to save his life, I'll do it."

Later in the sheriff's office, Sheriff Belknap explained his dilemma. "I may be getting old but I'm not over the hill. The townspeople know I was taken off guard, but my resolve is on the chopping block. To continue being this town's sheriff, I have to confront my attackers and arrest them." Mia looked at Palmer and said, "he has a valid point and I agree with him. Could we assist him to make the arrest?" "Of course, but I think there is more to his thrashing. I suspect this was all part of the plan to fulfill that threatening telegram. The question is how many gunfighters are we dealing with?" "Well, there are only three hotels that can handle a large band of men arriving at the same time, so, let's send Liam, Mistah and Missi to see where they spent the night and how many there are."

Mistah and Missi came back empty handed, but Liam hit jackpot. "Eight men arrived yesterday on the train from Deming. They did some heavy drinking last night, raised hell when they came back to the hotel. This morning, they raised more ruckus in the hotel's restaurant. Apparently, there was a shortage of tables, but the gang threw a patron couple out to make room for them. To make it worse, they left without paying their bill. As they were leaving, the hotel manager heard them say they were going to Sil's Place for a beer. The restaurant staff is still cleaning the place, since they were not only scruffy looking, but they smelled really bad."

"That's good recon work, now we know we are dealing with 8 ruthless pissants. We'll let them dull their reflexes a bit from alcohol, and then we'll be over to arrest them for assault and battery on a lawman." The team was not able to deter the sheriff from joining them, since he had the only power, as the victim and town lawman, to officially arrest them. Liam also wanted to join them, but Palmer said, "we never know how these confrontations will end up. If things go south, you'll be the only law left in town, so you need to stay out of it."

An hour later the team plus the sheriff walked into Sil's Place. Sheriff Belknap asked the bartender, "Sam, you got a scruffy bunch that smell bad?" "Sure do, and they look pretty dangerous! Last two tables in the right corner. I think their leader is the big guy with the white hat." "Yep, that's the one who coldcocked me. He's mine boys."

As previously arranged, Palmer and the sheriff stepped up to the leader's table as the Lightfoots stepped to the other table. Mia was watching everyone's back. Palmer had his pump shogun in his hands, and when he got to the table, he slapped the gun's metal receiver to the head of the closest gunfighter with his back to him. The guy was knocked to the floor as his buddy on the right went for his gun, and quickly got the same receiver in the face as he rolled backwards, butt over head, to the floor. Palmer sat down and asked the man to his left if he wanted the same mouthful. "I'm good, you'll not get a peep out of me, sir!"

Sheriff Belknap then said to the leader, "you're under arrest for attacking a duly elected officer— that will mean prison time, smart ass." Palmer added, "you coming peacefully or are you taking another route?" The man put his drink down and said, "I'm not going to jail, and you can't make me. I have seven good men to your four and an old man." "I'd say five, even if these two wake up, they won't be of much use to you. Besides, I've got four rounds in this shotgun and I can put four of you down myself." "Bullticky, once my men wake up, we'll be leaving." "We're giving you a half hour to reconsider, but if you step outside, we'll stop you any way we can—and that could mean gunplay!"

Waiting outside the saloon, with the sun at their backs, the sheriff repeated his need to confront the leader. "That bear of a man is going down hard, so, I'm replacing the two buckshot loads with these 1-ounce slugs—the only reliable load for a mad bear."

When the waiting time was up, the 8-member gang stepped outside and saw the team and sheriff holding their coach shotguns at cowboy port-arms, with Palmer's pump shotgun at his side. The sheriff said, "there is no need for this. Why?" Palmer added, "they won't tell you, but I suspect they were sent here to execute me and my team. Am I right? So, who sent you?" The leader yelled, "draw!"

As the gunfighters went for their guns, the shotgun blasts exploded. All the gunfighters, but one, were on the ground, everyone but the sheriff had emptied their shotguns—all ten rounds. The sheriff had fired only one shot but got a high hit on his left arm. The arm was amputated, and blood was pumping wildly. Sheriff Belknap felt it was a fatal wound and did not fire his second round. But the bear-man, after getting over the initial shock, pointed his pistol at the sheriff. Everyone went for their back up pistols, but there was no need, for Sheriff Belknap placed his second round in mid chest. The leader was stopped in his tracks, lifted up and thrown backwards in a heap.

As the team stepped up to see if anyone was alive, they were surprised to find one man alive with buckshot wounds to his right chest. Palmer said, you might live with good surgical care. We're going to give you that, but if you live, you owe us some answers. Commandeering a homesteader's wagon, they loaded the injured gunfighter. It was then that Palmer noticed that Mia was bleeding below her right hip. "I think it is just a flesh wound." "it doesn't matter, get in the wagon to get stitched up." Palmer was in the wagon with Mia as he spoke to the gunfighter. You're on your way to the hospital, but in case you don't make it, how about telling me who sent you?" The man hesitated but said, Lionel

Courtright out of Deming—The Crazy Eight Saloon and Gambling Hall.

At the hospital, Doc Sims took over the outlaw's case. When he saw that Mia was bleeding, he sent an orderly to find Doc Ross to take care of Mia. "No, no, I can wait, use Doc Ross to help you." "I don't need him to provide emergency care, I'll need him later to help with this man's surgery."

"Hello Mia, I see you've been playing gun games again. Let's take a look." After cleansing the wound, sterilizing it with carbolic acid, he placed the necessary sutures. While he was finishing the bandaging, Mia had to rush to the water closet. Returning she said, "that was ridiculous, I was convinced that I had a full bladder, but I managed to pee half-a- cup." "Really, lay down so I can check your bladder. Hu...um, I see" after examining her belly. "I better do an internal exam. Yes, I am sure. Why don't you get dressed and I'll go find Palmer and explain my findings." "Palmer, please come in." "How bad was Mia's wound." "Just a thru and thru wound through her love handle." Not realizing what Doc Ross had said, he asked, "is she alright?" "Yes, THEY both are." "What do you mean, THEY?" Mia answered, "I'm going to have a baby, Palmer."

Palmer was not registering things clearly as he added, "but HOW." Doc Ross came back with, "now really Palmer, you have been playing 'hide the pickle' for over a year, how can you be so surprised?" Once that registered, all three broke out in laughter. "Ok, let's now review things. When was your last monthly?" "I don't remember." "Well you were here almost four months ago because you were not ovulating. Have you had a monthly since then?" "No." Have you had morning sickness?" "Yes, once when I had to provide some bad news to a customer." "Have you had back aches when riding horses?" "Yes, when hunting down bank robbers." "Has your appetite increased lately?" "Yes." "I agree, by my scales you've gained four pounds. Have your breasts enlarged and do you have bumps around your nipples?" "Yes." "Any cravings?" "Yes, dill pickles," as everybody start laughing again. "So, do I need to continue?" "No, I believe you." "Good, by my exam, you are about 14 weeks along and your due date is mid-December."

Palmer finally realized, "we are having a baby, thank you Mia as he kisses her. Now are there any recommendations and restrictions?" "Yes, some early recommendations. One--Eat three meals a day. Have a good breakfast, a light lunch and a one-plate supper always with vegetables for your minerals and vitamins which the baby needs. You have to eat since you are feeding two people, but I don't want you to gain more than 20 pounds. Two--stop worrying about 'this and that' that might harm the baby. Worry raises blood pressure which is definitely bad for a pregnancy. Have a normal life but don't lift heavy objects because you'll pee your pants. Now for restrictions. I only have two for now. You are carrying a human life that is totally dependent on you. Mia, it is time to put your guns away, for a gunshot injury to you can be fatal to your baby. The other, get rid of those sexy tight jeans, that baby of yours needs room to grow, wear comfortable riding skirts till you are ready for maternity dresses. As a side, I see those jeans every day at home, one of our nurses and my fiancé wears them as soon as she gets home." "And who is your fiancé?" "You should know, Corinna Brewster—small world, heh? I will see you in 10 days to remove your stitches and I expect you to come in with a list of questions. With my new obstetrical bone-conduction stethoscope, I might be able to pick up a heartbeat."

Palmer added, "so the frequent peeing is caused by?" "The growing uterus pushing on her bladder—completely normal." "Does this mean no more playing 'hide the pickle?'" "I am certain that for the past 14 weeks it has not slowed you down, so why stop now? It is normal to continue relations throughout pregnancy as long as the mother is comfortable. Now go home and don't worry. You are healthy and pregnancy is a natural event. Reorganize your work schedule at home and the emporium. Stay active and even add a hobby. Enjoy these next months for they are a blessing."

***

CHAPTER 5

Planning a Factory

After their meeting with Doc Ross, the Duo was walking home, and both were quiet reflecting on their revealing news. Finally Palmer spoke, "it doesn't seem possible, we have spent our lives making our future happen, and this time, the most important turn of events simply happened when we forgot to make it happen." "That's because we were so busy with difficult capers, that mother nature could act without being controlled. How do you feel about becoming a father?" Palmer stopped in his tracks and said, "I'm the happiest man in the world, but it also means changes in our routine will have to come about. Let's get home and talk about it."

Once home, Mia went to change in a comfortable riding skirt with a loose blouse. "There, now the baby can breathe and so can I." "You know, no one can tell you're with child. So, until you decide to inform people, this attire will do till the maternity dresses are needed." "You're right, the waiting months are too long, to inform people of this good news." "True, but not for our parents, they need to know sooner than later." "I'll take care of that tomorrow night. But what about us, what are we going to do to keep us occupied and keep our minds off how this baby is doing. Remember what Doc Ross said, 'worry is bad, it raises blood pressure and that is very bad for a pregnancy.'"

"I see, well I'm going to pay a visit to this Lionel Courtright, get him taken out of commission, and hopefully put a final nail in this mob's coffin." "That's a two-day job, what about after that?" "Well I know that Harvey is working on a new project for me, but until he finishes his research, I get nothing from him." "What are you going to do about the Agency." "I don't think I want to continue without you, and you're definitely grounded. I think it is time for Sheriff Belknap to hire two more deputies and let go the day to day gun play—he needs to deal with politics, the city council, and do more administrative work for the judge." "So how are you going to spend your time?" "I really want to spend 'this time' with you, so how about I help with your project?" Mia stepped up to her husband and kissed him passionately, "how did you know." "It's been written all over your face ever since Waldo Steiner appeared on the scene." "You do realize this is going to cost a lot of money." "Yes, but we have it, and we'll do it 'right,' with room to expand and add all the modern technology that is available today— and we'll do it together, the three of us, heh?"

*

After dropping Palmer off at the train yard, Mia decided to go to the emporium shop and have a chat with Alice and Agnes. Meeting in the lunchroom, Mia started, "I am seriously thinking of building a factory and expand the business. As part of discovery, I want your opinions on what could be done differently—so this is your chance to get your two cents worth in the fracas, and possibly get somethings you wish you had at this work site."

Alice started, "We agree with you, it is time to strike when the iron is hot since you have an eager man who will do all the marketing and distribution of your product. So let's start, my list consists of:

1. Don't continue to rotate staff positions by bids. It is not working out. The new work requires getting use to, and it can take a

week or more for that station to be up to standard efficiency? A factory's function has to be based on maximum efficiency—not dilly-dallying on the job.

2. Our machines have been used over a year and need service. The gears are grinding and likely need some new ones. We need a maintenance man.

3. As a commercial business, please consider a retirement package. Separate in three categories of years of employment 10—15—and 20 years as an example.

4. Waldo wants you to add insulated work denim for those cold winters up north. It is simply adding a layer of flannel to the denim before sewing the pieces together.

5. Add more space for each stitcher, 6 X 6 feet is not enough.

6. Every stitcher needs larger 'in and out' boxes for their pieces in and the finished item going to the next stitcher.

7. We both suspect, it will be time to add an official 'boxing' person."

Agnes was next, "my list consists:

1. If you ever consider a second shift, we'll need artificial lighting. For now, daylight with plenty of windows is more than adequate.

2. The gals are worried about paying for medical bills. Would you consider medical insurance for the workers and their families. It appears that some of the husbands don't get this family benefit at work.

3. Cutting out patterns by stitchers is a total waste of their time. They are craftswomen that need to do their trade—sewing-sewing-sewing. We are going to need a separate department of pattern cutters and manually using scissors has to go by the wayside. There are new fabric cutters with peddle foot power that are more efficient and yield a better product.

4. We need a larger water closet for women and a small one for men.

5. More windows would be a benefit—like one between two stitchers.

6. Move the home accessory stitchers back into the shop. When we run out of certain items, Alice and I have to make them to keep the lines going.

7. With a commercial factory, we both believe that new employees will need to go thru a training program. They need a tutorial on how to run these commercial machines, and they need to see how they work sewing denim. The basics of sewing patterns our way has to be taught."

"Wow, these are all good ideas. Thanks for adding some thought when preparing your lists. For now, keep this quiet, but I want you to start working on three of your suggestions. First, order five fabric cutters and have the company reps teach the cutters how to use two of them safely—store the other three for later. Second, I like the idea of insulated denim mining pants. Order bolts of flannel and start making the patterns. Put the product into circulation asap. Third, cancel the rotating job bids effective immediately. We need to know if some gals will quit because of the change—better now than later. I always knew that this was an appeasement to keep everyone happy, but was not conducive to factory production lines. We will talk again, and any new suggestions will be welcomed. At some point, we'll get you involved with the development of a working floor plan. Thanks again."

On her way home, Mia stopped at Elmer's store. "Elm I need a roll of drafting paper, a 3-foot ruler, a 1-foot ruler, erasers, pencils, a pencil sharpener, and any tool or ink that Weber Construction uses to make blueprints."

Meanwhile, Palmer was arriving in Deming. His first stop was the sheriff's office to speak with Sheriff Wayne Stickney. "You probably heard of the shootout in Silver City?" "Heck, the entire state heard about it, and everyone heard how the old sheriff held up his end. That was big of you, sir." "Well beside that, my name is Palmer and while we were transferring the living outlaw to the hospital for emergency surgery, he gave up the name of the gunfight organizer." "Let me guess, Lionel Courtright. Is the outlaw alive?" "As of this morning, I heard that he had lived thru lung surgery and was stable in recovery."

"Then how do you want to proceed?" "I was given a court ordered arrest warrant by Judge Hawkins. I have been advised to bring this scoundrel back to Silver City for his trial." "You do realize that this man is part of the mob out of Albuquerque." "Yes, but this is not the first time I chip at their enterprise. The judge seems to feel, that if we take Courtright out, that they will move their underground operation out of state, because New Mexico has been such a financial drain. It's a chance worth taking, and besides, this man belongs in prison or dangling at the end of a rope." "Very good, I'll escort you to his saloon and be your witness."

The two men made their way to the Crazy Eight Saloon. When the sheriff asked the bartender where Courtright was, they were directed to an office behind the bar. Sheriff Stickney told Palmer, "I'll stand outside the office while you get control of Courtright. That way, no bouncer or bodyguard will come in to cause trouble." Without knocking, Palmer entered. "Who are you, what do you want, and close the door." Palmer responded by pulling a hunting knife and cutting off one of his ears. Courtright eyeballs nearly popped out when he saw his ear dangling off Palmer's knife. Screaming out loud, he finally said, "WHY?"

"That was for the two separate snipers you sent to kill me, the army of killer ambushers, and those eight men to kill me in a gunfight. They are all dead, except for one who will implicate you." "That will never happen, my lawyer will get your charges dismissed." "You sound like you were gifted with impunity. Let me tell you Judge

Hawkins is determined to do his part to affect your mob headquarters. Putting you away, seizing your business, or hanging you is his way of telling your mob to get the hell out of Silver City and New Mexico. So, here are the manacles, you'll still be able to put pressure on your ear. We wouldn't want you to bleed to death, heh? Now get up and let's go."

*

After getting home, Palmer walked in his house only to find it empty. He yells out, "Mia are you home?" "In the office." Palmer walks in and finds a huge paper covering the entire desk. Mia was walking on all sides making lines and adding names. "Woman, what on earth are you up to?" "While you were gone, I had a meeting with Alice and Agnes. They fired me up and I've decided to build a factory and double my operations. They gave me 14 great suggestion and I've already implemented three of them. Here is the list I prepared for you, note the ones about cancelling the rotating bids, buying power pattern cutters and start adding insulated mining pants with a layer of flannel inside."

"I like everything I read. Excellent! Well I admit I don't know much about the operations, but why don't you go over this fancy design and explain what this all means." "Ok, the plant will be 50 feet wide by 200 feet long—twice our present square footage. Starting at the rear of the plant is a large cutting room, next to shipping/receiving/boxing and the last room is for the designer/purchasing agent." "OK, so far."

"The next section is four lines of six stitchers each, and since each stitcher is allowed 8X8 feet, that means they will cover 32 lineal feet in width. In-between line 1 & 2 and line 4&5 is a 9-foot passageway for the expediter. This adds 18 feet which now totals 50 feet wide."

"The next block is four more assembly lines of another six stitchers each—plus the two passageways." "Good."

"This next block holds the water closets—eight stalls for women and a single stall with a urinal for men." "Good."

"Then the front end of the factory is a large meeting/lunchroom with a large commercial ice box for the ladies' lunches. The remaining space is for my office with a nursery and a receptionist/secretary office." "Wow, that looks well planned out, but why don't we add another 50 feet in case we ever want to add another four assembly lines?"

"Sure, why not, we never have enough room. We'll just push the water closets down 50 feet."

"Speaking of room, I see you are spread out all on one floor. I strongly suggest that we add a second floor, and leave it unfinished and completely empty except for ventilation panels in the walls and roof. We never know what the future will bring, and the extra cost is a fraction of the first floor and roof. Besides, if we ever decide to sell the building, it will command a much higher value." "True, but that may be useful to the kids, but I'll do everything I can to stay on one floor."

"Now what about all the other things we need to make this a modern building." "Well, here are my thoughts on this—let me list them:

1. A polished concrete floor.
2. A window between each stitcher.
3. Natural gas lamps.
4. Natural gas heating stoves.
5. Compressed air powered sewing machines and cutters.
6. Steel roof.
7. A separate gas-powered boiler and compressor in its own shed.

8. Our own concrete septic tank and leaching field."

"This sounds like an overwhelming project, do we have the energy to do all this, especially being pregnant and all?" Well actually, now that you have your floor plan, all you need is to find another 24 stitchers and a whole bunch of supporting workers. I will be your 'clerk of the works' and you'll only need to check on the progress of things a few times a day. We can do it, and remember what Doc Ross said, 'you need the distraction, heh'"

"Then, I'm all in, where do we start?" "Tomorrow morning we go see the town clerk. First of all we need a plot of land that includes city water and natural gas. Once we have the land, we see Marc Weber about building the factory; and find out who can install a compressed air system, indoor plumbing, and gas lamps/stoves."

"Ok, but tonight we go see our parents and tell them about being in the family way, putting the agency on hold, and building a factory to go commercial." "There is one more person who needs a heads up." "And who is that?" "Waldo Steiner." "Of course, I'll send him a telegram requesting him to come over for a special planning meeting."

After a fine steak supper at Grady's Diner, the Duo appeared at Mia's parents' house. Missus Myers was ecstatic with the news and started crying. She abruptly stopped tearing and said, "I am bored to death staying home alone, so I want to work in your shop, and help take care of the baby. I have a commercial college degree; and used to work in Ellsworth's bank before you came along. I will do your payroll, and assist the receptionist/ accountant to take care of the books, and I can watch my grandchild when you are on the floor. What do you say?" Palmer looked at Mia and said, "it's more than Ok with me if it's Ok with you." "Of course, what a fantastic idea." "Done, I'll be ready when the office is finished; and Palmer Bodine, my name is no longer Missus Myers, it is Helena." "Again, fine with me, but I prefer mom!" "That's even better."

On their way across the street to the Senior Bodines, Mia asked, "what do you think of moving your mom out of the emporium and into the factory?" "Once your mom hears the word baby, there is not a herd of buffaloes that will keep her out of that factory. So, be forthcoming, and ask her before she does." "Absolutely, I will."

"Hi mom and dad, we have some news for you, we are closing the agency, and building a factory to expand our business." Ella was surprised and said, "well what brought this on?" "Oh just a minor cog in the wheel of life—we are having you grandchild." The hollers, hugs, and hand shaking didn't appear to ever fade. It was Mia that said, "mom, would you consider moving into the factory. I have the perfect easy job for you working in dad's department. Dad would continue as shipping/receiving clerk and you would be the boxing clerk. All you need to do is write Waldo's address as well as ours, and label the contents of the box such as 'mining denim XL, waist 38 length 28." My mom will work in the office and . . . ." Ella could not hold back the tears, but managed to say a very clear yes. "The only hook is that when you need help, your helper will be dad—is that a problem?" "Well, after living with him 50 years, I can certainly get him to do whatever I want." "And if I need help with the baby, now I will have two moms to lean on."

After they got home and were in bed, Palmer said, "telling your mother will be like telling the telegraph." "No, I asked both our moms to hold up making this announcement for a while." "Hah-hah, that will last one week at the most."

*

The next morning after a light breakfast, the Duo headed for the town clerk's office. While walking, Mia asked, "what do we do if there is no place to build with water and gas" "We'll manage, Mia, we'll manage. Trust me!"

Walking inside, the clerk had a sign on the counter that read, 'Ike Harris, town clerk.' Palmer said, "hello Mister Harris, I heard the other day that the town council has developed a factory row, for small clean industry, that includes water and natural gas? Is that true?" Mia whispered, "you knew about this all along! I'll get you for that! All that worry for nothing."

"Yes sir, that is correct on all counts. Matter of fact, it went on the market two days ago. If interested, I'd be happy to show you the entire park layout." "We are." "Then follow me on a short walk."

Walking along the boardwalk, Mia added, "the idea of our home, our agency office, our emporium, and now our factory to be within walking distance is a plus for us, and most of our staff living in town." "Yes, but we'll have to include a pasture and barn for our many workers out of town on ranches."

"Here we are folks—Factory Row. We are standing on the graveled road entrance to the park. On the left-hand side are five ten acre lots, and the same on the right. The gravel road ends in a dead-end turnaround. All lots include a water and natural gas main line. The owner has to pay for an access line to their building. The lots sell for a pricey $300 but the yearly tax is only $100 for the next consecutive five years. Water is included for general use, is palatable, can be used in water closets, and horse watering troughs. The owner pays for individual gas usage as measured by meter. The lots being 10 acres allows you to build a concrete septic tank and a separate leech field. The city has no control over what you propose for an industry, as long as it is a clean industry, and you use natural gas for lights, heat, and steam energy to power industrial equipment. The council wants to avoid wood and coal burning plants."

The Duo both agreed that they could live with those restrictions. "May I ask what industry you would be bringing in the park" "A 12,500 square foot two story building to house a clothing manufacturing plant. We'll need a separate shed to contain the gas fired boiler and compressor to power the sewing machines. Other out buildings will include a barn and lean-to to hold saddled horses." "Perfect, that's just what the council is trying to attract—a quite clean shop to provide employment in our town. Are you interested in being our first residents?"

The Duo nodded in unison. Palmer answered, "we'll take lot #1 and #2 and #3 on the right-hand side. Our factory and power shed will be on lot #1, the barn will be on lot #2, and the horse pasture on #3. This will allow for future expansion and keep a buffer away from the #4 lot." "Yes, sir, if we return to my office, I'll write up a deed and contract for 3 lots. The cost will be $900 for the 3 lots plus $300 for the first year's taxes."

Walking home, Mia spoke, "wow, that is a perfect location and I'm so glad you bought three lots, it will give us freedom to expand, since we don't know what the future will bring." "Well dear, we have the land, but we now need someone to build the factory. What do you say we stop at the house, pick up you're your blueprints and floor plans, and go see Marc at Weber Construction?" "Great idea. If we can accomplish these two first steps, then we can move on and start building."

"Hello Marc, we have a construction project to offer you." "Those are pleasant words to my ears.

What do you need?" Palmer took over, "we need a 12,500 square foot factory with a second floor, indoor plumbing, a concrete septic tank and leech field, a separate shed for a power plant, a 30 horse barn with lean-to, and two eight-acre fenced in pastures. In addition, the plant has to be adapted to use gas lamps/heating stoves, and compressed air powered sewing machines." "Is this a joke?" As Mia opens her rolled up drawings, Marc adds, "I guess not, well, let's check this out."

Marc looked over every square inch on the layout and periodically made a list of items to discuss. "These are very clear layout plans that I can use during construction, along with my own blueprints. So, let's go over specifics:"

1. "Ground floor?" "Smooth concrete."
2. "First floor walls?" "You choose." "Ok, outside rough board and batten, 2X4 eight footers, inside tongue and groove fir at 45 degrees, walls filled with loose wool insulation filling.
3. "Second floor walls?" "Again, you choose. But we are not planning to use it yet." "Ok, same 2X4 eight footers but not finished

interior walls except wall ventilation panels with roof vents."

4. "First floor ceiling and second floor flooring?" "You choose." "This is where we use this new plywood—which are 1/8-inch wood layers glued together. The ceiling will use a half inch and the 2nd floor will be ¾ inch, with a good panel on one side. We'll also insulate this floor separation with loose wool filling—for heat insulation and 2nd floor quietness."

5. "Roof support and sheathing?" "Galvanized steel roof with trusses." Excellent choices for water proofing and structural integrity—this is not a place for ridge pole/rafter roofing.

6. "Second floor ceiling?" "Not finished till we use it."

"Any additional specifics" "Yes, we'll need some gutters in the concrete to accommodate air and water lines. Also who installs air lines, gas lines and sets up a power plant." "We will make the concrete gutters and we'll set up your water closets and sewage lines to the concrete tank and leech field. We do not touch gas lines, gas heaters, setting up a compressed air system and hooking them to each machine. You need your own mechanical engineer to do all that. We'll work with this individual to guarantee a finished system."

"Any recommendations for such an individual?" "Yes, there is an independent engineer that hires out for these projects. He does perfect work and is easy to work with, his name is Hollis Franklin on Wichita Avenue in town." "Great, I'll see him today. When can you start this project?" "Tomorrow morning with my 10-year-round carpenters and 10 extra project men that I've used before."

"Great, let's get to it. How much will this cost us?" "I have no clue. I've never undertaken such a large project. I can tell you that building a private 1,000 square foot house costs 60 cents a foot or $600 for a three- bedroom house. Now this commercial construction could cost $1 a foot or more. So, to get started, give me a deposit and we'll then go with the three standards—cost of materials, labor, and profit as the construction moves along and we'll try to keep ahead of expenses with regular payments from you."

Mia started writing a bank draft and handed it to Marc, "Mia, this is a $12,500 draft, are you sure?" "Absolutely, let's get started. We'll put the four factory corner posts on Factory Row Lot #1 so you can start building your concrete floor." Palmer added, "and I'll go talk with this engineer today."

After placing the four corner posts, they walked to Wichita Avenue only to find the office closed for the day. Mia left a note in the door requesting a meeting in their home, any evening, if busy during the day.

After a great home cooked meal, the Duo was talking in their parlor when they heard a knock at the front door. Mia answered the door to find a pleasant man in his late forties standing in the doorway. "Sorry to disturb you, but I believe you left this note on my office door." "Ah, Mister Franklin, please do come in and have a seat. This is my husband Palmer." After the usual pleasantries, Palmer started, "the long story is that we start building a clothing manufacturing factory on Factory Row and we need a certified engineer to lay out gas lines to lamps and heaters as well as build a gas fired boiler to activate an air compressor to power some 50 sewing machines and possibly triple that in the future." Mia added, "plus we have 24 sewing machines that need to be overhauled and rebuilt. Plus a total of 50-100 machines that need monthly maintenance."

"Well, I am certified by the state to do such installations and I'm available to jump right in. For references I can give you a dozen of local customers........." "Not necessary, Marc Weber says he would enjoy working with you again, and that's all we'll need. What pay would you need for this work?" "If I may be honest, work has been rather scarce of late. My wife and I were thinking of moving to Albuquerque, but were dissuaded by the city council when they developed Factory Row. So, I need the work and I'll take whatever you offer me!"

"Well we are willing to pay your going rate." "Well my best job involved such work as establishing safe gas systems and setting up gas fired power plants—and that job paid me 40 cents an hour—but I haven't seen that hourly rate for several years." "Very good, we'll be glad to pay you $5 a day, but anything over 40 hours is time and a half—and we know that during construction, prolonged hours are common. Plus we also provide family medical and worker accident insurance."

"Oh, I forgot, the state of New Mexico requires me to maintain a liability insurance which I am current in dues." As they were talking, Mia was writing away, and suddenly hands Hollis a bank voucher for $300. "What is this for Ma'am?" "First of all, in the future we are Mia and Palmer as you are Hollis. Secondly, this is a bonus for signing on with us. We want all our workers to be free of encumbrances such as old credit accounts or overdue bills that need to be cleaned up. Welcome aboard and see you at the plant. You'll be needed tomorrow to lay out channels for air, water, and gas lines in the concrete. Actually, you'll be on the ground floor of a new family enterprise—Bodine Manufacturing."

***

CHAPTER 6

A Transitional Time

The next morning the Duo was notified that Waldo was in town. After his meeting with the staff at the emporium, Waldo showed up at the Bodine home for a business meeting. "To my pleasant surprise, Ella told me she was moving to the production portion, so, what is going on, Ella will be a great loss in the emporium." Mia started, "we'll replace her, but for now Ella wants to join our family in our new venture. We are building a factory, doubling our stitchers, and doubling our production."

"Whoa, I thought this day would never arrive. Well, here is my bank draft for $10,000 as I promised." "And what do you want for this deposit?" "A guarantee that I will be the only distributor of your product for the next two years." "Really, but are you aware that we are adding new products such as: men and women denim vests, shirts, slim jeans, and men's denim overalls and insulated mining pant. Later we'll add summer and winter coats—with or without a 'rear slit' for riding."

"Oh boy, this is a completely new ball game. I have the salesmen staff that will start advertising your new products. It is now time to expand beyond New Mexico and Colorado. We'll start in neighboring larger communities to include Arizona, Nevada, Utah, Kansas, and Texas. First, we'll start on cities closest to the New Mexico/Colorado borders, and we'll expand outward as the market allows. Will you agree to a year as your sole distributor so I can justify my expansion costs?"

"Do you really think you can handle our proposed 1,600 pieces a week." "Heck, I'm now handling 800 pieces a week, and my retailers are asking for more—I know we can handle that volume." "Ok, then as long as you can process all our products, then you will have exclusive distribution rights. If we start building a surplus, then you can still have all you want, but we'll be looking for a second distributor."

"So, as long as I take your products, pay for them, I can store them in my Deming warehouse and you won't have a surplus, heh?" "Correct." "So, what are you going to do with that $10,000 draft." "This will go into an escrow account; in case you fail to make your payments to us. Once this reserve is used up, our contractual agreement is null and void." "Agree." Palmer finally spoke, "we had our lawyer draw up this contract and if you care to sign it, we'll get my mother-in-law next door to witness our signatures." "Great, let's do it!"

*

That afternoon, Mia started looking for new employees. Agnes and Alice were already looking for some +-30 new stitchers as well as planning a new employee introductory class to commercial denim sewing. It was Mia's job to find all the other accessory workers to include:

- Designer.
- Purchasing/inventory agent.
- Three more power cutters.
- A second expediter (man).
- Boxing agent (Ella).
- Shipping and receiving agent (Ralph).
- Mia's secretary.
- Accounting and payroll (Helena).

- Boiler supervisor (man).
- Wrangler for barn (man).
- Equipment maintenance (part time engineer).

Palmer was looking at her list and asked, "how are you going to find all these people?" "Advertise in the local newspaper." "I see, well tell me about some of these people. What's this about a designer?" "We are adding so many new lines, that we need new ideas. Alice and Agnes are too busy with production and we cannot keep up with competition without our own designer on board."

"What's the job function of a purchasing/inventory agent?" "We need many things other than many rolls of denim. We also cannot function without many items to include: thread, needles, rivets, brass and ceramic buttons, sewing machine spare parts and oil, and of course countless cardboard boxes just to name a few. Of course, it's not just a matter of ordering these items, it's also a matter of knowing when the supplies are going down before they run out."

"I see, now what is an expediter?" "We have two main corridors on my floor plans. In each, a man brings denim to station one's left box, then moves each station's finished product, out of the right box, onto the next station left hand box and so on. The sixth station makes the final piece that is then loaded onto his wagon, which is then brought to the boxing station in the rear next to shipping and receiving. Plus, don't forget that he has to handle two lines that lie to his right and left down the corridor. This is a high energy job that requires healthy men."

"Ok, lastly, what are accessory stitchers. "We presently have two of those working home. Agnes and Alice want five that work in the shop. These gals need to handle power cutters and sewing machines. They make parts that are added to pieces such as inside and outside pockets, belt loops, knee patches, hammer loops and the like. These workers use up all the leftover pieces from the pattern cutters, so we don't waste any denim."

"I have to admit, you are organized, and you know your business. Why don't you get your ad ready, we'll drop it off and then go see how the concrete floor is coming along." "Fine, plus I have my order ready for 30 new sewing machines, a couple more power cutters and brass button/rivet installers. I've already paid for this with a bank transfer, so we are good to go. Plus, we can go to the bank and deposit Waldo's draft."

After making all three deliveries, Palmer suggested they get a light lunch, of soup and sandwich at Grady's Diner, before they go to the construction site—"remember Doc Ross said not to skip meals because our baby is hungry even if you're not!" "Right, lead on McDuff!"

Stepping in Grady's, the Duo saw Waldo sitting at a table reading the local paper. "How come you're still here?" "The next train doesn't leave for another hour. So, after our meeting, I went to your construction site. Marc Weber has 20 men working—that is quite a scene. Of special note, watch a man by the name of Franklin. He appears to be the clerk of the works and is working closely with Marc. That man is giving you 110% and is clearly on the ball, as well as knowing what he's doing."

"Really, we just hired him yesterday as our resident mechanical engineer." "Other than that, I forgot to mention two things at our meeting. First, when I said we will be expanding to nearby states, I meant to nearby cities on the railroad lines. I only ship your product by covered boxcars and I do not use open freight wagons where your clothing will be exposed to rain and dust."

"The second thing is your prices. I honestly think it is time to increase your mining pants by 10-15% before you add insulated pants. In addition, all new products have to be carefully priced to match competitive products. My salesmen drummers will be able to help with competitive prices as they see these prices at all retail locations. The key is to keep your quality products priced below the inferior products—a ploy that no retailer can disregard."

"I see, but if we raise our current prices, that means that you have to also add your 15% on top of our new higher prices?" "Of course, that the way business is done, and don't forget, the local retailer also adds his 5-10% over my prices." Mia added, "but why, we are already making more money than we deserve."

"For two reasons. First, the only reason to be in business is to make money—irrelevant whether you need the profit to survive. Secondly, you have to pay for your new factory!" There was a pause when Palmer added, "thanks for your advice, it is very sound, and we'll try to listen to you more carefully in the future." Mia added, "actually, during the construction, would you consider coming over twice a week for two weeks, and check out the changes, you might pick up some problem we had missed."

"Why I'd be happy to, see you in three days when the shell will be up and before the floor partitions go in. For now let's order, I don't want to miss my train."

During their meal, Mia asked, "I'm curious why you charge 15% for your marketing and distribution services?" "I charge 8% as my profit which is the trade standard but also covers the cost of maintaining my staffed office and warehouse in Deming. The 7% covers railroad shipping charges and salaries for my two, but soon to be, five drummer/salesmen, who will be pushing your new products. If expenses go over the 7%, then the extra expenses are taken out of my 8% profit. Yet, fear not, your new products will make both of us rich."

After a worthwhile dinner with Waldo, the Duo walked over to Factory Row #1. On arrival, it was stunning to see 20 carpenters busy at work, and half of the concrete floor finished. Marc came over, "thank God, Hollis was already here waiting for us. We arrived before dawn with gravel, cement, water tank, and lumber. Hollis looked at my final blueprint and immediately found a problem."

"I had forgotten to add a gutter for three lines— water, gas, compressed air, and a side smaller gutter for the compressed air to each sewing machine. So, once the coal fired steam plant was started, we've been cutting a 2X6 with sides cut at 30 degrees inward—making the top part wider than the bottom part. This allows placing them in concrete but easily pull out once the concrete sets."

The Duo looked around. They had three cement mixers rotating continuously under the steam power plant and six men handling the wheelbarrows. Marc added, "the concrete is the same from mixer to mixer—24 shovels of gravel, three jugs of water and five dispensers of cement. As you can see, every man has a job. We have three men feeding the cement mixers, three men on leveling and spreading, one on smoothing, several digging out an edge trench so we can make the edges six inches thicker in concrete to support the wall, several men making 6 inch walls to hold the concrete pad, several men to continue hauling gravel, cement, and water to the site from my warehouse, and of course Hollis laying down the large gutter wedged timbers including the smaller wedged timbers to the individual sewing machines."

"Wow, I can't believe you're half done." "Heck, we'll be done by dusk tonight and it will include the 15x25 ft. pad for your power plant. Tomorrow, all we do on the building is to remove the gutter wedges, starting with the edge ones in the morning, and the centrally located ones in the afternoon— done by my skinny carpenters, heh?" "So, what will the other 18 men do all day?" "Haul lumber, build a truss jig, and build 53 foot wide trusses. With a truss every four feet, we'll need 62 plus two ends—guess we'll be busy, heh?" Mia asked, "don't you mean 50- foot trusses?" "No, 53 feet, you need an 18-inch overhang over the walls."

"What do you do with all the wedges you made?" "After cleaning them off, that's what we'll use to make your 15X25 ft. power plant shed."

Anything else we need to discuss before our daily visit tomorrow?" "Yes, Hollis asked me if we were installing a service elevator like the one in the emporium. He suggested, that if you weren't planning to use the old one, that he could convert it to compressed air operation, so he has laid out a compressed air gutter to where the elevator would be located." "Fantastic idea, and we'll move it after the shop is moved to the factory. Anything else?" "I've added a stairway to the second floor, since I suspect you'll use the second floor for storage, especially with the stairs and elevator." "Great idea, see you tomorrow and express our thanks to Hollis."

*

That evening while sitting in their parlor, Palmer asked, "this morning you told Waldo that the factory would produce 1,600 pieces a week, can you review where that figure came from?" "Sure, when we started with six stitchers, they could put out 170 pieces a week and generated a weekly profit of $160. Do you remember cyphering out the numbers?" "Yes." "Well continue, after we doubled the stitchers to 12, we generated 400 pieces a week at a profit of $400 a week. Then we expanded the shop and doubled the number of stitchers to 24, yielding 800 pieces and a profit of $800 a week." "I see, now 48 stitchers would likely produce 1,600 pieces and a profit of $1,600 a week—but that's a profit of $83,000 a year." "Not if we increase our prices, heh?" "Wow, I'm impressed, heck we'll pay for that factory in one year and still make a profit—at-a-boy, lady!"

"On a different subject, can you again go over what each worker does on the six stations to make a pair of mining pants?" "Sure, but keep in mind that it varies according to each worker's needs; and the process starts after the patterns have been cut out. The first three stations utilize less experienced stitchers, whereas the last three stations require more experienced workers:

Station 1. Sew two rear parts from beltline to crotch.

Station 2. Sew two front parts from beltline to crotch.

Station 3. Sew both front legs to rear legs—both on the outside and inside seam.

Station 4. Make a doubly lined belt backing, install the belt loops and hammer loops, and build the pants cuff to varying leg lengths.

Station 5. Sew premade inside front pockets, outside rear pockets, the knee patches and build the fly.

Station 6. This station requires special power machines to install brass buttons—belt button, fly buttons, and suspender buttons. It also includes installing rivets to the entrance sides of all four pockets, and attaching the leather company logo that includes the size and dimensions of the piece."

"Well that's it for me for now, do you have any questions?" "Yes, I also have two questions. First, what is natural gas." "Natural gas is a gas that was formed millions of years ago. It is a fossil fuel usually located in fields over oil lakes. Since we have oil fields nearby, it is not surprising that there are natural gas fields. If it is not used up, it has to be burned off and that's a waste. The local oil company has piped this gas to a central plant, and then piped it to town."

"The composition of the gas is 85% methane with minor gases of butane, propane, ethane, and pentane. The gas is odorless, but the central plant adds a substance that smells like rotten eggs that will indicate a leak in the line. Without the smelling of rotten eggs, a leak would lead to symptoms of headache, fatigue, dizziness and nausea." "I thought natural gas can kill you?" "Well, if the gas replaces all the air in a plant, then everyone will suffocate, but that's in theory and not realistic." "Isn't it explosive?" "Yes, but again who is going to light a match if the plant air has been replaced with methane. Although, we'll have 'no smoking' & 'no match lighting' signs in the factory. The key to natural gas safety is in the proper installation of gas lines to our lamps and heaters with shutoff valves to every unit. I will be speaking to Hollis about that."

"Good answer, now I'm not so leery about modernizing to gas. My last question is, what are we going to do with the shop once we move out?" "Wow, that's the most important question of the day. To give you a quick answer—apartments. We are going to convert the entire 10,000 square feet into four 1,000 sq. ft. family apartments and twelve small 500 sq. ft. units for single people. But most important of all, we are renting these units to our workers." "Why, our present workers are all locals." "I may be wrong dear, but I do not think that Alice and Agnes are going to find another local 24 experienced home seamstresses. If that's the case, we'll need to advertise in the Deming newspapers, and that will mean people moving into town—here come our rentals to facilitate the move." "Let me kiss you, you deserve it for such planning. What do you say we take a walk; Alice only lives a block from here. We'll find out how the interviews are going?" "Sure, let's go."

"Come in, such a pleasure to see you." Alice did a double take and exclaimed, "Mia, you're pregnant?" 'Yes, I guess my bump is beginning to show." After the congratulatory hug, the Trio sat down. "We came to see how the new interviews were coming along." "We have hired ten very experienced ladies who are widows, homesteader's wives or spinsters in the 40 to 55 age group. There are many young women and newlyweds that have no experience, but we don't feel these are the workers to start in a factory. I'm afraid we're going to have to go out of town, we just don't have the time to teach a sewing course to newbies; we have enough just to show the experienced people how the commercial sewing machines work, and now how to use a compressed air activated machine."

"I agree, I'll place the ad in the Deming Times, and arrange for a meeting place in Waldo's warehouse for interviews. Palmer and I will take care of these interviews. You have enough to starting insulated mining pants, and preparing an introductory course on commercial machines. We'll report to you when we have another 15-20 workers— yes, we're going to get you a half dozen extra workers to fill in where needed or to replace sick workers."

*

The next day, after placing the Deming ad, Mia started her interviews for new accessory workers— designer, purchasing agent and personal secretary. Palmer was meeting with potential workers for the boiler supervisor and wrangler positions. Mia's first interview was for the designer position.

Mia met her first applicant, "I see by your application that you are Josie Robinson from Albuquerque. What do you have for a background, training, experience, and why do you wish to leave the big city?"

"I was born in Denver 22 years ago. My parents died from the fever when I was a baby. My spinster aunt raised me and sent me to a two-year college to study art and clothing design. After graduation, I went to work at Corduci's Design. For two years as the newbie, my ideas were passed over as being too modern. I quickly realized that it would take ten years to gain enough seniority to put my ideas through. I am ready and want to work independently. So, an old college friend, who lives in your town, saw your ad, and notified me. In addition, she told me that a rumor also suggested that you were planning to add some new clothing lines—so here I am."

"Perfect, do you have any samples of your work?" "Yes I do. Here are samples of overalls, slim jeans, vests, summer jackets, and winter coats—all in denim. Mia looked at each sample in fine detail and finally said, "these are very nice and useful designs. How would you like to move to town and work for me?" "Ma'am, I would be so happy to." "Before you decide, tell me what your present salary is?" "I presently make $2 a day and can get by because I live at home." "That's not a living wage in town. Here is my offer:

- I will pay you $4.50 a day. We will have small size one-bedroom apartments at $25 a month to include water, heat and a water closet.
- Benefits include medical insurance, and maternity benefits of your full salary for 4 weeks.
- The work week is five days a week, eight hours a day.
- Beyond designing and making your own patterns, you may be asked to help cutting out the denim using a power cutter which we'll show you how to operate. Our employees will help those who need help, and in your case, my mother-in-law is the boxing agent, and you may have to help her along.
- If you are offered overtime, we will pay time and a half.
- You will likely have weekends off and this will give you time to socialize. You are no booglin, and will likely meet some young man. Were you to marry and become

pregnant, we hope you will work thru your pregnancy as long as you are capable, and your doctor agrees.

- All your designs have to be approved by me and my two supervisors—but we'll be happy to work with you to get the proper design for our line."

"Now, do you have any questions?" 'Yes, what is a booglin?"

"Short, fat, and ugly!" "Oh, I see. When can I start?" "My new factory won't be ready for three weeks. The apartment won't be ready for another five weeks, since we are converting our old shop into furnished apartments. I would like you to start working in my old shop and start working on designs and cutting patterns. We will put you up, free of charge, in a boarding house till your apartment is ready." "Great, I'll be here in three days." "Oh, I forgot, my name is Mia, not Ma'am. My husband's name is Palmer as well. To make your move, and as a bonus for signing on, here is a voucher for $100 to cover train fees, storage of your stuff, make a wardrobe update if needed, and other incidentals. Come see me when you arrive, and I'll introduce you to the staff and set you up in

Miss Waterford's Boarding House for ladies. And by the way, don't change those vest designs, they are perfect. Welcome aboard!"

*

Her next interview was for the expediter position. "Hello, Sir. What is your name, how old are you and what is your work history?" "My name is Nigel Watson, I'm 55 years old, and I've been working in a mercantile for 20 years. When my boss sold out, I was forced to retire. That was six months ago, and I'm bored to death. I need to work for my sanity. I'm looking to work five days a week. Evenings and weekends off is enough for my hobbies, home repairs, and time with my wife."

"Ok, well here is the job. Eight hours a day and five days a week. Your job is to service two rows of stitchers. You bring the cut patterns to the first stitcher, keep moving each stitcher's finished product to the next stitcher. When the sixth stitcher is done, you load the finished piece onto your wagon, and bring the load to the boxing agent. Basically, stitchers sew and it's up to you to keep them in pieces without waiting. It is not heavy work, but you have to move about at a good clip."

"Heck, I can do this work. I am a punctual worker, have a strong work ethic, and will give you my best." "Great, what do you want for a salary and what were you making before your forced retirement?" 'I was making $15 a week, but I'll take whatever you offer me—I really want this job." "The other expediter, Wally Crimshaw, has been with us for over a year and he now makes $22 a week. I will start you at $20 but if you stay with us for six months; I'll match Wally's salary. If you work overtime, it's time and a half." "Ma'am, I suspect the expediter will end up prepping for the next day, and I'll gladly do this at no charge—I consider this part of the job."

"Fine, let's have you start next week at the Emporium shop, and we'll have Wally show you the ropes. And by the way, you're Nigel, I'm Mia and my husband is Palmer. Here is a $100 bonus for signing on—pay off creditors and buy a new wardrobe. Welcome aboard!"

Her last interview was for the secretarial position. After the usual introductions, the applicant started. "My name is Gloria Balinger. I am a local girl with a two-year business degree at an Albuquerque college. I am 24 years old, married four years to a town barber, and no kids yet. During the past four years, I have been the private secretary to the president of the National Bank. My boss is retiring in a month, and the parent bank is sending in a new president with his own male secretary. So, I'm out of a job. We live in town, and I'd like to find work within walking distance. I have a reference from my boss at the bank."

Mia read the reference and was pleased to find such high recommendations. "Very nice Gloria. This job requires a few skills such as typing, writing business letters, accounting, payroll, reconciling bank books, filing, preparing invoices and bills, writing shorthand, and get along with your helper— my mother, Helena Myers." Gloria cracks up and adds, "yes, I do all those jobs every day and I know Missus Myers. I don't see any problems. I'm easy to get along with."

"You're hired. The factory won't be ready till three, or at worse, four weeks." "That's Ok, I'll wait to give my two weeks' notice." "What salary do you want?" "I presently make $20 a week if that is Ok?" "I'll give you $25 a week, plus this $100 bonus for signing on—pay off creditors. We also include medical insurance and a maternity benefit of four weeks full pay. We hope you will work during your pregnancy if you are capable and your doctor approves. Welcome aboard."

Palmer joined Mia for a light noon dinner. "How did your interviews go?" "Great, hired all three of my applicants. How did yours go?" "Hired both of my applicants. Kip Turner will be our boiler supervisor. He has experience working with boilers and compressed air in underground mines. He really wants a 'top of the earth' job. He's a single young man, pleasant and polite. I got good vibes when I told him he would be working with Hollis. He'll make a fine worker." "Great, how about the wrangler?"

"Mel Johnson is a 60-year-old livery worker, who wants to slow down and work regular hours and days. I told him the job involved unsaddling the workers saddled horse when they arrive, and saddling them at closing time. In-between, he can feed horses that need extra nutrition, watch the herd in the pasture, repair broken saddles, or even reshod those that need it, keep the barn clean, order hay and grain, or take a nap. The man was happy to take the job. His easy and pleasant nature will work well with the ladies. In case overtime was needed, he was fine with it."

"That sounds good. How much are you paying them?" $25 for the boiler supervisor and $20 for the wrangler—per week."

After their light lunch. Mia laid down for a short nap. Palmer took a quick walk to Elmer's mercantile. "Say Elmer, my mine manager may have been here to order some books on an alternative mining method!" "Why yes, he ordered five and I ordered an extra one, just in case!" "May I see it." Elmer hands him the book, the title was, "Everything you need to know about Open Pit Mining for Copper." "Oh really, may I buy it?" "Of course, who else would be interested in such a wild venture—ha-ha-ha?" "Remember, hush is the word."

With Mia still napping, Palmer started reading. In an hour's time, it was clear that this mining method needed further investigation. Hiding the book, he planned to finish reading it when Mia would introduce the new designer to her two floor managers and sewing staff.

Their daily site visits were always revealing. Today the walls were going up. Marc came to greet them, "we have half the walls up and should have them all up by the end of day. We are bracing them with posts in the sand, and adding a few second-floor studs to secure them. Tonight, before we leave, we will temporarily X, with 2X4's, the four corners and a few sections midway down the long side walls. Tomorrow, half my men will start adding 'board and batten' to the outside walls, as the other half will be finishing the second-floor studs. After that we'll be adding your first- floor ceiling using the new plywood. Once completed, poured in wool insulation will follow, and finally the second-floor flooring with the thicker plywood for weight bearing. This will give us a work area to build the second-floor wall framing." "What is Hollis doing outside?"

"He's working with three of my men laying a water and gas line from the mainlines to your power shed. This reminds me, to avoid driving wagons over these lines, you will need two entrance ways. One to the rear for shipping and receiving, and one to the front for anyone else, including workers being dropped off or continuing to your barn." "That makes sense, now what is going on the other side of the factory?"

"I have subcontracted the building of a concrete 1,000-gallon tank and pipes to your building and to the leach field—this includes a steel rain bonnet. They do everything, we'll only help them lift and drop the prefabricated framing, for the concrete walls, into the hole."

"One last thing, I see a center beam and posts. Are these the only posts on the first floor?" "Yes, every 20 feet we place a 6X6 inch posts that supports a 6X8 top beam. These posts and beams are spliced together 2X6's for extra strength, and will support the double 25-foot spliced 2X6 ceiling/floor studs. This design will give you two 25-foot wide swath of open work area. Likewise, the second floor will also have the same design of posts and beam system to support the trusses which are 26.5 feet long and will sit on the center beam and be spliced together—53-foot trusses would have been unmanageable, especially on the second floor!"

Mia had been letting Palmer ask the questions. Yet, she liked what she saw. Finally, she asked Marc, "we have scheduled, starting tomorrow, two days of business in Deming. Where will you be after two days?" "We should be putting up trusses, if not close to done." Palmer agreed, "then this is a perfect time to take care of that issue. If sudden plans need to change, then make the decision and move on. See you in two or three days."

***

CHAPTER 7

Setting up Operations

The train ride to Deming lasted 90 minutes. Upon arrival, the Duo took a room at the Deming Silver Queen and went to a local diner for a noon meal. Waldo had sent a message at the hotel that things were ready for interviews at 1:30 PM. After a light lunch, the Duo made their way to Waldo's office and warehouse.

"Hello Waldo, how are things shaping up. Do we have any applicants?" "I had to sit them down in the warehouse to wait for their individual interviews, which you can hold in my private office. There are fifty ladies out there for 20 positions. How are you going to weed out the few special workers you need. "Simple, watch me work the crowd." "Let me warn you, I've heard the small talk, these gals are expecting big bucks for their work."

Mia stepped in the warehouse and said, "thank you so much for coming today. We are looking for stitchers to work in our clothing factory. I will now go over job requirements, benefits, and a chance for you to ask question. At any point, if you are not happy with my conditions of employment, please feel free to walk out, for these conditions are not negotiable. To start, this job is in Silver City and we require you to live in town in one of two ways. You move into town or you arrive Sunday evening and you leave Friday evening. Either way, you need lodging in town so you can walk to work. (four ladies got up and walked out). We are hiring women, either widows, spinsters, or wives but with five years' experience making clothing for yourselves or others. (three ladies got up). This is an 8-5 job, five days a week, with 45 minutes for lunch and two 15-minute breaks. (two more ladies left). You must work with a compressed air powered commercial machine." (three more ladies bit the dust). Your workstation and sewing machine is your working location—there is no rotating to another station for a different job. (another three ladies walked out). We'll hire Indians, Mexicans, Negroes and Whites. (two ladies got up in a huff).

"Now for benefits. The job pays \$4 a day. (six ladies left). We provide apartments: 1-bedroom 500 sq. ft. for \$25 a month or 750 sq. ft. for \$35 a month. 2-bedroom 1000 sq. ft for \$45 a month. That includes water, water closet, gas lamps, heat, and fully furnished. (no one left for the first time). We include medical insurance and maternity benefit of four full weeks' pay after the birth—including guarantee that your job is secure when you return. (no one left). Overtime is voluntary and pays time and a half. (no one left).

"Now are there any questions?" What is your work dress code? Trousers, dresses or riding skirts—that includes jeans. Shirts or blouses with short sleeves for safety reasons." "Do you allow working when pregnant. Of course. If you are healthy, capable, and your doctor agrees; you may work up to your delivery." (one lady left) "Do you pay for sick days?" "Never have but will likely add this as a benefit in due time."

Palmer gave Mia a signal then whispered, "there is only 26 left!" "Thank you ladies; we will now conduct individual interviews and review your applications." The first interview was a single lady age 51. "I have thirty years' experience working for a seamstress in Colorado Springs. I have a recommendation from my old boss. I moved to Deming to care for my dying father, and I cannot survive on $3 a day working for Miss Daisy's shop, when my rent is $40 a month and no overtime. I know no one in Deming, owe no one, so moving to your town is acceptable especially with a rent of $25." Mia looked at her letter of recommendation and read words like, fast and efficient stitcher, pleasant and easy to work with, a reliable employee. Mia looked up and said, "you're hired. We will notify you when it is time to move. Until your apartment is ready, we'll house you in a boarding house at no charge. Here is a bank draft for $100 as a bonus for signing on. Please use it to pay your moving costs and for a wardrobe upgrade if needed. Welcome aboard."

The next applicant was an enlightenment. A young woman was moving to town because of her husband's work. I have been working making clothing for private customers and I believe I'm capable of handling my own station. We would like your 2-bedroom apartment, since I hope to raise a family. Eventually we would buy a house in town." "What does your husband do and where will he be working?" "Oh my, you don't know?" "No." "Stan is a dynamite expert and has been hired by

Mister Elliot to work in your gold mine." Palmer's eyebrows arched up in total surprise as he added, "wow, that's almost an embarrassing development. I'm sure there's going to be a heck of a story behind this." Mia smiled and said, "more than happy to hire you. Here is your $100 bank draft as a bonus to sign on. Use it to pay for moving expenses and a wardrobe upgrade if needed. Welcome aboard."

The next applicant was a 50-year old spinster by the name of Miss Daisy. "I have been running a tight shop with four employees. I am tired of fighting with lazy employees. $4 a day is not enough, I would prefer $5 instead. I need my hot tea during the break and 15 minutes is not enough. I also want a retirement package..........." "Whoa, I thought you accepted the job requirements. Why are you here?" "Well, I assumed you needed someone to supervise and keep these lazy workers on the assigned quotas. That's a necessary position if you want to be successful with your factory, my dear!" "Well Madam your services are not needed. Thank you for coming in and I'm not 'your dear.'" "What, you are dismissing me, how dare you?" "Well it is rather simple, ma'am. You are bossy, demeaning, a snob, and I want nothing to do with you. So get the hell out of here before I kick your ass, you hypocritical shrew."

After Mia cooled off, Palmer called the next applicant. I'm a 48- year old single woman and I've been working for Miss Daisy for five years, but I can't work for her anymore." "You're hired, wait right here." Mia stepped out of the office and said, "any of you ladies work for Miss Daisy?" Two hands went up as Mia said, "you're both hired, wait here for your personal interviews." After the three were given their bonus and given final instructions, Mia needed a break.

"It appears we have accepted six, one left from the waiting area and we have 17 to go. Are you Ok to continue, or do you want me to take some myself? "No, I'm fine. Let the next one in, please."

"Hello, I'm a 53-year old widow. My husband died from old gunshot wounds he suffered as a stagecoach jeju. For three years he received a $40 a month disability. When the stagecoach line closed, because of the railroad, his disability stopped. That was two years ago, and we've been living on my income sewing clothing for customers. My husband died six months ago, and I'm in debt. This job means a lot for my survival." "At your age, do you think you can handle the rigors of factory life?"

"Ma'am, I'm now working 10 hours a day, seven days a week, and still cannot pay my bills. I am healthy and not afraid to work." "How much do you owe creditors?" "$91 to the local mercantile, $80 to my landlord, and $56 to the doctor who took care of my husband. But with this job, they will know that I'll pay them back in full."

"I will be honored to have you as my employee. You're hired. Here is your $100 bonus for signing up. Now, we have a Benefactor Fund that helps people like you. Here is a bank draft for $500 for you to do as you wish. Pay your bills, buy a new wardrobe, pay for moving or whatever you need. Come to work without any worries or encumbrances. And do not mention this gift to anyone." After all the business details were finished, Mia added, "welcome aboard."

The remaining interviews were very similar. A single woman, young and old, unable to find work, cannot survive on waitress work, happy to leave Deming, want a better life with more income, want the security of a regular job with a regular paycheck, and looking forward to the camaraderie of coworkers. Mia used the Benefactor Fund five more times when there were creditors to be paid. All in all, Mia was pleased in the moral character and work ethic of these new workers. Most important of all, Mia knew these ladies would mix well with her present workers.

After supper in the hotel restaurant, the Duo walked the major commercial district doing some window shopping. Seeing a furniture store, they walked in and went straight to the nursery section. The Duo chose a crib, dressers, changing table, and accessories for their nursery. Mia also chose a crib, changing table, and accessories for her office. Afterwards, they went to a garment store for children and bought all the necessary clothes for a baby and up to six months of age—as starters.

Returning to their hotel, both of them were too tired to perform their domestic duties. Palmer jokingly promised a double duty come morning. After a restful night, both were eager to resume love making. After an overwhelming first round, Mia saw to it that a second round would follow. With her hand on the subject matter, things went into full attention. Without prolonging the glow period, both participants were then rushing to get to the breakfast table before the restaurant closed—and a replenishing breakfast was enjoyed by all.

*

Taking the noon train to home was a comfortable 50-mile trek. Mia took a nap, and Palmer read more of his book. Arriving home, the Duo changed into casual clothes and headed for the work site. Arriving, it was clear that the trusses were all installed, the end pieces built, and men were adding cross pieces to secure the trusses as well as provide a backing for the steel roof. Marc saw the onlookers and came to talk to them.

"Welcome back, as you can see, things are going well. We'll have the trusses secured by the end of the day. Tomorrow we put up the steel and secure the building against rain." Mia stepped inside and was staring at the finished wall of tongue and groove slanted at 45 degrees, and meeting every 8 feet. "Don't that look classy—I like it. How come you started the finish work inside?" "Because Hollis is ready to lay pipe and wants the walls finished before he starts—he doesn't want workers stepping over his pipes or sawdust entering the pipes. But that's Ok, because the finish carpenters don't do well working on roofs."

"So what is on schedule for tomorrow?" "As I said, the steel roof and the inside wall. I'm also trying to find a plumber to help him thread and cut pipe. I don't have much hope since my own plumber is out sick." "Hey, I can help him, if he shows me how to do it." "Why not, let's go see him."

After a long discussion, Palmer finally summarized the situation. "If you spend the time to show me, I can learn how to do it correctly. I am a meticulous person and want to do things the right way. If I don't work out, you can fire me, heh?" "You have a deal. Can you start now?" "I certainly can."

Two hours later, Palmer was putting out perfect threads to a standard depth. After threading the pipe, he placed a finishing knife thru the threads, then a triangular grinding stone in the inlet and steel brushed the dust and steel chips. Hollis looked at the last three pieces he had done and said, "that is truly fine work, I could not have done any better. You're hired, boss. Be here at 8AM sharp and plan to work till 5PM."

That night, Mia reminded Palmer that she had a doctor's appointment in the morning and would be introducing Josie Robinson to the workers as the new clothing designer. Palmer was up early, made a stack of flap jacks and coffee. Got Mia to eat her share, and took off with a bag lunch of cold roast beef on fresh bread.

Hollis was already on the job measuring the gutters. "Good morning Palmer. Today we lay pipe from the intake line to the drinking fountain and the water closets. Then we'll connect the eight women's water closets, the several sinks, and the men's water closet and urinal. Once that is done the carpenters might be done the inside walls so we can tackle the compressed airlines, and finally the gas lines. All three lines will be using these galvanized pipes of varying sizes. My job is to measure, cut, and add fittings. Your job is to make perfect threads like you did yesterday." "And whose fault is it if there is a leak?" "If the thread is good, then it's likely caused by a defective fitting that I failed to detect."

The day moved along well when using 12-foot sections with unions till Hollis got to the water closets. There, many measurements were needed to reach the sinks and the overhead tanks for all of eight toilets. It was 8PM when the water pipes and bathroom plumbing was done. As Palmer was leaving, Hollis hollered out, "that was great work you did today, I know you're beat, but look on the bright side—you just made three hours of overtime!" "Funny, ha—ha."

After a late supper, Palmer fell asleep waiting for dessert. Instead of sitting in the parlor after supper, Mia escorted her limp husband to bed—while undressing him, she verified that his pickle wasn't going to do any hiding tonight.

The next day was piping for compressed air. That meant 8-foot sections with a T-fitting and another section to get to the sewing machines. They had a total of four such lines and each one was at least 200 feet long. The first day on the job, they were able to lay out two full lines but again finished at 8PM because darkness was approaching—not because they had met their goal like yesterday, but because they couldn't see.

The next day was the same. At one point, Hollis kept staring at the job Palmer was doing. "How do you get such perfect threads and how do you always end up with 18 threads?" "Here is the trade secret. Once the threading head is applied, I add 3 drops of cutting oil. That allows me to make 9 full turns. Another three drops give me 9 more turns. Then I break off any finishing teat and ground your internal cutting flashes. After brushing off dust and chips, I give it a final inspection. When there are defects, I pass the threaded cutting knife until the threads are all clean." "Well, after today, we start gas lines. And that is not a place for leaks I assure you. You're now a master thread man, and that is what we need for gas line. See you tomorrow."

That night, after supper, Palmer was the first to suggest that he wanted to go to bed. Mia asked, "this is the third night without extracurricular activities—how many more before we play hide the pickle again." But Palmer had fallen asleep in his chair.

It took three days to lay out pipelines to a dozen heat stoves and that many days to feed ceiling lamps.

*

During those six days, Mia had been busy receiving Josie and introducing her to Alice and Agnes as well as to all the staff. Jose was taught how to take her patterns to Weber's shop to make permanent wood paneling patterns. She was also taught how to operate a power cutter to help maintain a good supply of pieces ready to enter the production lines. It was Alice who reminded Mia that they would still be short of power cutter operators; and so Mia decided to find a person that could do all three jobs—purchasing agent, inventory monitor, and part-time pattern power cutter operator. She had three local applicants for the position but one was from a ranch three miles away.

The first two were disappointing. Neither had living skills, or basic eye to hand coordination. The third lady was a real find. Jan Henderson was a 22-year old lady who had just married a rancher and was bored staying in the house all day. She had a 10th grade education and had worked in a harness shop where she had used power cutters to cut straps of leather. Mia quickly offered her the job.

The applicant had one comment and one question. "I'm looking forward to the interaction with other ladies—this is something I never got working in an all-male harness shop or on a cattle ranch. As for questions, I'll be riding three miles twice a day, are there any other workers that live on my road?" "Yes, six others, and I'm sure you'll be joining their riding group." "Great, when can I start? "How about tomorrow, I'll go over the present inventory, and Agnes will teach you how the power cutter works on denim instead of leather."

Josie's first design was to modify the ladies' jeans. Once approved, a line was assigned the task of producing the final product that Waldo was waiting for. The next pattern she presented was the vests. Mia had already seen this one, and said nothing as Agnes and Alice criticized every aspect but, in the end, accepted the pattern with a modification on the pockets—these had to be wide and deep enough to hold in place a pocket watch, change, paper currency, or the fixings for a twirly. After the permanent pattern was made, another line was given the new pieces and Alice supervised each of the six stations till the end product was perfect.

That same day, Alice expressed a thought. "We are now producing standard mining pants, extra space mining pants, insulated extra space mining pants, ladies' slim jeans, and men/women vests. I think we should stop there and perfect our stitching before adding new lines. Once we move to the shop, we can add men's work shirts, men/women casual shirts, work overalls, men's slim jeans, jackets, and winter coats. But I really think Josie needs to get these patterns developed, approved, and turned to permanent wood panels—and make shirts the next priority."

"I agree, but if we approve the shirts, let's try to start their production and assign a line that can start making them in the old shop. That way, they'll be ready to continue their work in the factory. I may be wrong, but I think this shirt project will keep Josie up at night."

During those six days, Mia was a regular visitor at the building site. She would meet with Palmer and then together, they would check the progress, and talk to Marc. The Duo saw the workers: add many first-floor windows, finish the angled tongue & groove, finish the outside board & batten to two floors, finish the steel roof, build soffits and facia boards, add wool insulation to the first floor walls, build ventilation units in the second floor walls, add numerous doors, add a front and back porch, and build the shed for the power plant. It was at the end of the sixth day that Palmer asked, "what's next?" "I split my team, 10 framing/rough construction men will now build your barn, corral and lean-to, while the other 10 finishing carpenters will build your partition walls, work tables, shelving, sewing machine boxes, stairway, elevator, painting, and set acoustic panels. This is when I prefer you show up in the mornings and every noon—that way we can plan the mornings and afternoons. Besides, you'll want to watch the barn go up."

"We'll be here, but what is this about acoustic panels?" "Well, with 12,500 sq. ft. of wood walls and ceilings; what do you think a hundred sewing machines will sound like?" "Oh, of course. What do acoustic panels accomplish?" "It's a new experimental material that absorbs sound. Their engineer has worked out the square footage and noise factor, and have sent us the proper pieces to screw into the ceiling. If things are still too loud, we'll add more panels to the top three feet of the walls. Besides, it will add a decorative, while still a functional, feature."

The next morning at daybreak, Mia was up preparing a welcomed replenishing breakfast. At the factory, partitions walls were on the agenda. The rear of the shop was divided in four sections. The far left was the pattern marking and cutting room. The middle porting was for shipping, receiving, and storage, the next on the right was for boxing and holding, and the far right was for two offices, one for Josie to work on designing patterns, and one for Jan's files and work area.

The middle partitions were for the water closet walls and stalls, as another crew built the stairway to the second floor. The front portion of the building was separated in a large lunchroom, an entrance foyer, a supervisor's office, Mia's office/nursery, and a secretary/business office.

The second day a 5-foot-high full-length wall was added in the center of the sewing area and anchored to the floor and ceiling beam. This was part of noise control but also a way to add cabinets and lockers to each worker's space. The third day was the actual building of cabinets and lockers that were attached to the building's side walls and center wall.

The next day, tables and shelves were built for the rear pattern, shipping, boxing room, and offices. In the afternoon, large dining tables were built as well as shelving and cabinets for the other front offices. It was impossible to list all the finishing touches that took another week to finish, as the barn was built.

Meanwhile, a gas fired boiler and air compressor were delivered by a local company bearing the name Henry's Equipment. Hollis spent days on end adding the valves, gauges, and pipes that were required to convert steam to workable energy. To help him with this project, Kip Turner (the power plant supervisor) was brought in to be involved from the ground up. Once the system was installed, it was fired up to test the integrity of the pipes. Hollis and Kip's last job was to install the heating stoves with a direct wall exhaust as well as the many overhead lamps. Once installed, the gas mainline was activated. Each heating stove and lamp was checked out for proper function without gas leaks.

So, at the end of three weeks, the factory, barn, shed, and septic system were built and ready for occupancy. Before the big move, Hollis was given the task of moving the 30 new machines from storage to the factory, and installing a transmission to each machine that converted air pressure to usable power. Fortunately, Marc's men moved all the machines to the factory and Kip Turner helped Hollis do the final installations. Once the power plant was started, Alice and Agnes came to test each machine to be certain that they all worked properly. With this final test a success, it was time to move the shop to the factory.

*

Palmer had settled his bill with Marc and had to add a bank voucher for another $2,165 over their deposit of $12,500. Included in this final payment was hiring the 20 carpenters to dismantle the elevator, move the +-30 sewing machines, 50 rolls of denim, endless boxes of supplies, and install the elevator in the new factory.

Mia had prepared for this move. She had taken a recent inventory and knew how many items had to be moved. The goal was to empty the shop 100% and leave no inventory—that included the elevator. The morning of the move, the stitchers had to pack their shelves, cabinets, and anything in their station. Each stitchers' boxes were labeled to duplicate their place in their specific line. Once their boxes were picked up, they were free to wait outside the factory until their boxes were unloaded and brought to the labeled line and station. Then they had to unpack their stuff and wait for further instructions from Agnes and Alice.

While the old sewing machines were being installed, it was now clear that the old workers had been assigned the new machines. The new workers would be using refurbished machines as soon as Hollis had the time to rebuild each machine. When Alice was asked where the new workers were, she said, "the new workers are all settling down in their temporary housing, and would start working in three days."

The move continued at a good pace. Two men were moving each sewing machine into place as Hollis and Kip were installing transmissions. During this time, Alice and Agnes started explaining how this compressed air would work. The gals all learned the three speeds of slow, medium, and fast. Their job for the day was to practice sewing while using the power mode only. By lunch time, the gals all gathered in the lunchroom for the first time. In the afternoon, they started making their products. The first pieces had over-sewing defects and were given to the accessory stitchers to make parts. It took all afternoon to start making pieces that were not rejects. By the end of the day, the stitchers were happy with the new powered machines.

During the afternoon, the men brought in boxes of supplies and 50-100-yard rolls varying from 36-60 inches wide and of varying thickness from 8-16 ounces. The Duo was watching the men as they filled the storage room with rolls of denim, boxes of supplies to include thread, brass buttons, rivets, wood or ceramic buttons, large and extra strong commercial needles, scissors, sewing tools, sewing oil, and many other miscellaneous items.

Palmer commented, "you certainly have plenty of boxed supplies, but you don't seem to have much denim ahead." "Our old storage space was too small, and 50 rolls was all we could store. Our new storage area will hold 200 rolls, and we have 350 more rolls stored in boxcars. The freight company will bring 150 of them today. Jan will keep 200 rolls ahead in boxcars at all times. Without denim, our factory is closed. The same will hold on other boxed supplies." As they were watching the moving, the hardware store arrived with wagon loads of chairs for sewing machines and the lunchroom. The other wagons included furniture for Mia, Gloria, Josie, Jan and the floor supervisors. It also included secretarial and business equipment. The last item was a large ice box to keep the ladies' lunches fresh till lunch time—and included a weekly ice block replacement.

By the end of the day, the factory was completely stocked, and the stitchers were putting out perfect finished products to include mining pants, vests, and ladies' jeans. The expediters were functioning well, as everyone was settling in their offices.

That evening, while sitting in their parlor, Palmer wanted to know more about denim. "Ok, here is what I know. Denim is 100% cotton. It is a weave of inside white threads called the 'weft,' and outside died indigo blue thread called the 'warp.' It comes in different thickness and stiffness from 8 to 16 ounce—which means the actual weight of one square yard." "So, a square yard of 16-ounce material weighs one pound?" "Correct, now mining pants use 16-ounce, men and women jeans and vests use 12-ounce, work shirts use 10-ounce, and casual shirts use 8-ounce material. Usage wise, mining pants take a total of 2.5 to 3 yards and shirts will take 1.5 yards with sleeves, as vests take a single yard."

"Good info, now why so many different size rolls?" "First of all we buy denim by rolls, not bolts. Bolts are fabric wrapped around cardboard and are used in retail stores. Our rolls vary in length, width, and weight to maximize the pattern fit and minimize fabric loss. For example, mining pants are best cut out of 42-48-inch wide rolls with minimal remnants that are used by the accessory stitchers to make pockets and other parts."

"I noticed that your rolls are actually rolled onto a wood dowel; why is that?" "Easy to handle a roll by one man or two, then the rolls are stacked on racks and held by the dowel handles that stick beyond the denim. Otherwise, the rolls would be stacked on top of each other and would end up in crushed shapes making it more difficult to handle. The dowels are returned to the mills for a refund— then reused."

"If you leave 200 or more rolls in boxcars, what happens if you run out of one material?" "We call

the freight company to go get us a load, I guess?"
"Why don't we have Marc build us some racks upstairs, and keep those 200 boxcar rolls upstairs That plus good inventory work will keep you in available denim. With the compressed air powering the elevator, that's an easy way to store all our material in the shop and at no cost."

"Agree, not only cheaper, but more accessible for Jan to maintain her inventory. We'll investigate this after talking with your dad." "Speaking of dad, handling rolls, and railroad crates is not easy work. Seeing he's getting on in age, what do you say, we hire him a strong helper?" "Of course! I should have thought of that!"

The next morning, after a replenishing breakfast, Mia went to the shop and Palmer went looking for his dad's helper. Once the shop started rolling, Mia spent a long time with Jan in organizing her inventory. Once Jan was set, she decided to check on Ella. "Would you explain what you do since your job was set up by Agnes?" "When the finished products start coming in, I separate them in categories. Let's take this pile—they are mining pants with extra thigh room, waist 34 and length 28. The label will say **B-MP X W34 L28** (B is for Bodine, MP is for mining pants, X is for extra thigh room and so on). So, I collect them till I get a dozen and then box them in these extra strong paperboard boxes. I then interlock the bottom and top flaps and add a string across the flaps as insurance that the bottom flaps won't let go."

"Before you add them to the railroad crates, how do you label them?" "I have three stamps prepared by the newspaper printing shop. These stamps hold the ink from the pad. The first stamp states, To: W. Steiner Distribution, Deming NM. The second stamp states, From: Bodine Denim, Silver City NM. The third stamp is the most important. It describes the box's contents under three categories. Here, take a look. Under product, I write MP-X or R. Under Size, I write W 34, L 28. Under Number, I write 12. This labels the box and makes for easy classification once the crates arrive in Waldo's warehouse." "Ok, so how would you label vests, say men's for example." "Under Product, I write MV. Under size, I write L (for large and M for medium). Under Number, I write 20. And by the way, I write this with my fountain pen that has indelible ink."

"How often do you ship out to the railroad." "Their three wagons arrive every morning before opening and take all the full crates to the closed boxcars. They arrive the same day in Deming. I give Gloria the product invoice of today's shipment, she telegrams the invoice to Waldo, and we receive a telegram voucher for full payment—the same day." "Wow, I like it and that's why we do business with Waldo."

At noon, Palmer arrived at Mia's office. "I found dad a helper. Before I went looking, I asked dad if he knew of a possible candidate. He told me of a railroad worker who picks up their daily crates. I went to find this guy, made him an offer and three things were the clincher—working for dad, $20 a week, and working around 100 women!"

During their lunch break at Grady's, the telegraph messenger delivered a telegram. Palmer read it and said, "Harvey wants to meet with us about a new business venture?" Mia answered, "I would like to spend the afternoon at the shop to clear up starting problems. Let's meet with him for breakfast in our home, before he heads to the mine." Palmer wrote his answer and gave it to the messenger as well as four bits for payment and tip. That afternoon, Palmer would finish reading his book on "Open Pit Mining."

***

CHAPTER 8

What is Open Pit Mining

While helping Mia preparing their breakfast, Palmer added, "you know I've been reading that textbook on Open Pit Mining. Now I plan to let Harvey talk freely without my interruptions. Since you know nothing on the subject, I would prefer that you ask all the questions you feel you need an answer. We're not going to mention the book I read till he's done talking. Then I will ask my own questions if Harvey or you did not cover my issues. Is that Ok with you?" "Sounds like a sound approach, I'm all in!"

It was a great breakfast with Harvey. They reminisced about their early days at Mine #4 and how the mine was still making a fortune with their rich gold vein. With the men's second pot of coffee and the dishes cleaned up, Harvey started.

"I've been researching this subject for weeks and it's time to talk about it. Let's start with 'what is copper?' Copper is a metal gaining popularity and industrial use. Historically, it has been used in jewelry, lamps, tools, bells, sinks, and sculptures, as an example, the Statue of Liberty. New uses that have increased its value and demand are pipes for plumbing and electrical wires."

"Unlike gold, found in hard quartz rock, copper is found in soft sedimentary rocks as the sulfide mineral ore called chalcopyrite. In its natural form, it is a red-brown-orange color. When exposed to air, it oxidizes to a green color like the Statue of Liberty has."

"Now, for your information, let me digress onto the subject of how it is processed before we talk about how to mine it—which is what this presentation is about. The steps are:

1&2. Rock crushing and grinding. These are done by steam powered hammers and grinding mills which we'll discuss later.
3. Concentrating. By a process called froth floatation, the slag(rock) sinks to the bottom.

4. Roasting. Using heat to 900° F, the ore is exposed to charcoal to produce CO from carbon. The CO removes oxygen and sulfur.
5. Fluxing. The roasted ore is fluxed with limestone to release the metal from the ore.
6. Smelting. The fluxed metal is added to a blast furnace at 2000° F—which is a coal fire enhanced with a massive blast of air to raise the temperature. The metals separate at different temps: as tin 450, lead 650, yellow brass 1660, silver 1761, gold 1945 and lastly copper at 1983° F."

"Now how do we mine it?" Mia interrupted and said, "didn't you once mine it in our underground mine, and why did that fail?" "The yield was one pound of Copper, worth $3.50 a pound, in a ton of ore. It was not financially feasible to even come close to pay for the labor. The only way to do it is with large volumes of ore extracted each day. So how do we extract these volumes of ore? By mining on the earth's surface called Open Pit Mining. After using dynamite, we load the ore directly onto open boxcars by using heavy equipment."

Mia interjected, "wow that was a mouthful, guess you'd better cover each one separately, heh?" "Sure, the earth's surface is covered with sedimentary rocks—formed eons ago as the earth was developing. These are soft, weigh +-150 pounds per cubic foot, are formed from deposits of minerals, organic matter from living things, and inorganic chemicals. To impress how soft they are, on Moh's scale of rock hardness, diamond is 10, quartz is 7, sedimentary rocks art 3, fingernails are 2.5 and Talc is 1."

"The process of Open Pit Mining starts with removing the 6-12 inch of dirt, sand, and vegetation overburden to expose the rock. This is achieved with steam powered earth movers. The next step involves drilling holes in certain patterns and adding dynamite. The explosions release large amounts of rock fragments of differing sizes, and the smaller the rocks, the easier it is in extracting the copper."

"Stop there. Can you give us an idea, worse scenario, what a ton of this ore is worth?" "At a very low yield of 1%, multiply 2000 pounds by .01 and that will yield 20 pounds of pure copper per ton of ore. At $3.50 cents a pound, the ton of ore is worth +-$70." "But that cannot be financially worth it?" "Yes, it is, consider we can expose, load, and fill a full open boxcar that holds a minimum of 75 tons of ore. Now in my book, 70 times 75 equals +-$5,000." "That's a fortune, but what are the expenses?" "I have computed them in detail, but for now the expense breakdown comes to:

"Labor $500, supplies $250, Stamping and grinding $750, and smelting at $1,000. That totals $2,500."

"Are you saying there is a profit of $2,500 per 75 tons of ore in one boxcar?" "Yes." "And how long to load it with a couple hundred men—a week or more?" "No, with heavy equipment, we can load a full boxcar every and each day." "Whaaaaaat, that's nuts. Harvey, have you lost your senses. What kind of equipment can load a boxcar in a day?" "A massive machine called a coal fired steam shovel." Mia just looked at Palmer with a look of total confusion. Palmer finally spoke, "It sounds like this entire operation is based on steam shovels. Tell us about these things."

"Steam shovels are manufactured by two companies: Bucyrus Foundry out of Milwaukee and Marion Industries in Ohio. They are used in digging large ditches, dredging lakes and loading dirt. Recently they have been sent to Panama to build the Panama Canal. The newest use in this country is in open pit mining as used in Utah. They are massive machines weighing 100 tons, are 50 feet long, 10 feet wide and extend as much as 25 feet high. You'll only appreciate these dimensions when you walk up to one. They're built on a railway chassis in two parts. The rear unit is a cabin housing a coal fired boiler generating the steam to power the many winches that wind up, half to one inch, steel cables."

"The front part holds the working units: the main boom, the dipper stick and the bucket. These front working parts sit on a rotating platform that spans 240° since the boom cannot clear the rear cabin. The dipper stick holds the bucket and slides 'to and fro' on the main boom. The bucket measures 30 inches, with hardened steel teeth, and when fully loaded can hold a ton of rock per bucketful, and can do this in five minutes. Now, even with partial buckets, in an hour some 12 buckets get loaded and this comes to +- 9 tons per hour or +- 75 tons per eight-hour day, heh?"

"Yes, I see what you mean. How do you move this machine since you did not mention what kind of wheels can hold this thing?" "In this day, the only wheels that can hold 100 tons are railway steel wheels, which is why it travels on railroad tracks. It propels itself by using the dipper/bucket—pushing or pulling off the ground."

"How many men are needed to keep this machine operating?" The shovel itself needs three men. One to feed coal and keep the steam pressure up, one to operate the gears and winches, and one to operate the boom/dipper stick/bucket. Plus six men on the ground laying double tracks for the steam shovel and the boxcars getting loaded."

Mia was pensive and finally said. "I can see that with the overburden removed, it is feasible to remove the first 3-4 feet by using dynamite and steam shovels. But what happens when the first layer is removed?"

"Ok, let's take a cleared plot measuring ½ mile by ½ mile. Once the first 3-4-foot layer is excavated, we start a second layer. The key is to leave a 40-foot bench of rock as the bed for the shovels and open boxcars. The idea is to build a terraced pit with 40-foot benches around all levels. Years down the road, you'll end up with a pit that looks like a roman colosseum."

"So that means that the railroad tracks laid on the benches stay there for now—being the only access to lower levels?" "Correct, for now!" Palmer finally spoke, "assuming we are interested where to we start and what do we need?" "Ok, here is a list and we'll discuss each one—we need to: buy land that has tested holes, build headquarters, find a dynamite man, hire a civil engineer/clerk of the works, buy rails and cross ties, rent an earth moving tractor and a steam shovel, buy a portable steam powered air compressor for drilling holes, and we need a dozen men to make the project operational."

Palmer smiled as Mia said, "that's a heck of a long list, I didn't think you were ever going to stop! So, without land we don't have a mine. Where do we find tested holes that assayed at 1% copper content"

"Not to be corny, but that's why you pay me the big bucks. The railroad travels 16 miles east of Silver City to a town called Santa Rita. There, a group of men are mining surface rocks for copper. So we know that the sedimentary rocks hold copper in this region. Now only four miles from town, along this rail line, is an area proven to have copper. An old prospector drilled 3-ft holes and the assay was 1%. I had some drilling teams extend those holes to 8 feet and the assays came back 1.5%; as is common for the copper content to increase as the depth increases."

"Now this prospector is an old eccentric codger. The bank has it listed as $2,500 for a full section of 640 acres, and there are three sections for sale all along the rail line. Only the central section was tested, but all three will likely hold the same amount of copper. The problem is that, once negotiations were started, the owner decided not to sell, and was about to pull it off the market when he heard the name Bodine. Does the name Rufus Whitlow ring a bell?" The Duo looked at each other in clear recognition. "Yes, we know the gentleman." "Know, heck he said you saved his butt. Anyways, you can now have one or all three sections at a reduced rate of $2,000 per section."

Palmer looked and saw Mia's countenance as she finally spoke, "I have my hands full with the factory and you need something to keep yourself occupied. It's up to you, but it sounds like a sound and innovative idea. My vote is for you to jump in with both feet and make it work."

Palmer looked at Harvey and said, "buy all three sections. We'll need room for the overburden, and room for expansion. Besides, we don't want neighbors complaining of the noise. Now let's go over the other requirements."

"Once we have the land, we put our ducks in a row and arrange to rent the earth mover and steam shovel. Then we hire the men. We need six to lay railroad tracks, three to drill and blast, one to operate the mini engine that moves about the boxcars. Then we buy rails, cross ties and a portable coal fired air compressor/boiler with a man to operate it. Finally, we need a dynamite man, a civil engineer/clerk of the works, and a manager." "Didn't you forget the men to operate the steam shovel and earth mover?" "No, they come with the rental. More later on this."

"Let's start with the manager. That would be me. Your gold mine is self-sufficient, and I can divide my time between the two places every other day. While away from the gold mine, my secretary can take care of things as you can take care of the digs over here." "Ok, does that mean more money for you?" "No, I am well paid. Now for a dynamite man, Liam Johanson is moving over. I have found his replacement as you know from your hiring factory employees. He is ready for a change and his wages won't change as well." "Good, a great move for us as well."

"The real problem was finding a civil engineer to be the clerk of the works. Ever hear the name

Emmett McGivern?" "Yes, he was the wagon-master relocating a bunch of Colorado miners to New Mexico." "Correct, but you forgot how you saved the wagon-train from an Indian attack, and also left a fortune at an Alamogordo mercantile to help the miners, heh?" Palmer just waved it off. "Well, come to find out this wagon-master is a well-qualified and recommended engineer working in Santa Rita with those miners I mentioned. When I offered to hire him, he declined. Again when he heard the word Bodine, he changed his mind and said he'd take the job without even negotiating a salary. He wants to meet with you first." "Will do, now what about headquarters?"

"We need a building for a lunch/break room, offices for me and you, a business office with a secretary, and an engineering office. We also need a shed for tools and a coal bin. A separate dynamite storage shed, a privy and a barn. Since this is desert country, there is no stream nearby. We'll need to truck in water for horses, the steam plant for drilling, and running the steam shovel. The reserve tank should be next to the barn for easy access to horses. We'll also need to build a fenced in pasture for us and employee horses."

"That does it, it's a go. Set up the closing for the land, buy everything we need, and I'll hire Marc Weber to build our buildings." "Great, I'll get on it, but you have to go to Henry's Equipment to arrange to rent the earth mover, steam shovel, buy a portable air compressor, and pay for your shop's complete power plant and air compressor which Hollis got for you—in other words, bring your bank book, heh?"

*

The next day, after Mia spent a few hours at the shop, the Duo had an appointment with Henry's Equipment. As they arrived, they were totally mesmerized by the largest equipment they had ever seen—a steam shovel was parked in front of Henry's business. After examining the item in detail, the Duo finally understood what Harvey was talking about. Entering the premises, the receptionist escorted them to Henry's office. Mia did a double take when she saw the receptionist, but could not place her in her past. Stepping inside the owner's office, the Duo was asked to have a seat. In front of them was a name plate that said Henry Brubaker. Mia had a flash of times gone by as her eyebrows arched upwards. The receptionist noticed Mia's recognition as she placed a finger across her lips and then whispered something in Henry's ear.

Henry started, "so, we finally meet. I have heard the name Bodine almost every other day for the past two years. Then a few weeks ago, I got an invoice for a gas fired power plant. I knew that if I didn't put a charge that you would be contacting me. Then Harvey Elliot came to see me regarding a steam shovel. And here we are." Henry looked at Palmer and said, "you don't know who I am, do you?" "No sir, but by my wife's face, I suspect she does." "I see, well Mia, go ahead and start the story from the beginning."

"When we stripped the emporium's upstairs to build a shop, I had a furniture sale out in the rear parking lot. There were three cook stoves for sale. A lady was looking at all three and said that her barrel stove was falling apart, and it became impossible to cook for a family of five kids. She desperately needed a stove. Of course, she fell in love with a real kitchen stove with a water tank and an oven. When I told her the price, she nearly collapsed. Her homesteading husband freely admitted that they barely had enough money to eat, so he would find a junk barrel and build another stove. It was then that

I saw the five barefoot kids, clothing falling apart, and two adults skinny as rails to save food for their kids. That is when I had my first epiphany—how I had so much, and so many people had so little. So, I called two strong men to pick up the real kitchen stove and had them load it in the homesteader's wagon. The husband pleaded to take it out for he could not afford it. Instead, I had the entire family enter Elmer's mercantile, and after giving Elmer directions I went back to my furniture sale."

Henry interrupted, "that's fine Mia, so let me continue the story. To shorten the story, we came out of the mercantile with new shoes for all of us. The kids had three changes of clothes, their first individual bags of candy, toys for the first time, my wife had three new dresses and I had three pairs of mining pants with store bought shirts. On top of it all, we had enough food for a month, and I had a new double barrel shotgun, a Winchester rifle and a Smith & Wesson pistol—including ammo for all three guns. My credit was paid off and we had a bank draft for $1,500."

"After cashing in the bank draft, I gave my wife $750 to cover the household expenses, and I went prospecting for gold in a mountain stream that went thru our land and eventually petered out next to the barn. The first day I came back with a pound of gold nuggets. My wife was totally mortified. The next day all seven of us went looking for gold nuggets and came back with three pounds worth $900. Over the next weeks, the girls continued picking up nuggets, and we set up a sluice box on a flatbed wagon. Our twin boys added the gravel and water, as the Missus and me picked up the visible gold. We saved the sludge and bought a machine that extracted a portion of the 'fines.' To shorten the story, after two months we had a bank account worth $100,000."

"By then, the stream was played out and it was time to excavate our one section claim of the mountain where the stream jutted out. That meant heavy equipment, building tunnels, and dynamite. Not certain what to do, a large mining corporation offered us $100,000 for our homestead and our mountain claim. We sold out, moved to town and bought a large home."

"After two months, I was going nuts with nothing to do, so we bought this dealership and continued making money. This fall my two twin boys are going to college in Albuquerque, and will stay in their own house close to the college. In two years, our two high school daughters will be joining them, and we'll be left with our 8-year-old baby girl."

Missus Brubaker interjected, "normally I don't work here since Henry has his own secretary. But today is a special day, so I gave his secretary a day off. Do you remember my promise to you, Mia?" "Yes." Looking at Palmer she added, "when this family was about to leave, the lady said to me, 'remember the name Henry Brubaker for one day you will hear it and we will be able to repay you!'" Henry added, "and how does Missi enjoy her new home?" Palmer acknowledged with a smile.

Henry took over, "and this brings us to settling your account. Your charge for the factory power plant and the portable air compressor is $2,000. My cost is $1,300 and that is what you pay. Now the rental for an earth moving tractor is $50 a week and the steam shovel is $300 a week—that includes three men on the shovel and one man on the tractor. We are giving you both pieces free of charge, for three months on the shovel and until your site is cleared of the overburden. This will allow you time to get your mine operating, and able to pay these rental fees."

Palmer objected and added, "this is not right, you are losing a fortune!" "Do we look like we are destitute? Actually, this is a business advertising ploy on our part. In return, we would like you to allow people to watch your heavy equipment in operation. We feel this will push that group in Santa Rita to rent the tractor and steam shovel."

"You see, I was able to buy two steam shovels from Bucyrus. They had a contract to deliver 70 shovels to the Panama Canal but were strapped for cash since they had to pay the freight to Panama— that's 1,200 miles of rail service to Galveston and 1,500 miles by sea freight to Panama Canal."

"So, I presume this deal is not negotiable" as she wrote a bank draft for $2,000 and added, "as this amount is not negotiable." Henry smiled and showed the draft to his wife who added, "Ok, finally we can go to sleep in peace, knowing that we repaid our gratitude." Henry then added, "Harvey will be adding a rail line to your site as soon as you pay for the land and get your deed. The shovel/tractor will follow and good luck."

*

That afternoon, Harvey had scheduled the closing at the town clerk's office. The Duo walked over and as they entered were greeted by Rufus Whitlow. "Well, we finally meet again." After pleasantries and reminiscences, Palmer asked Rufus, "what are your plans for the future?" "I have abandoned my digs since the gold vein has run out. I bought a house in town and will officially retire at the age of 65. With my lifelong savings and this sale, I have more money than I will ever be able to spend." "What are you going to do to pass the time?" "Eat at diners. drink coffee and beer, play cards and wait for the end, I guess!" "Hu-um, well try it, but if you are too bored, we need a man to drive a preloaded water wagon to the mine every day of operation—that will chew up half your day!" "I have already tried it for two months and I am already bored. Using the morning up every day sounds like the solution. When do I start?" "As soon as the holding tank is built in a few days—see Harvey for the details."

The paperwork was completed, a prepared new deed was signed and registered. Harvey was headed to the railroad office to arrange for a switch and side rail to the excavation site. He had hired six men who would help the railroad workers laying the new line, and learn how to do the job properly when adding rails for the steam shovel and open boxcars.

The Duo then went to Grady's for dinner. Waiting for their order, Mia told Palmer she was planning to go back to the shop till closing. Palmer in turn would visit Marc Weber to arrange the headquarters' construction, and would finish the day, meeting with Emmett McGivern at Palmer's house.

"Hello Marc, how are the renovations coming along over the emporium?" "The 'rough crew' finished your floor plan partitions and the plumbing. The 'finishing crew' will now start." "So, is your 'rough crew' available?" "Yes, got anything else to build?" "Matter of fact, I do." After describing his new venture, Palmer said, "I need headquarters built. The main building will include a large lunch/break room, offices for Harvey and me, a business office, and one for our resident engineer. In addition we need a tool shed with a coal bin, a secure dynamite shed, a privy and a barn to hold at least 30 horses with an enclosed pasture. Most important, and first to be built, is a 500-gallon water tank attached to the barn. This water will be used by the steam shovel and tractor boilers as well as for watering the horses." "Great, we'll start tomorrow, just write down the directions and who will meet us there? "I will." "Then tomorrow, with the workers, I'll bring plans for your buildings."

Palmer then walked home to meet with Emmett McGivern. Arriving, Palmer saw a man sitting on the porch. Stepping up, he offered his hand and said, "Shades of the past, who would have thought a wagon-master was a college trained civil engineer?" "And who would have thought that a saddle bum/ Indian fighter would become a detective agent, an underground gold miner, a co-owner of a clothing factory, an open pit miner, and let's not forget a philanthropist, heh?" "Ok, well this 'jack of all trades' needs a civil engineer. So let's talk. Tell me what you've been up to since that fateful night in Tularosa."

"Once we arrived in Deming, the miners farmed out to different mines and I got a job with the railroad. I've spent the last two years building railroads. I've worked with land scouts, surveyors, ground leveling crews and trestle builders. Once the local lines were built, I decided to try mining. For six months, I've worked in Santa Rita with surface copper miners. It is a tough group to work for, since they are afraid to modernize and use heavy equipment."

"So, what are you after?" "I want to be involved in building an open pit like they have in Utah. It sounds simple, but I assure you it is quite involved, in assuring that every bench is solid and fuses with lower levels thru a safe railcar grade. Worse of all, every bench has to be built in such a way that the rail lines do not slide off the benches. You can imagine a 100-ton steam shovel next to a 75-ton loaded railcar, and the catastrophe if the rails slip off the benches. This requires careful planning and a close relationship with a good dynamite man. Harvey assures me you have such a dynamite man, and for this reason, I would like to work for you. I know I can do the job and keep your workers safe."

"Wow, now I know what your job entails. Harvey already told me that you were the man for the job. So, I would like to offer you an employment package." After reviewing the insurance benefits, Palmer addressed the living situation. "I would like you to live in town, or in the country close to the work site. Is that possible?" "We now live in a poor neighborhood in Santa Rita, as we lived in similar locations when I worked for the railroad. My wife has been tolerant, but it is time for us to live in town where she can socialize as I work long hours."

"Great, you can rent a house, till you find the one you like, for $50 a month, and I will pay for that as one of your salary benefits. Now, what do you want for a salary not related to hours worked."

"I want this job at all costs, and my wife deserves to live with people. I'll take whatever you offer me."

"Well, let's start with your railroad salary and your present salary at the surface mine." "For the railroad I was making $80 a month without benefits. For the surface miners, $75 without benefits. With the benefits and housing allowance, I'm willing to take less Mister Bodine."

Palmer came off his chair, first of all my name is Palmer, my wife is Mia, and you are Emmet. Secondly, those were abusive wages for a professionally trained college man. To start with, what do you need for equipment?" "Nothing, I have all the drafting tools, a perfect transit, and all measuring tapes and markers." "Very well, I will offer you $125 a month, the housing allowance and your own office in the headquarters' building. The work is five days a week. It includes working late at night if necessary. If you end up working Saturdays, which I doubt, I will pay you $10 extra for the day." "If I have to work Saturdays, there is no charge for I feel it is part of the job." "We'll see." "Do you accept the job." "Of course. When do I start?" "Tomorrow morning, Harvey is laying a rail line to the site and he'll need your help." At that point, Palmer writes the usual bank draft and hands it to Emmett. "Hey, this if for $200, what is this for?" "Every new employee gets a signing on bonus to cover moving expenses and a wardrobe upgrade."

As they were standing, they shook hands. A noise was heard, and Mia entered. "Emmett, I would like you to meet my wife, Mia. Mia this is Emmett McGivern, our own resident civil engineer." After the usual pleasantries, Emmett departed. Mia then said, "that man looks sound, so tell me everything you know and how the interview went, heh?" "For sure, have a seat my dear!"

***

CHAPTER 9

Getting Started

That evening, Mia was too tense to appreciate Palmer's advances. After a fretful night of tossing and turning, Palmer was up early to make breakfast. The smell of bacon must have gotten to Mia who showed up after the usual morning ablutions. "Well, dear lady, what got you so tipsy turvy last night. You rolled and kicked, and I have the bruises to prove it." "Oh, today is the day we all dread. We have 30 new ladies who are starting today. It's going to be a one-hour training session on the powered commercial sewing machines, followed by an all-day training for each stitcher to learn her station. It could go smooth, but I suspect it will become a zoo!" "Sit down and enjoy your breakfast, I'm sure that Alice and Agnes will have everything well organized. As for me, I have Harvey, Emmett, and the railroad crew coming to lay a rail line to the excavation site; as well as the steam tractor arriving to start removing the overburden."

As Mia arrived, the shop was full of stitchers—30 regulars and 30 new employees. Alice blew her whistle, and after welcoming pleasantries, assigned each of the new ladies to their own new machine as the regulars started their usual work routine. "For an hour, I will go over this commercial machine. First, this is a powered machine. Look at the floor, there are three pedals. The left one is for slow speed, the middle one for medium and the one on the right for fast sewing. Place a piece of denim under the needle, drop the needle arm, and press on the slow pedal." Whirr............. . "As you can see, the machine draws the fabric and you don't need to push it along. Your fingers, kept 4 inches from the needle, are to fold, guide and align the denim. If you push or allow your fingers to follow the denim, you will put the needle thru your fingernail and finger—and that is an experience you will never forget! Now keep practicing all three speeds." Whirr........... .

"Remember the safety features. You have to take your foot off the pedal to stop the machine. If you lift the needle arm, the machine will stop. If there is a power failure, lift the red arm on the transmission and you will hear a pop as the air is release. Then you can peddle the platform manually like your home machines. Try it—pop..pop..............pop. If you break a needle, and you will, loosen the retaining screw and replace it—this is common when you are sewing three or more layers of denim. Now, practice folding the fabric and guide it in place. We'll watch you and verify that you are doing it right." Whirr...................... . Mia, Agnes and Alice walked around and verified that the operators were doing things correctly.

Alice blew her whistle as everything stopped. "Remember, when you hear our whistle, immediately stop and look up at us. Mia will now take over." "It is time to move you to your assigned station. When we did the interviews, we assigned you a station based on the type and years' experience you had, plus our assessment of your manual dexterity. When I call your names take your place on Line 1 for regular mining trousers. Dixie, Station 1. Lynn, Station 2. Claire, Station 3. Jean, Station 4. Diane, Station 5—these are all sewing stations. Sandy, Station 6—this is a station that includes three machines: a brass or ceramic button installer, a hole maker that weaves the edges to prevent fraying, and a rivet installer for all pockets." The next line was for extra wide mining pants, the third line was for men and women's vests, the fourth line was for ladies' jeans and the fifth was for accessory parts—with all stations filled.

"Turn around and introduce yourselves to the lady standing behind you. She will be your tutor for the remainder of the day. With that, I give you Agnes." "Watch your tutor, she will show you how to fill the bobbin and thread the five loops on your machine. Note that you have four bobbins, the thread spools are 8 inches high and 4 inches across, and the thread is the standard gold color. This thread is heavy duty and is the only thread you will use in this shop. Actually, it is like a small string or cord and it is what helps the durability of our products. You cannot break this thread; you have to cut it with those short fancy scissors. The standard long scissors are for cutting denim."

Alice took over, "Next, watch your tutor demonstrate how to sew your pieces. She takes the pieces from the inbox, sews them, and then places them in the outbox." Whirr...... . After the tutors sewed two pieces, Mia rang the bell. "This is the 10 o'clock 15-minute break. This is when you use

the water closet, fill your bobbins, or have a snack."
After 15 minutes, Mia rang the bell to resume work.
Agnes took over, "it's now time to sew your first
piece. Good luck." Whirr......... . Most of the first
pieces did not pass the tutor's inspection and went
into the pail of failed pieces, instead of the outbox.
Alice spoke up, "we expect you will be making
seconds all morning. We don't sell seconds, so
these pieces will go to the accessory stitchers to
make parts such as pockets, belt loops, hammer
loops, knee pads, and others."

The morning continued as the seconds' pails
filled up. At noon, Mia rang the bell and said,
"this is your 45-minute lunch break. Sit with
your line workers to get to know them." During
lunch Mia talked with Alice and Agnes. "How
are things going, have you found any workers who
will never pick this up?" Alice said, "no, everyone
has the potential for being excellent stitchers. It
is interesting that our assignments were right on.
For example, the least experienced ladies were put
on vests, and they are doing very well. The ones
we considered fast workers do belong in accessory
parts since they have to cut patterns as well as sew
edges. The ones in ladies' jeans are very particular
and do extra clean stitching. The ones in mining

jeans are strong workers which is needed to handle 16-ounce fabric." Agnes added, "I suspect that by 2PM we are going to see finished products in the outbox—instead of the seconds' pail."

Mia asked, "do our regular stitchers know what is going to happen tomorrow? Alice answered, "they know that Josie has been working on new designs, but they don't know that the wood panels are all made. So, as planned, our five regular lines will have new products to sew, and again the second's pails will fill up, heh?"

The return to work bell was sounded. Alice announced, "you are now on your own and your tutors will let you drive solo, unless they see you heading for a crash." Lots of laughter. "So good luck, watch your fingers, enjoy, and everything will turn out Ok."

*

That same morning, Palmer arrived at the land only to find no one there at 7AM. Palmer used the time to walk the middle lot and sort of set in his mind where the access rail line would be, the barn and water tank, the headquarters, and of course the approximate location of the pit. At 8AM, Palmer heard the rumble of an incoming train. Since this line ended 12 miles east in Santa Rita, he knew that the train was coming from Silver City. The train consisted of the engine, the coal tinder and water tanks, a passenger car, and four flat cars full of rails and accessories to include: straight and curved rails, switches, crossties, boxes of spikes, and tie plates. Once the train stopped, a dozen men stepped out of the passenger car. The apparent man in charge introduced himself to Palmer. "My name is Sylvio Dunhead, I'm a track laying engineer. I'll see to it that we have a working line to your steam shovel and open rock boxcars." Last to jump off the passenger train was Harvey and Emmett who had hopped onto the train for a free ride to the pit.

While the foreman was working with his team to install a switch off the main line, the team of Sylvio, Harvey, Emmett and Palmer started walking around. The layout was set for the barn and headquarters as well as the water tank, privy, barn lean-to and pasture. The biggest demand for space was the curved rail lines that took a lot of room before they entered the pit area. Once the stakes were laid out, Sylvio set up his transit and started laying out the track guiding posts. Emmett had worked for years laying out railroad tracks, but this was a bit different. This would require some variations to secure tracks to rock-beds instead of on the ground, and Sylvio would be the one to help Emmett out.

The next group to arrive were the six men hired to lay tracks in the pit. Palmer didn't know that Harvey had hired two of those men with past experience working for railroad track laying crews. The other four were young strapping muscular men to ease lifting rails. The rails that Emmett was planning to use were 15 feet long and weighed 800 pounds each—the rails' grade of steel that could hold 75-100 tons.

With everyone working on the switch leading to the access tracks, Harvey and Palmer waited and shortly, Marc Weber arrived with a cavalcade of wagons carrying, lumber, gravel, cement, steam powered cement mixers, a prefab double privy, a premade form for a water tank, and every trade carpentry tool imaginable. Marc was shown where the building markers were located. The privy was then unloaded, the work was started on the water tank, and two men were installing a sign by the road that said, "Bodine Open Pit Copper Mine."

The bulk of the carpenters were making concrete for the barn, water tank and the headquarters' building. For every wagon emptied out, others arrived with water, gravel, and cement. Amidst the pounding of rail spikes and the rotating cement mixers, an engine was heard chugging along the tracks from town. Everyone looked up in awe as a huge tractor, with a coal fired steam plant and a 4X12 foot front blade, sat in its majesty on top of a flatbed rail car.

Two men were apparently taking care of the unit. One to add coal, water and keep the gauges at optimum pressures, and one to operate the earth moving machine. The entire unit sat on four massive steel wheels mated to steel spokes and axles. With expert finesse, the men unloaded the tractor using special flatcar ramps.

As the earth mover was being driven to the pit site, Rufus Whitlow arrived with a wagon-tank full of palatable water. Palmer asked, "how did you know we would be needing water?" "Because Harvey told me the wagon-tank was loaded, and you would need it for that tractor, cement mixers, forty thirsty workers as well as some horses. I have a manual transfer pump and I'm ready to start filling your buckets. Once my tank is empty, I'll come back with a second load this afternoon." Palmer asked, "where does this water come from?" "There is a company on Lake Kroil that pumps clear filtered water into the tank and fills me up while I watch. Ironically, this is my first job at age 65, thanks to you, and I love it, heh?" "For sure, Rufus, for sure!"

By lunch time, half the concrete was done, and the tracks were coming along nicely. After lunch, Sylvio went to see how the earth mover was working out. After examining the surface rock, he called Palmer, Harvey and Emmett over. "Notice how smooth the rock surface is. This won't do. You cannot lay track on this surface—the tracks will slide and lead to a catastrophe." Emmett added, "I had the same problem working for the railroad when covering rocky surfaces. We had a solution, but I would like your opinion in case methods have changed."

"No, I'm certain the same holds. You need to have your dynamite man do some shallow drilling and lay down blasting caps. The explosion will produce small rock fragments that you can use as ballast between the railroad crossties. It's amazing when the space between crossties is filled with rocks, how it stabilizes the tracks. And also, the explosions now roughen up the rock surface, plus the addition of 'rock chip' ballasts, your tracks will never move."

"Out of curiosity, how wide are you planning to make your benches?" Emmett said, "forty feet wide and the walls to the next bench as deep as the steam shovel bucket can reach." "I agree with the depth, but may I suggest making your benches at least 50 feet wide. The reason is how much to make the dipper stick travel to reach the boxcar. If you are too far, then you make the dipper stick travel way to its end, and if you are too close, then the opposite is true. My past experience working with steam shovels in Utah is that there is the greatest safety, and the least wasted time, with 50-foot-wide benches—and time is money."

The day continued and the entire complex was becoming alive. By the end of the day Harvey said he would skip tomorrow to work at the gold mine, but would send Liam Johanson to the pit tomorrow. Sylvio estimated he had two more days work to lay all the tracks needed. Marc would split his men tomorrow. Half would start building the barn while the other half would start the headquarters. The tool and dynamite sheds would be last. The water tank would be ready to hold water in 36 hours. Once both trains went back to the yard, Palmer called it a day and went home.

*

That evening, after a home cooked meal, the Duo was sitting in their parlor. Mia said, "I left work early today for a quick visit with Doc Ross." As Mia places Palmer's hand on her belly, Palmer exclaims, "Jeeeezze, what is going on in there?" "I noticed that all day, and Doc Ross called it the 'quickening.' The baby is kicking, stretching or rolling over. I'm at 24 weeks and this is completely normal." "Oh good, and you are really beginning to show, maybe it's time to change your expandable riding skirts to dresses." "Yes, I agree, will do starting tomorrow."

"Now, tell me how your day went." "As hectic as it could have been, it actually went quite well. We only had one accident when a lady punched her fingernail with a needle. We had warned her three times to not let her fingers follow the material into the needle. I guess, a word to the wise is not always sufficient, heh?" "Or is it that you cannot fix stupid?" "Well, I think this lady learned her lesson. Otherwise, we broke 8 needles, usually when doing the backstitching. As expected, we made seconds' all morning, but as of 2PM the perfect pieces started appearing in the outbox."

"At the end of the day, Alice and Agnes were very pleased and both felt that all these gals would make permanent workers. I listened to these new gals talking as they were leaving, and the consensus was that this could likely become a long-term employment—or at best, I didn't hear anyone complain or grumble." "Great, but the real proof is how many return tomorrow morning, heh?"

"So what is the plan for tomorrow?" "The newbies will be on their own and the oldies will have all new designs to build—including men's slim jeans, overalls, work shirts and casual shirts. We'll start making seconds again, but probably for just a few hours."

"So, are you saying that you will have 60 machines in operation." "Heck, we had that many already today, why do you ask?" "Because, that means that Hollis had to have been working night and day to get all sixty machines connected." "Well, that will be reflected in his overtime." "Should, but don't be surprised if it doesn't—let me know either way. What is he doing now?"

'He has commandeered Ralph's work bench. He has boxes of sewing machine parts and is rebuilding the old machines one by one. He exchanges three new spare machines, and works on those old ones till they are upgraded. Apparently, this is just metal fatigue from 18 months of continuous daily use—as expected. The parts cost $79 dollars which is a bargain considering the new commercial machines cost $300 each. Once upgraded, they work and sound just like the new ones. Hollis is rebuilding three a day, so he's got 10 days of work ahead." "Well, I have to plan a meeting with him soon, the question is whether we keep him on as a regular, share him with the pit mine, or just use him on a 'as needed basis.'"

"On an aside, are these commercial machines overpriced?" "Ten years ago, my mother bought her first domestic treadle machine and paid $100 at a time when the average income was $500 a year. Today, these machines are made for daily use and are guaranteed—any broken parts are replaced and installed on site free of charge. This is the company that gave us the best price and their service has been good." "Perfect."

"Now, how did your day go?" "Hectic but well organized. I had a peaceful hour then all hell broke out. A train arrived with a dozen railroad workers, rails, crossties and equipment. Then Marc arrived with his 20 men as our six rail installers arrived to work with the railroad men. Rufus arrived with a tank of water, and then Henry delivered that massive earth moving tractor with two men to operate it— one to work the controls and the other to feed the coal fire and keep the steam pressure up."

Emmett worked with the railroad engineer and got valuable tips on how to lay tracks on solid rock. The work continued and by the end of the day, half the tracks were done, all concrete floors were done, and the water tank prefab walls were filled with concrete." "So, what is next?" "By tomorrow night, most of the rail tracks will be done, the barn and headquarters will have walls or more, the water tank will be filling, and some of the bedrock will be exposed—plus whatever else Harvey is planning to spring on us." "I should be able to leave work early tomorrow, so, if you get my buggy ready in the morning, I'll have Mel, the wrangler, take care of my horse and he'll hook up the buggy for me. I'll meet you at the pit around 4PM."

"No way, we're only a few months away from our agency days. There may still be some miscreants out there who may still have ideas of revenge on their mind. I'll have Rufus Whitlow pick you up on his second water run to the pit. He will pick you up at 3PM and bring your Bulldog. Rufus carries a pump shotgun and I know he is good with it. Plus he's a tough wiry old coot that will protect you and our baby—I trust him." "Ok, but we'll eventually have to let go this tight security." "Probably, but let's have more time elapse before that time."

Meanwhile, in a house rental across from the Bodine Factory, three out-of-towners dressed like city dudes were moving in. They had their horses in the barn out back and had brought enough supplies to last a week. "So boss, tell me again what the Califano family wants us to do?" "The family capo, Lou, wants us to capture Bodine's wife, and hide her in this house's cellar— right under Bodine's nose. After ten days, we'll just release her and get out of town real quick. The lady will carry a prepared letter from the family, warning Bodine that any further interference from him will result in a poorer outcome next time. A real simple job. Starting tomorrow, we'll watch the workers as they arrive and leave, and start simply documenting how Bodine's wife gets to work and back home—and with who. That way we can plan her kidnapping."

*

The next morning after a replenishing breakfast, Palmer led his horse and walked his wife to the factory. He then got on his horse and headed east.

Meanwhile, watchful eyes were busy at work. "Well, it figures that Bodine would walk his wife to work as he continues east on his horse to his pit mine. Now if he picks her up at night, we may have to resort to plan B." "Which is?" "No idea, guess we'd better start working on it."

Mia got to work, and things were bustling with 60 or so ladies chatting away. The expediters were busy stocking up the inboxes as the steam plant was being fired up for making compressed air. On time, Mia rang the start bell. Agnes got the new gals settled down in the same stations they were yesterday. Alice addressed the old workers. "Today we will be making new products, and on the brand-new machines. Line 1 will be making slim men's jeans in 12-ounce denim, so take your places in the same station positions you normally work. Line 2 will be making 16-ounce overalls, Line 3 will be making 10-ounce work shirts, as Line 4 will make 8-ounce casual shirts."

"Now line 5 will have some old and new parts to make. The old ones are belt loops and slim jeans pockets. The new ones will include: an overall bib panel to make useable slots, a new deep pocket on the left hip to hold a collapsible measuring stick, and a wider hammer loop for framing hammers on the right hip. Shirts will require varying lengths of banded or flip down collars, sleeve cuffs, and shirt pockets."

Agnes then takes over. "Alice and I will go thru line 1 and 2 and show you what you need to do on every station. Then we'll do line 3 and 4. Mia will go over the accessory parts with line 5."

After breaktime, all the workers were ready to sew their assigned pieces. A few ended up in the seconds' barrel, but for the most part, finished products were coming off the lines. At lunch time, Ralph came to see Mia. "The upstairs racks are finished, and I've arranged for the freight company to start bringing our rolls of denim." "Good. Now, do the freighters unload their wagon, and if so, where do they leave the rolls?" "They do unload the wagon, but they leave the rolls on the receiving porch. My new helper and I load them on the elevator and then transfer them to their racks upstairs." "No, no-no. You and your helper have enough to do. I'll hire the freighters to do the work. Better still, offer them each a silver dollar to do the job above their wages. Here is a bag of silver dollars, let's give it a trial, heh?" "Hell, Mia, these men will be fighting at the office; to go on the job. I am certain that a dollar almost doubles their daily salary."

The afternoon went quite smooth. Mia was spending time with Ella in the boxing department. They both examined the new products and finally Mia said. "This is quality. Please join me with Agnes and Alice. We need to set prices on the new products and raise the prices on old ones. You've got retail experience and know how customers react to prices. Waldo wants me to raise the prices on old products as much as 15% and to make the new products comparable."

Once things were going well on the floor, the four ladies gathered in the lunchroom. Mia had all eight products displayed on lunch tables with the old prices attached to old products. "This is the time to make up our minds. I would like to start with a discussion on your personal ideas in regard to pricing. I will start. I need to raise prices and be competitive with new products because I have a big investment and our products are already known for quality. I am hoping we can achieve a price that is still a good bang for their buck." Ella was next, "During my time at the emporium, I heard many times that the prices were too low. I know this is good material and well-made clothing. I think we can get good prices without much complaining." Agnes was next, "I know how much work goes into making these pieces, and although I don't know the bottom line, I feel we can get better than competitive prices." Alice was last to comment, but she kept looking at the new products. Finally she spoke up, "I am totally amazed at these new designs. You did good to hire Josie and I think you should set her loose to redesign our old products. If the old products are changed a bit, it will be justification to increase prices. As far as the new products, they are way above the quality as set in Sears Roebuck or Montgomery Wards for standard cotton or canvas products."

Mia pondered and finally said, "let's put down the competitive prices next to each product. Then, we all put a new price on each product and place the paper upside down next to each item. We will then tabulate the four prices and come to a consensus."

For the pricing, Gloria had prepared four packs of 8 voting stubs. An hour later, each person had added her preferred price—for a price that Waldo would have to pay for the product. Each lady was aware that he would add a middleman's fee of at least 10%, and as high as 15%, to pay for shipping, salesmen, warehousing, and a reasonable profit.

Gloria collected the votes and averaged each pile to the 25-cent level. As explained, an average of let's say $3.44 would be listed as $3.50. Whereas an average of $3.35 would be listed as $3.25. As it happened, all eight products went for one of four prices: $4.00, $4.25, $4.50, and $4.75. At the end of the meeting, Gloria was asked to telegram Waldo and inform him of the price changes on his next order.

At the end of the gathering, Rufus appeared at the lunchroom doorway and was totally enthralled at the shop full of women. "Boy, I will stop and pick you up anytime, just to revitalize my eyeballs. Your taxi is ready Ma'am."

Meanwhile, in the house next door, the leader said, "well speaking of luck, the

Bodine woman is in the water-wagon with that old coot. He must be bringing her to the pit. Let's saddle up, we'll shoot the old fool and take her captive. It's midday and that road east is not heavily traveled." Another man said, "yeah, but that woman is knocked-up. Are we going to still kidnap her?" "Hell yes, we're not going to hurt her, and besides, she is a double reason to bring Bodine to his knees—his wife and kid!"

Rufus and Mia were on their way at a comfortable trot for the team of geldings. "You're going to like what you'll see at the pit. The conversation continued as galloping horse were heard. Rufus turned around and saw three men riding their horses hard. He knew that this was not a good sign. "I don't like what is coming behind us Mia. Keep your Bulldog hidden with your dress but in your hand. Rufus pretended nothing was amiss as he turned his pump shotgun around and pointed the barrel in the wagon's floor with the trigger next to his right hand.

The riders, now clearly wearing face masks, overtook the water-wagon, and held up the wagon's team. The leader pulls his pistol and yells out, get out of the wagon you old coot, we want the lady, not you. If you don't get down, I'll shoot you dead where you sit!" "Go to hell!" Rufus drops the reins, grabs his shotgun and even before Mia pulled her Bulldog free of her dress, she heard BANG, kaching BANG, kaching BANG. Mia looked up and all three would be kidnappers had been knocked out of their saddles, and the leader's horse was also down. Without any hesitation, Rufus put his shotgun down, grabbed the reins and yells out, "hold on tight, we're out of here. Rufus slaps the reins on the horses' backs and yells, YAAAH--GET GOING, YAAAAAAAAH."

***

CHAPTER 10

Ending the Mob Threat

Palmer was talking to Emmett when, over the noise of the workers, the water-wagon was seen coming. The wagon was moving excessively fast and the horses were covered with lather. Rufus brought the wagon to a stop in front of Palmer. "Rufus, what's wrong, you look like you've looked at Beelzebub in the eye!" Mia answered, "we were just waylaid by three masked men. They wanted to kidnap me at gunpoint. Rufus pulled his pump shotgun and knocked all three out of their saddle as well as putting a horse to the ground."

Mia started crying as Palmer helped her off the wagon, and held her in his arms. "You were right, it's still too early to be away from the agency. We owe Rufus for saving my life and the life of our baby." Palmer walked over to Rufus, "where did you find the willpower to stop those men?" "All my life, I've been free of dependents, and I never had any one to protect until today. Today I had Mia in my charge and I was determined to shoot those three men, and I knew I would do it, even if they shot me in the head before I fired my first shot."

Palmer walked to Rufus, took his hand, and said, "to the end of your life, I will be grateful beyond words. I promise you this, if you ever need anything, the answer will be unquestionably, yes. I'm going over and check on those outlaws. While you are unloading your water-wagon, Mia can walk around to see what is going on. Afterwards, would you bring her home?" Emmett was standing by Mia and said, "I'll show her around and explain the goings on. Afterwards, I'll escort Rufus to make sure Mia gets home safely." "Great." Palmer kisses his wife and says, "I'll see you home, and still keep your Bulldog handy, although I suspect that the danger is resolved."

Palmer made his way to town, when he came on the gunfight site, two outlaws and one horse were dead on the ground, as the third outlaw was trying to get up in his saddle but was not succeeding. Palmer came up to him, took his pistol out of his holster, and said, "you have a bad shoulder wound and have lost a lot of blood. I'll help you up on your horse, and bring you to the local hospital. Then we're going to have a serious talk before the sheriff shows up."

Arriving at the hospital, Doc Sims took over. "Let me check out his wound and stabilize him. Then I'll come out and talk to you." Palmer waited and a half hour later Doc Sims came out of the emergency room. "This man has a shattered shoulder with buckshot still in the bone. I'm going to put him under and operate." "Before you do that, this man tried to kidnap Mia, and I need to know who he is and who ordered the kidnapping. Can I have 5 minutes with him?" "Certainly, and good luck. Is Mia alright?" "Shook up, but Ok, thanks to her elderly determined bodyguard."

Palmer walked in and said, "you're in a pack of trouble. Kidnapping is a hanging offense—if I press charges against you. Now I'm sure we can come to an agreement to save your life. I need to know your name, the name of your two dead partners, and the name of the man who sent you to do his dirty work." "I can't say, because if I do, I'm a dead man." "Well as it now stands, you'll hang if you live to even get to your trial. I'm sure who ever ordered this deed won't want you to divulge his name for a reduced sentence. Either way you're dead."

After allowing the outlaw time to digest his situation, Palmer added an alternative. "There is another way; if I don't press charges, give you $1,000, put you on a train, change your name, and head north, preferably to Canada—there you can restart your life under a new identity." The outlaw looked at Palmer and said, "why would you do this for a man who tried to abduct your wife?" "Because I suspect this kidnapping was ordered by the New Mexico mob. With names, I'm going to put an end to this—once and for all."

The outlaw was pensive for a while when he suddenly said, "my name is Gino Demelli, my partners were Marco and Flavio Bonatti. The man who ordered this is Lou Califano, a mob capo, and he lives at 1444 Bernini Drive in Albuquerque." "Deal. You'll be in the hospital for a few days recovering from surgery. I'll ask the doc to keep you here till I come back in 2 to 3 days, and I'll put your horse in a livery."

Palmer left the hospital and went straight to Sheriff Belknap's office. "What brings you here, Palmer?" "Two masked outlaws just tried to kidnap Mia. Fortunately, she was riding the water-wagon with Rufus and he put down both outlaws with his pump shotgun. Their bodies are on the east road to the pit. One horse was accidentally killed, so bring a rope to drag it off the road. You may also want to bring the undertaker. I'll settle with you later; Rufus and Mia will bring you their report. For now I have to go out of town on business for a few days." "Ok, Liam and I will get on this right away."

Arriving at the house, Rufus was just arriving as Emmett had just went home. "Rufus, come in the house a minute." Palmer explained his arrangement with the third outlaw; and why the event could only have happened with two, now dead outlaws. Both Mia and Rufus understood Palmer's deal, and would write their statements accordingly.

Later, after supper, Palmer told Mia the name of the man in Albuquerque who had ordered the kidnapping. Palmer then said, "I will be leaving for 2-3 days with the Lightfoots. I will make this Califano capo an offer he won't be able to refuse. This is the only way we can put an end to this mob threat. While I'm gone, please walk to the shop with mom and dad. Bring your Bulldog and ask dad to bring his pistol or shotgun, even if you have to explain this day's events." "Well in that case, they'll insist that I stay with them till you return."

"That's a great idea."

The next morning, the Trio took the train to Deming and connected to the northern route, through Truth or Consequences and Socorro, to Albuquerque. It was a 7-hour trip to cover 280 miles and include two meals. They decided to bring their horses, to get to Bernini Drive to avoid a taxi, and to have in case a quick escape was needed. For firearms, they elected to rely on hidden Bulldogs in shoulder holsters; as well as the Lightfoots' war clubs, knives, and Palmer's sap—plus moccasins for all.

During the trip everyone was reading. Palmer was reading several books on pit mining, hammer mills and smelters. Although the Lightfoots were financially secure and officially retired, they had started a small business to keep busy. They had a lead melting shop where they poured molten lead in molds to make bullets. Along with this they had all the modern reloading presses to make ammo. They had an arrangement with the gun shops and mercantiles in town, as well as the same retail locations in Deming. Their reading materials covered the current literature on these trades, as well as books on business management.

The Trio arrived in the city at 4PM. They got their horses, went looking for Bernini Drive, and found the mob's mansion at 1444. They rode by, and noticed that a gunman with a shotgun sat on the front porch. Mistah went back on foot in the woods and scouted the back of the building. He came back and said, "the windows are all barred, there is a shotgun bearing guard at the rear door and a side delivery door is also guarded. There is a huge black dog without a tail that roams the perimeter fence, and he don't look very friendly."

With this information, the Trio went to see a vet and picked up a tranquilizer used in shooing unruly horses. Next, they went to a mercantile and picked up several handkerchiefs and a roll of strong twine. Then they went to a diner for supper where they had their special—beefsteak, baked potatoes, carrots, hot rolls, apple pie and coffee. Before leaving, Palmer ordered a large steak, cooked rare, and to go."

With plenty of time to spend, the Trio elected to stay out of the public's eye by going to the train yard and purchasing three tickets and horse tags for the 6AM train south. Afterwards, they stopped at a livery to water and feed their horses. With nightfall, the Trio made their way to the woods area behind the capo's mansion. After leaving the horses tethered away from the mansion, the Trio made their way to the perimeter fence with the steak and extra paraphernalia.

By 2AM, the three guards and the black dog were sound asleep. Palmer throws the laced steak over the fence. As the steak hit the ground, the black dog's ears perked up. Quickly thereafter, the dog started sniffing, got up, and started walking around. When he found the steak, he started to tear it up and eat it. The dog never finished the steak before he laid down and fell either asleep or dead.

The Trio, wearing moccasins, slowly made their way to the three guards. Mistah was ten feet away from the first one when he woke up. Without a choice, Mistah hurled his war club and got a perfect face hit. He then gagged him with one handkerchief as he used the second one to secure the gag in place. He then tied his hands behind his back, tied his feet together, and walked away with the guard's shotgun. Missi had an easy time and got right behind her guard, knocked him out, gagged, and tied him up. Palmer was bolder. He got right next to his guard, tapped him on the nose to wake him, and said, "you'd be wise to get another job."

After knocking him out with a solid sap hit on his forehead, he secured him in place like the others.

The Trio made their way upstairs. There were four bedrooms. Two were empty, one had a woman and the last had a man who was snoring loudly. The Trio went into the lady's room, gagged her and tied her in place. They then entered the man's room. Palmer took his Bulldog and tapped the man's front teeth. The capo woke with shock on his face. The Lightfoots quickly tied his hands together onto a bed post, as well as spreading his legs and tying them to separate bed posts.

"Well Mister Califano, we finally meet. My name is Palmer Bodine and you tried to kidnap my wife. Palmer then put three round punches on the man's face, flattened his nose and pushed two teeth out. Califano was spitting blood and teeth as he said, "you're a dead man." "Nope, I 'm very much alive and I'm going to prove to you that it's time to leave the Bodines alone, or I'm going to maim you for life."

Without warning, Palmer takes his right hand and breaks all five of the capo's fingers on his right hand. Califano screamed his heart out. "Are you ready to make a deal?" "Go to hell!" "Too bad, Palmer grabs his sac, squeezes it, makes a slice and pops out one testicle. He then grabs it and yanks it out with full force. Califano was too shocked to scream and just kept looking at his bleeding sac and his jewel in Palmer's hand.

Palmer spoke, "I strongly suspect that you know I mean business." As he was speaking, Mistah stepped up and quickly cut off one of his eyebrows, and quickly followed by whacking off the opposing ear. Califano was now begging, "STOP-STOP-STOP!". "Next, on the agenda, my Indian friend will now scalp you like Indians do so well. Afterwards, we're going to pop one of your eyes out. And if that doesn't work, we'll take the other jewel—"Ok, Ok, Ok. What do you want?"

"It's rather simple, I want you to forget this vendetta, you lost the fight to add human trafficking to Silver City. You will not win by sending assassins and kidnappers after us—in short, I want you to forget the name Bodine, and move on with your life and crime syndicate. If your attempt to hurt us does not stop, we will return, and scalp you as well as take both your eyes out. Do we have a deal." "Yes, on my parent's grave, I promise you will never hear my name again, nor will I ever raise a hand against you or your family." "Good, we'll now release that women in the next bedroom so she can get you some medical attention."

"Oh, and by the way, your tool will still work with only one jewel, heh? To save face let your hair grow to cover your missing ear and eyebrow. That is a lot simpler than hiding a scalped bald head with a wig. You made the correct move just in time to save your scalp."

The Trio then made their way to their horses, headed for the train yard, and took the train home. Once on the train, Missi said, "well, I would say that went pretty well." Mistah grumbled, "yeah, but I again lost my chance to scalp a white man!" Palmer added, "For sure!"

*

That evening at home, Palmer reassured Mia that the mob threat was resolved without going over the gory details. Mia accepted that and then expressed disbelief as to the speed the pit mine project was coming along. "Rufus brought me again today, and you won't believe where things have progressed since you left. The barn is finished, and I like it that it's one floor with the hay/grain room easily accessible to the feeding racks. There is a well-organized tack room and a nice private corner for Mel Johnson, your wrangler. The nice feature is a lean-to waiting area for saddled horses before closing time. The water tank is conveniently placed to fill the outside and inside water troughs, and easily accessible to the earth moving tractor."

"The tracks and switches are all installed, and the railroad team is gone. Emmett and his six laborers are now laying tracks for the steam shovel and open boxcar over the rocks. Liam Johanson and his drillers are making a lot of stone chips for ballast. Liam seems to work well with Emmett. The carpenters will finish your headquarters' building tomorrow. Then they build a tool shed and coal bin. Out of need, the dynamite shed has already been built and full of dynamite for storage—far away from the pit and buildings."

"The neatest thing is a six-foot high free-standing wall of massive timbers next to the pit." "What is it for?" "For the men to hide behind when the dynamite explodes, heh?" "Anyways, we both need to be at the pit tomorrow at 3PM for the arrival of that massive steam shovel. Liam has been drilling all day today, and is blasting away all day tomorrow to yield some ore for loading. We'll be able to see a demonstration of this thing in a live setting."

"It is nice to know, that I wasn't needed for the past two days, and things got done." "That's because we have good men with strong work ethics." "Enough about the pit, what's new at the shop?" "Stepping back, days before the kidnapping attempt, I had sent Waldo three boxes of all our new products—with our new prices. Waldo has three salesmen that cover three districts, and these men will now peddle our products in several new locations. I suspect that the results are available since Waldo is coming tomorrow morning for an emergency meeting; and I would like you to be there."

"Sure, besides I'll be there afterwards to talk to Hollis about his future with Bodine Manufacturing. Other than that, how is production coming along?" "We're producing at optimum levels. Waldo pays us the day he picks up a load and we haven't touched his $10,000 deposit. The gals are making top quality products and at maximum production rates. We are going thru denim as fast as we can order and receive the shipments. Alice and Agnes are very satisfied with all the workers and are tweaking and distributing the workload of each station."

"What does this 'tweaking' mean?" "Let's say a gal has a difficult part to sew, or too many parts to sew, then Alice will take some of these duties and move them down the line till every station workload matches the others. That is the ideal way to get a steady flow of products and not have idle workers waiting for products in their inbox." "Ok, how is Dad and Mom doing?" "Mom is handling the extra products very well. Your dad is happy working with Billy, his new helper. He has recently succeeded in paying the denim delivery workers, my idea, an extra dollar per man per load, and they are unloading the rolls, placing them on the downstairs' racks, or on the elevator, and stacking them upstairs in their appropriate racks." "Good for you and for Dad—that was money well spent."

"We do have a potential issue. We have four workers, cutting patterns, using the power fabric cutters. The fifth machine is needed to keep the stitchers supplied. So, Josie, Jan, and Billy spend two hours each on the power cutters, and they do a very nice job avoiding over cutting that requires trimming with hand scissors." "Why is that and who does the remaining two hours?" "We think because short term cutter operators don't develop equipment fatigue. And I'm the fourth cutter operator. I enjoy it and I'm good at it—unlike the poor job I do on sewing machines."

"Sounds to me like you need more power cutters and operators." "I agree, but I'm waiting for tomorrow's meeting with Waldo. If we need more machines, we get the biggest discount with large orders. For 2-4 machines we get a 5% discount, 5-9 is 10%, and 10 or greater gives us a 15% savings." "Whoa, that's good planning! Now in case we need more workers, do you have a waiting list of preapproved people?" "Yes, I have dozen ladies ready to jump in, but keep in mind that we only have six extra machines and three are being used when Hollis has three in the shop being rebuilt. New workers mean an emergency machine order." "Ok, well let's get some shuteye, Waldo's train from Deming arrives at 7AM and he'll be at your doorsteps before opening time." "What kind of shuteye do you have in mind—one or two eyes?" "For me, both eyes open to stay the course, heh?" "For sure!"

The next morning the Duo was up by predawn. After a replenishing breakfast of fried potatoes, bacon, eggs, toast, and coffee; the Duo made their way to the shop by 7:30. As expected, Waldo was sitting on the porch talking to some of the early workers. "Come in Waldo, I'll put the coffee on while we wait for Alice, Agnes, and Ella."

Sitting in Mia's office, Waldo started. "Since you sent me those three boxes of new items, my three salesmen have been beating the bushes. We now have three districts of new customers. District 1 is two old sites in Albuquerque and a new one in Santa Fe. District 2 covers Tucson and Phoenix Arizona, and El Paso Texas. District 3 is Pueblo and Denver Colorado. Denver has three big stores, one garment and two department stores. These three stores encompass almost 40% of our orders. I can say that the orders are coming in faster than I can fill them."

"Now, your new prices are more than fair. The good news is that I just negotiated a new contract with the railroad. In view of the new customers on their lines, they reduced my freight charges, they are charging me $5 per crate that measures 48X36 inches and holds up to 100 pounds of merchandise—that comes to eight of your boxes totaling +- 50 items. The retailers have to order that many items to get the minimum freighting charge. With this good news, I'm tacking on my 10% instead of the old 15%."

"Now, the demand for your clothes has changed. The biggest seller is men and women's slim jeans— or a package of slim jeans, vests and shirts.

The demand for mining pants is way down, and incidentally, we now call them work pants. The next popular item is denim overalls for homesteaders— now over-selling canvas overalls."

"Adjusting for the demand, stop making work pants. I have a supply that will last at least two months. Replace those two lines with extra lines for slim men and women's jeans." Alice interjected, "we now have 10 lines for a total of 60 stitchers. We can change the 10-line makeup as follows: Slim jeans-4, vests-1, work shirts-1, casual shirts-1, overalls-1, and accessories-2."

"Now, the problem at hand. I desperately need to build up an inventory surplus of these new products. What is the potential for your ladies working on Saturdays for the next 6 weeks?" "That means a $6 pay for overtime. Plus, the 60 stitchers and dozen ancillary staff willingness to work. Many have families and have household duties to do over the weekend." "I will pay the $2 overtime over standard pay out of my $10,000 deposit. Now let's ask them if they are all willing to work."

Alice blew her whistle and explained the situation. When asked to vote with a show of hands, seven hands were down. Waldo spoke up, "how about $7 a day for everybody?"(I'll pay the extra

$3 for overtime)." Loud cheers and applause were heard, and those seven hands went up.

Returning to Mia's office, Waldo addressed his last issue. "I see that you have six lines not being used. What is the potential of filling those empty lines." "That means 36 more stitchers and three more pattern cutters. We only have five single apartments left to rent, and the boarding houses are full. There are no more locals we can hire, so we are restricted by housing. Palmer has a big investment in developing a pit mine that, without housing, we are not planning such an expansion."

"A housing deficit can be fixed. Take my $10,000 deposit and have Marc Weber build us two separate 15-unit apartment complexes. I will pay the balance of expenses and will become a landlord with a good solid investment. This is such a boom town, that I can't lose. The extra workers will guarantee my business expansion. It is a well-known fact that there are plenty of unemployed people in the cities we are dealing with. Advertise as you have done in the past--$4 a day with five years-experience, housing at $35 a month for a single furnished apartment, $45 for a two bedroom furnished unit, applicant must be willing to move to town, and a sign on bonus of $100 to cover moving expenses and wardrobe upgrade."

Mia looked at the other people in the room. Agnes started, "you built it to hold 96 stitchers, heh?" Alice added, "it can be done, and it's certainly better than a second shift. However, we're going to need a third supervisor, and Agnes and I know which stitcher is capable of doing the job." Ella was thinking and said, "I hate to say it, but I'm going to need a helper. If so, I'm all for it." Mia added, will do Ella." Palmer asked, "is there enough room in the pattern cutting room to add three new power cutters?" "Yes." "Then, it's up to you Mia, I think it's the thing to do."

Mia asked, "Waldo, are you sure you can distribute all our products?" "I know I can, but if I start building an excessive inventory surplus, I will do one of two things. I will extend our customers to new cities, or contact Sears Roebuck or Montgomery Ward myself, and schedule an appointment with one of their executives. Mia, you have nothing to lose." "Alright, but we're going to do this differently this time. We are not hiring 36 more stitchers as one block. We are going to advertise out of town, I will hire 6 stitchers at a time, then give them to my supervisors to get them matriculated. We will follow the status of your apartments before we hire people to move to town. And I will order ten machines at a time. This gradual increase in production should allow you to meet your order commitments, or add new customers if necessary."

"Great, how long before Marc is finished with your project?" "Probably available as early as today. Stop over at his office, if not there, I'll give you a ride to the pit where you'll find him."

On their way out, Waldo asked, "I'm certain you have new products planned for the future. What is Josey working on?" "Actually, she is designing short summer and fall jackets, short winter coats, and long riding winter dusters—but don't count on them by the next moon cycle."

*

Palmer drove Waldo to the pit where he could meet with Marc. He returned by mid-morning to meet with Hollis before they returned to the pit to see the steam shovel's arrival. "How is it going Hollis?" "I have about three more days to finish rebuilding these sewing machines. Then I'm done. Kip Turner is very capable of maintaining the power plant, as well as turning on the gas lamps and heating stoves. If there is anything he can't handle he will call me. So I guess, I'll shortly be pulling my wages and will return once a month to service your machines. I will come at 5PM and will work till dark. These gears have to be greased once a month and this is the kind of work I do. The gals will oil their machines every morning as I've instructed them. If a machine breaks, your service arrangement will bring a repair man to fix it."

"So, there is not enough work here to keep you on full time. What about work at the pit?" "Not really, Henry maintains his steam shovel and earth moving tractor. If there is a breakdown that his men cannot fix, he calls me for assistance. Your mini engine that moves about railcars will be maintained by the railroad company. So, this has been a fantastic place to work. The job has been good advertisement for me, as I have two big jobs waiting for me." "Very well, leave your bill with Mia's secretary, and we insist on seeing all those extra overtime hours we know you put in." "Thank you, you are very generous." "More like appreciative, for sure! If you need a future reference, feel free to use my name."

After a small lunch at Grady's, the Duo left for the big event at the pit. While waiting for the train's delivery, they went into the headquarters to see how the finish work was coming along. The workers said that Marc had left with Waldo to look at some land and work on floor plans. The Duo started looking around.

The break room was insulated, the walls finished with tongue & groove, a coal heating stove installed, and tables built in place. Emmett's office was being finished as they toured the two office spaces for Harvey and Palmer's offices. A secretary's reception area was added with a customer service counter. Basically, the finish carpenters would be done in two days. Mia made a note to have office furniture, chairs, and other items, presently in storage, be delivered in two days.

As the Duo walked to the pit site, a whistling/chugging steam locomotive was heard coming down the tracks. All the workers moved to the main line switch to see what was arriving. The locomotive was pushing four empty open boxcars, one tarp covered boxcar full of coal, a flatbed carrying a steam powered tractor/locomotive to move cars around the pit area, and the last flatbed was carrying the massive steam engine.

Everyone was in total disbelief, despite looking directly at the monstrous machine built by a plant in Wisconsin. Mia said, "it's inconceivable how a plant can manufacture such a 'huge' structure.

Where do they get a 25-foot boom in one piece?" "In one 'huge' steel plant." "To think they are using these to build the Panama Canal—how do they get a steam shovel to Panama?" "By train some 1200 miles to Galveston. Then 'huge' 1,000-ton sea faring freighters transport it another 1,500 nautical miles to Panama." "I'm beginning to get the message, when dealing with steam shovels, everything is HUGE!"

There were four separate side rails controlled by several switches. The far right was the parking area for full boxcars containing coal or copper ore. The next on the left was a holding area for empty boxcars. The next was the line to bring the steam shovel onto the bedrock tracks. And the furthest on the left was the line to bring boxcars for loading.

Once the tractor/locomotive was unloaded and coupled to an empty boxcar, the boxcar was placed on the bedrock for loading and the tractor was shut down till the filled boxcar needed to be parked and replaced. The last item to be rolled onto the tracks was the steam shovel.

Because these shovels did not have their own propulsion, the main operator was putting his bucket on the ground and pulling himself off the flatbed. Once unloaded, the machine made its way slowly next to the empty boxcar. To the right of the shovel was an extensive spread or large stone pieces from the dynamite excavation—ready for loading. At that point, the fireman let the steam blow off with a loud whistle, and the three men walked down to introduce themselves to the workers.

"Hello folks, my name is Lou West, this is my brother Skip, and that is Mortimer McClusky. We are the operators, which means that every day we switch jobs so we can do all three jobs. Since I'm the oldest I'll be the main operator sitting on the rotating platform, Skip will control the winches and gears, and Mort will be the fireman and steam plant monitor. Tomorrow I will be the fireman as Skip becomes the main operator, and so on."

Palmer asked, "what do you need from us?"

"Nothing, as long as your 6-man team keeps laying tracks ahead of the shovel and boxcar, we are completely independent. We start the day by filling our coal tinder by wheelbarrow transport from the coal boxcar to our tinder. We will take water out of your tank to fill our own tank. As long as there is an empty boxcar ready to load and your dynamite man keeps breaking up the bedrock, we'll load a 75-ton boxcar every day—even if we have to work late some days."

Harvey asked, "this unit, as huge as it is, seems to be smaller than the 150-ton units sent to the Panama Canal." "That is correct. This shovel has a 24-inch bucket. It's smaller because of the heavy weight of rock compared to dirt. This unit weighs approximately 95 tons loaded with water and coal. The two advantages are: the three hardened teeth on the bucket that tears sedimentary rocks apart, and the altered gear ratio makes it a fast turning boom and moving dipper stick."

Harvey had an interesting question, "I see that cables control the works. Do these cables ever break?" "We've been using these shovels for three years, and no cable has ever broken. You need to realize that the one-inch cable that holds the boom, dipper stick and bucket is rated for 40 tons which is way higher than the actual tension on them. What does rarely happen is that the cable connections slip and let go. That will put us out of commission till we cut off the stripped end, bend it over the u-track and apply three new bolted clamps—usually a one-hour job. By not filling the bucket, we tend to avoid this event."

Mia asks, "I've heard that these steam boilers on riverboats have been known to explode. What are the chances that could happen here and kill several men?" "Like the earth moving steam tractor, the steam plant is never left alone. There are fail safe valves that will automatically open if the pressure gets too high, but you know how these valves can fail. A man who is trained to watch the double gauges can thwart a potential catastrophe if a release valve sticks closed. So, at lunch, one man is left in the steam plant to maintain the coal fire and watch gauges. The other two will be glad to use your break room."

Emmett was next, "when do you do the daily maintenance?" "In the morning, it takes an hour to build up the fire and steam pressure to operate this thing. That is when we replenish the coal and water as mentioned, do the gear greasing and oiling, as well as other maintenance for the day."

Liam had the last question. "What are these red sawhorses, with connecting ropes, surrounding your equipment and boxcar. That's to keep all workers 30 feet away from our equipment. To prevent injury from falling rocks, and falling booms in case steel cables let go."

Liam quickly added, "in the same regards, we blast rock at noon and at closing. We require all workers to stand behind the blast wall with earplugs in place. That includes you three as well, Ok?"

"You'll get no arguments from us. Well, it's 3:30 and with the steam pressure still up, we thought we would give you a demonstration of what this baby can do."

Lou lifted the boom, rotated 90 degrees to the right, and dropped the boom. The dipper stick positioned the bucket as Lou filled the bucked to a ¾ level, lifted the boom, turned 180 degrees to the left and placed the bucket over the boxcar. The shovel's bottom opened, and its load fell in the boxcar. Lou yells out, "by my watch, it took 3 minutes to load a half ton of rock. That means we can load 20 buckets in an hour which is 10 tons per hour. And that is how we can load a 75-ton boxcar in one day."

Emmett was impressed as he added, "they say this thing is equal to 100-125 men—as if you could get that number of men around a boxcar and fill it in one day when the rock being loaded is 2-6 feet below surface. Unreal, totally unreal." Palmer adds, "It's clear to me that without a steam shovel, pit mining is impossible." As Mia adds, "and with less than 15 employees: 6 track layers, 2 drillers, 1 steam/air compressor operator, one tractor/locomotive operator, 1 engineer, 1 dynamite man, and 2 office staff. Now what is wrong with this picture; I have 100 women to your fifteen men, and I will make a quarter of your income!" "True, but I won't be any more satisfied or productive than you will be—I think, heh?"

***

CHAPTER 11

Operational Changes

Six weeks had passed, and the Duo was again having a business discussion in their home parlor. Palmer started, "well how are things going at the shop and what is new?" "I finally have the first financial statistics that I can share with you. Ella said that the last 5-day week, with 60 stitchers and 12 ancillary staff, produced 2,000 pieces. Now if we fill the remaining six lines with 36 more stitchers, our production will go up to +-3,000 pieces a week—at a low $4 a piece, that's $12,000 a week."

"I also have a tentative weekly expense list to include: Cost of denim and other materials=$5,000, labor for 115 workers=$3,000, investment payback=$500, operating expenses=$500, and other unscheduled expenses=$500. That comes up to $9,500 a week in expenses—or a profit of $2,500 a week. Is that realistic?"

"Yes, it can be real. Just to remind you that Harvey is predicting the same profit margin for the pit mine. Your figures will be more realistic if based on a month, and closer to reality when it includes six months. But for now this is a reassuring early analysis."

"Second issue, do you really think that Waldo can peddle 3,000 pieces a week, now with a well built-up inventory?" "I have no idea, but if his payments come in, you need to wait him out." "Money is always there by telegraph voucher the day he receives his shipment." "Then, keep supplying him. When the payments are late, Sears and Wards are only a telegram away, heh?"

"How are the interviews going?" "We brought in the six local ladies on our waiting list that don't need housing. Alice and Agnes are now putting them thru a training program. Every day, I conduct 2-4 interviews. As soon as I have six strong candidates, I will bring them to town. That will occupy the five apartments we have vacant plus one recently vacated boarding house room. After that I will continue building a waiting list and bring them in as Waldo's apartments open up."

"For your information, I went to see how the apartments were coming along. The first floor units are now finished and will be furnished this week. That will give you 6 single apartments and 2 larger double bedroom ones. The finishing crew is now on the second floor as the rough crew is framing the next unit." "That is good news."

"What is new on the shop floor?" Alice and Agnes have chosen the 3rd supervisor. They chose a gal that started with them in our first shop—one of the original six. Her name is Agatha, and from now on I will refer to my three supervisors as the A-Team—that's a lot simpler than to refer to them by name: Alice, Agnes and Agatha. As a preparation, Agatha is spending a week with each line to learn how to master each station. So in 10 weeks or less, she'll be helping Alice and Agnes. Agatha will share an office with Alice who had the largest office."

"All good news, what's new with the cutters?" "Hollis installed the three new machines. Two weeks ago, I hired the 5th worker. It was a middle-aged lady, by the name of Sheila, who admitted she was lousy at sewing. Yet, some of her physical attributes made her a possible candidate. We put her on a powered cutter, and within a half hour, she was working as fast and accurate as my other experienced cutters. She was a natural talent and was hired on the spot."

"When we went back to fill out her employment papers, she gave me her last name as McGivern!" "You don't mean..........naaw, it couldn't be?" "Oh yes, Emmett's wife. She's been at it for two weeks and is doing a perfect job. Plus the lady is happy as a lark, she now has lady friends for the first time in her life. This may be good for both our businesses—for if the wife is 'on solid ground,' then the husband will be as well. For satisfaction breeds contentment, heh?"

"So that is why Emmett just refused a job with twice the income. Yesterday, the railroad engineer came to do a courtesy visit. He was impressed at the quality work Emmett was doing to secure the tracks from sliding on bedrock. He offered Emmett twice his income, but Emmett refused. He would not take his wife on the road again. They were both happy where they were, and that was not about to change."

"How are Mom and Dad doing?" "Your dad is fine and seems happy with his work. Your mom just found her own helper. She stole Miranda from my Emporium. Miranda was easily replaced by a worker's friend. And there is no doubt, that Ella and Miranda are not just friends, they really work well together."

"Well, we've covered most of the bases, now what about you. How are you doing with work and the pregnancy?" "I am fine. Doc Ross says that the baby is growing on schedule and I remain free of complications. I am now 7 months along and Doc has not placed any restrictions. What is about to change is my appearance. I will move from being 'just pregnant,' to being 'heavy with child.'"

"Now what about you, how is the mining coming and are there any problems?" "The mining couldn't be any smoother. Liam and Emmett get along very well. The shovel men are operational masters, the railroad is picking up the loaded rail cars on a regular schedule, Emmet is staying ahead of the boxcars and shovel, and Harvey and I are handling the business aspects. We even have a business secretary. Things could not be any better." "Yet I detect that there is an issue, to block the wheels!"

"Yes, we supply the hammer mill with a full boxcar each day. But they are unable to process the incoming ore, and so we have 8 boxcars waiting in their parking lot. Every week, they now park two boxcars in the lot, but parking space is soon to be full. That means we'll have to shut down for intermittent weeks at a time. The holdup is the first stage in the hammer mill—the rock crushing stage. Actually, the second and third stages are waiting for crushed rock. In other words, the entire plant is held waiting for the rock crushing first stage, while my boxcars wait in the parking lot."

"Why doesn't the hammer mill install a second rock crusher." "You see, the entire plant is powered by that 10-foot water-wheel. The water flow turns the wheel, which in turn is geared down, to perform the rock crushing, hammer stamping and roller grinding. Apparently, the mill cannot afford another rock crusher's demand for geared down power—for the mill will fail. Yet, if I could deliver crushed rocks, my boxcars will be able to bypass the mills slow step, and thereby solve our problem."

"Now husband, I know you never present a problem without a feasible solution, so spit it out." "Correct, the solution is a mobile steam powered unit that converts the flywheel energy into the force needed to crush sedimentary rocks. In other words, we need our own rock crusher that does the job before loading the boxcars." "Really, and whose idea is that?" "Combination of Liam, Emmett, Harvey, the shovel Trio, Hollis, Henry, and me."

"Whoa, with 9 cooks stirring the pot, this is going to cost big bucks. Tell me more!"

"The mobile rock crusher is like the shovel. The crusher is built on a railway chassis. The rear portion is the coal fired power plant. The steam's power is converted to gears that gear down the power to the point that it activates the steel plates to crush rock. The steam shovel drops a bucket load into the crusher. The steel plates close and crush the rock. The small rocks fall thru grisly bars, and the large leftover pieces get crushed again on the next pass. Once the crushed rocks get thru the grisly bars, the receiving bucket lifts and dumps its load into the boxcar."

"So, looking back, I went to see Henry, who called in Hollis to design this machine. Once the design was accepted, Hollis went to Ohio to have the massive steel crushing plates manufactured. At this time, the steam plant is built with its own housing, the gears are now being installed, and the dumping bucket is installed along with the grisly bars. As soon as the steel plates arrive, we'll have our own rock crusher, as I already have two men lined up for the job."

"It sounds like this will now require three sets of tracks." "Yes, one for the boxcars and one for the dumping crusher—both on the first level. This means that the shovel is moving down the lower excavated 2nd bench on a third set of tracks. Emmet is already setting tracks on the next bench, and making a graded access to the lower level. Liam has meanwhile changed his blasting to provide the shovel some accessible rocks."

"How deep is this next bench?" Every blasting involves drilling 4 feet deep and the blast disrupts rock for 6 feet. So, the steam shovel will now be 6 feet below the first level—more than enough for the boom to reach above the crusher's top edge. These three tracks will continue around the ½ mile circle. The shovel will now stay on this lower bench, and allow it to excavate ahead and to the right before moving ahead."

"This appears to be a financially sound and well-planned addition. How much for the total project?" "$5,000—which is peanuts compared to the parked boxcars full of ore worth some $40,000 before expenses. Now they will eventually be processed since we only plan to bring crushed rocks to the hammer mill."

*

Two months later, the Duo had just finished an agenda for an unscheduled meeting with the sewing staff. Afterwards, they discussed the current status of both businesses. Mia started, "It took three weeks to fill the last six lines. Now, being well trained, the shop is putting out some fine clothing. Josie designed some fine new items to include loose ladies' riding pants; and a full-length, front buttoning, and general use ladies' dress. Both these items use 10-ounce denim for comfort and durability. With the extra stitchers, we resumed building regular and extra wide work pants."

"As of a month ago, we are producing a solid 3,000 pieces a week. Waldo finally admitted that 2,000 pieces a week was all he could handle. So, we already have 4,000 pieces, boxed, and stored upstairs. Waldo has contacted the two large mail-order catalog companies. Sears is not currently interested since they have two clothing manufacturers and their next catalog is not due for another 8 months."

"What about Montgomery Ward?" "The message I got was that they were very much interested. Apparently, there are only 30 days left to include an advertisement page in the next catalog. For this reason, we're having two top executives visiting in two days. This visit is what has become my utmost concern. I really want to nail a contract to take up our surplus before my maternity leave. If it isn't Wards, then Waldo will look for non-competitive distributors on the west coast to include California, Oregon, or Washington—which will take a month and another 4,000 surplus pieces."

"Well, good luck." "How about things at the pit?" "Everything has centered on this rock crusher. After it was built, Hollis came to get three one cubic foot rocks weighing +- 150 pounds each. When they placed one rock in the crusher, the machine pulverized it and all the chips went thru the grisly bars. The same happened with the other two rocks. When they brought the unit on site, the shovel operators quickly realized that if they slowly opened the bucket and spread the load in the crusher, the results were much more effective. The loading process was not delayed since the crusher could crush and dump its chips in the boxcar before the shovel arrived with the next bucket-full."

"For other news, the earth moving tractor has stripped the overburden and is now back at Henry's. On that same note, we are now paying Henry's $300 weekly fee—and we can afford it. That steam shovel has worked every day without breakdowns.

The hammer mill has finally processed our boxcar backlog—ironically their rock crusher is now down half the time, and we save on our crushed ore deliveries. And last, we are now shipping 50-pound copper bricks regularly to recycling and distribution centers in Tucson and Albuquerque"

"This all sounds great. Out of curiosity, did your free use of the steam shovel and tractor turn out beneficial for Henry?" "Oh yes, I have been entertaining 'big wigs' in the construction industry—especially those involved with large community projects. That second steam shovel has been on loan to big cities since my unit was on display. To Henry, distance is not important—he will ship it hundreds of miles on a train flatbed to get the $300 a week fee."

"What ever happened to the miners to our east?" "They couldn't get together in time, and the second shovel went to construction projects. Now they regret being procrastinators. Instead, they bought one of Henry's rock crushers and are loading it with wheelbarrows on a moveable ramp to follow the crusher."

"Well, you've always said, 'the time to strike is when the iron is hot!'" "Yes, and when you are in business, those challenges come around regularly.

So, what is the theme of you meeting tomorrow?"
"Longevity."

*

Without warning, Mia rang the closing bell early at 3:30PM. Alice then yells, "everyone in the lunchroom." After everyone was seated, Mia started, "before we start the business portion, I want you to meet our current staff at the emporium. Three gals stand and introduce themselves. Mia then adds, "I consider you part of this family, and whatever benefits I announce today, will include you."

"As you can see, my time is near. After the birth I will take 4-6 weeks of leave, and Alice will be the temporary manager." *Applause.* The other announcement is the fact that Waldo's wide starving mouth has been satiated. We now produce 1,000 surplus pieces a week over Waldo's 2,000 pieces. Tomorrow, I will be entertaining two executives from Montgomery Ward as a start in our search for a second distributor."

"Now for the theme of this meeting. 'Longevity means security!' As a business, we firmly believe that keeping our trained employees is an important key to success. For this reason, we believe in the 'trickledown effect—meaning, if we make money, then the employees should be able to share a portion of the profits. Well, we are making money, so this is our profit-sharing proposal: First, bonuses for longevity. For those original six stitchers, $200. *Applause.* For the next six to join us, $175. *Applause.* For the next group to join us after we expanded the original shop, $150. *Applause.* For everyone else, $100. *Applause, cheers and hoots.* Now, feel free to pay up your lines of credits, for we want the merchants to know that our employees have good paying jobs and are a good credit risk."

"Secondly, every worker gets a permanent pay raise of one dollar a day. *More applause and exclamations.* We will also celebrate three holidays, 4th of July, Thanksgiving, and Christmas, with a paid day off."

"Third, we have decided to close this factory one week a year and provide you with a paid weeks' vacation. The question is whether it should be at Christmas time, or the 4th of July. So please take that 2-inch paper in front of you and write your choice down as Gloria picks them up for tabulation."

"Now, moving away from salaries, let's get back to longevity and its benefits. For any employee that is with us for one year, we will provide the worker short-term disability for any illness or injury. We will pay your full salary up to 8 weeks. If the disability extends beyond 8 weeks, but less than 12 weeks, we will pay half your salary. Beyond 12 weeks, we will guarantee you a job when you are ready to return."

"For employees who are with us 5 years, we will offer you long-term disability. That means, if two doctors state you are no longer able to work in this factory, we will maintain your full salary for life. As some examples, if you are blind, have cancer, had a paralyzing stroke, or crippled with arthritis, you would be considered fully disabled."

Palmer was watching faces, and it was clear that no one ever anticipated this type of benefit. "The last benefit is retirement income. If you are with us 15 years, at age 55 or later, we will guarantee you a life-long yearly income equal to 35% of your retirement year's salary."

After more prolonged applause with happy faces, Palmer had a closing announcement, "Gloria's tabulation reveals, 92 votes for July and 23 for Christmas—guess that no one likes the heat, heh?" *Plenty of closing applause, hoots and THANK YOU'S.*

*

The Montgomery Ward advance team had spent the night at a local hotel. They were on the factory's doorsteps before any of the employees' arrival. The two were mingling with the ladies as Palmer and Mia arrived. Eventually, a gentleman came to Mia and introduced himself. "Hello, my name is Wendell Biddy and I carry the money. My associate is Claire Aubuchon, still talking to your employees. She is the marketing and advertising specialist. Actually, she tells me whether our company can make money with your product."

"Very good, let's bring everyone inside, start the workers, and pull Claire free of the potential complainers, heh?" As per routine, Alice got the sewing machines activated with compressed air, oiled, bobbins filled, and started the production. Wendell was looking at how the machines were powered, visited Kip in the power plant, visited the cutters, shipping and receiving, boxing, and talked with Josie and Jan. Satisfied at what he saw for a supporting staff, he then started to watch the stitchers themselves. He was impressed in their use of the "in and outbox" system, and was amazed at their dexterity. Mia heard him ask what the stitchers did with junk pieces. The bold stitcher said, "Sir, we don't make seconds or bad pieces. For the rare accident, we give the piece to the accessory cutters for parts." Like Claire, he examined every finished product and basically liked everything he saw. Yet, Claire had not yet spoken.

Palmer had been following Wendell around to answer questions, as Mia was following Miss Aubuchon. Claire was examining every final piece in detail. Mia realized that she was actually scrutinizing every detail down to the quality of buttonholes, buttons, rivets, and even down to the quality of stitching. This lady shocked Mia when she took a pair of riding pants and went to try them on in the ladies' bathroom. She came out wearing the riding skirt, stepped over to the vests, tried on a lady's model, took a man's vest and told Wendell to try it on. All Claire ever said was hu-um repeatedly. After two hours, the 10 o'clock bell rung for the morning break. Claire again mingled with the workers as Wendell stepped outside to enjoy a local cheroot.

After the resuming bell, Mia asked if they wanted to resume their inspection. Claire finally spoke, "no, we're done." Mia then handed her two boxes as she said, "during the break, my super prepared these two boxes of samples of our products, in case you would like to bring them to your superiors." Wendell simply looked at Claire as she said, "ma'am that is not necessary, but we'll bring them of course, because no one would ever believe what we saw here today. Ma'am, this is the most beautiful and well-made line of clothing I have ever seen—and this pair of riding pants are mine forever!"

Claire looked at Wendell and added, "Wendell, this clothing line will sell like hotcakes and will likely end up in the top 20 bestselling products in our catalog. If you don't sign a contract today, I'll have you examined by a head doctor, after you find yourself picking up beets in Wyoming. You see Ma'am, he may say he carries the money, but I make the final decisions."

Wendell spoke up, "so what are your prices like, and what financial arrangements would you like—keep in mind we know you have a significant surplus upstairs."

Mia was bold and said, "as far as the surplus, it is denim and not tomatoes or bread—it don't go bad! The surplus has no bearing on prices, since you're not the only fish in the pond. In addition, Mia pointed out that this 'full-line' of clothing offered four major categories: a work category to include pants, shirts and overalls. Casual wear to include jeans, shirts, and vests. A riding garment category to include riding skirts, and jeans. And finally a lady's category of jeans, riding pants and full- length dresses."

"My prices for every item fall in one of four-dollar amounts: $4, $4.25, $4.50, and $4.75. I ship 50 pieces, labeled in six or eight boxes, in a 48X36 standard railroad crate weighing 100 pounds. The railroad charges my current distributor $5 but going to Chicago, the freight may be more. I do not pay for shipping my product to you, I will only ship an order of 1,000 pieces (20 crates) or more, and I expect payment by telegram voucher the day after you receive the order."

Wendell asked, "are any of these conditions negotiable?" "No, Sir!" Claire, exploded in applause and laughter as she adds, "good for you Ma'am, stick to your gun. You have a fine product at fair prices. We can add our 10% as well as paying for shipping like we do with all our other suppliers. Money transfer is a bit quick, but we can live with your demands. Any questions Wendell?" "No Claire, this is the rare time that I can agree with you." "Fine, I want 2,000 assorted pieces for the first order, so pay the lady with a bank draft, and let's see if we can start loading the crates. We will send you a copy of your two advertising pages within ten days and your catalog thereafter."

"On your next orders, are you planning to order assorted pieces like this first order?" "No, certain items sell more than others, and we would specify this in our subsequent orders." "Ok, so in that case, allow us two days to get your order to the railroad, since we cannot prepack those railroad crates till we get your order." "Agreed."

Once the standard business contracts were signed, money transferred, and the Ward's Executives gone; Ralph and Billy were upstairs moving assorted boxes to the elevator to bring downstairs for packing in the railroad crates.

*

That night, after supper, Mia went into labor. After two hours in the hospital, Doc Ross came to the waiting room. "Mia was in false labor as is common with the first pregnancy. All is well and expect a few more weeks till her time."

Mia spent the first week getting the nursery organized. After the furniture was in, all the baby clothes and diapers were laid out. Meanwhile, Palmer had hired Hollis to redo the plumbing in the scullery. A state-of-the-art washing machine with manual agitator and ringer was plumbed with hot and cold water—with the used water drained to the outside.

Palmer was staying close to the house, and only made short visits to the pit when Missi came by to spend time with Mia. The second week, Alice showed up with a 2-page sample of their ad in the upcoming Wards catalog. Mia was surprised to see actual photos of their products and several actual live models—Mia laughed when she recognized Claire modeling a riding skirt with a casual shirt.

The next week, Alice arrived with a telegram from Claire Aubuchon. Mia read:

Catalog out one week—unbelievable STOP

Selling out of your products— unbelievable STOP

Need an emergency delivery of 3,000 assorted items STOP

Have made arrangements for quick delivery STOP

Express train leaves 6PM daily in town STOP

Enclosed is preliminary payment for this order STOP

Please send ASAP Claire

"But Alice, it will take two days for Ralph and Billy to load 60 crates and then a week more to get to Chicago. By the time 9 days goes by, Claire will be completely out of our clothes and will be taking backorders only!" "Well, that is not quite right. You see I sent Billy with a sign that said $4 for a short day's work. He came back with six cowboys. They loaded the sixty crates, the railroad freighters hauled all day, and our crates took off tonight on the 6PM express train. According to the railroad office, this train travels 24 hours a day, only makes freight delivery stops and pickups in big cities, and at 40 mph, it will cover the 1,500 miles to Chicago in 48 hours. And I can just imagine the look on Claire's face when the receiving department notifies her of our 60 crate's arrival, heh?"

"Nice job, lady. Anything else new?" "Yes, lately some of the old machines are breaking down. The repair man came to fix four of them and when he realized it was the same part breaking, he got Kip involved. There is a link that is breaking from metal fatigue. It is a drop-in part that Kip can change in three minutes—which is much quicker than exchanging machines and hooking up the air transmission. The company is now manufacturing this part with a higher carbon content. Until these are available, the repair man left us 10 old style links for temporary repairs—that's service and that's why I went with this company."

After Alice left, Mia went for her afternoon nap. Waking up to the smell of a sizzling steak, Mia said, "that smell is fantastic, but I think we'll have to put them aside, I'm in labor again—and I think for real this time."

Palmer went next door and informed the Bodines and Myers. After Mia was brought in the hospital's maternity department by Helena and Ella, the two grandpas and the dad were left in the waiting room.

After waiting an hour, Doc Ross finally showed up. "Mia is in early labor and all's well. She is 2 centimeters dilated, so it's going to take a while. I'll keep you posted in an hour."

Once the doc left, Ellsworth asks, "what's this '2 centimeters' all about?" Palmer answers, "the birth canal is only open the width of your index finger." Ralph asks, "and how wide does it dilate for the birth?" "10 centimeters!" "Boy, it's gonna be a long night, son!"

An hour later the doc showed up. "Mia is 4 centimeters and all's well. I just broke her water and her labor will now pick up. Any questions?" Palmer thought and said, "Why do we put ourselves in these stressful situations?" "Because it is part of living. In as much discomfort Mia is experiencing, she is still smiling. She can see the difference between temporary pain and lifelong happiness."

After the doc left, Ellsworth asked, "what's this 'breaking water,' is it like 'breaking wind' or a 'dam busting?'" "It's about releasing the fluid that the baby is in." "Never mind, I liked the old way of the men waiting in the barn till the baby came." "Just for your information, Doc Ross said that there is current thinking that fathers will one day be allowed in the labor and delivery rooms." Ralph and Ellsworth both objected. Ellsworth said, "I've heard that giving birth is natural, but messy and can tear a woman's genitals." Ralph added, "and I've heard that older doctors think that witnessing a birth can turn a man's sex urges off for a long time."

The next hour seemed to last so much longer. Palmer was beginning to pace around and showing signs of stress. "When I think back of the two kidnapping episodes, at least I could do something about it. Now this waiting, when there is nothing I can do to help my wife, is pure torture for me."

On schedule, Doc Ross popped out of the maternity ward. He didn't realize that he pushed the door hard enough to hit the back wall—as he saw the three waiting men look like they had seen a ghost. Waiting for them to settle down, with a slight chuckle, he finally spoke. "Mia is now 6 centimeter and is in hard labor. All's well, and things will start moving much quicker." Ellsworth couldn't take it any longer and said, "Doc, do us all a big favor and don't tell us anything else till Mia is 9 ¾ centimeter dilated and delivery is imminent." "Can do, gentlemen!"

Half an hour later, with a totally silent waiting room, all three men heard a piercing AARHH...........ARHH. Ellsworth suddenly passed out, Ralph fell off his chair, and Palmer instinctively jumped out of his chair with his fists in a ready fighting position. By the time Ellsworth woke up, all three heard SLAP, SLAP, SLAP....... BAAHH, BAAHH.

Doc Ross eventually came out and said, "congratulation Palmer, you have a beautiful healthy baby weighing 7 pounds 6 ounces. One of the grandmas will come and get you when Mia is presentable." "What is it Doc, boy or girl?" "I consider this the mother's right to inform you and the rest of the family, friends and employees." "What employees?" "Just look out the window in the street." Palmer moved the curtain and saw the street full of factory and pit workers. "Is Mia Ok?" "Absolutely!"

Half an hour later, Ella came to get Palmer. As the door opened, Mia was holding a beautiful baby in a blue blanket, "Palmer, say hello to our healthy son. Helena brought a chair for Palmer to sit in as she picked up the baby and placed him in Palmer's caressing hands. In their silence, they both realized that they were 'truly blessed.'

***

CHAPTER 12

Bodine Bodyguards

Palmer stayed with Mia 24 hours a day for the next two weeks. When Mia slept, he kept watching their son. When Mia nursed, Palmer slept in naps—and that was every two hours for 20 minutes to a half hour. This routine was their way of protecting, providing, and bonding as a family. Every morning Helena would come to cook meals and tidy up the house. Every evening Ella would come to clean the supper dishes and then do the laundry for the day.

After these initial two weeks, the schedule relaxed. Palmer would visit the factory and the pit on a regular basis when Helena was in the house. In the afternoon, Helena would go to work, and Palmer would be the resident helper. Palmer would nap with Ella in the house, but as soon as she left, Palmer was back on the job till morning—although the nights were not as long, with increasing naps, as the baby was a good sleeper.

By the fourth week, Mia had regained her strength, was spending most of her day feeding their son, preparing meals, and started to do her own laundry. The baby was quite alert, and spent most of his woken hours in his 45-degree slanted swing or in his portable chair—and basically following mom throughout the house. The Christening was scheduled for the weekend and the proud parents had chosen their son's name. Winston Ralph Bodine would stand for power and leadership if he ever followed his dad's footsteps, and could be shortened to Winn as a child's and young man's nickname.

Meanwhile in a camp outside of town, Big Dick Barber was meeting with a group of sycophants. None had any leadership skills and so tended to follow Big Dicks lead. "It's high time we start making big bucks. This breaking and entering is not productive because we can't sell furniture, clothing, and even jewelry. Cash is in short supply, so we're changing our routine. From now on, we are kidnapping the rich man's family. We all wear masks and we do not harm our catch. Once the ransom is paid, we release our hostages, and we get out of town. Now for our first caper, we're going to kidnap a rich man's wife, child, and mother-in-law. The ransom will be $5,000 for the old woman and $15,000 for the wife and kid. This is what you will do, where you will go with your hostages, where I will collect the reward, where you will release the hostages, and where we'll eventually meet."

As the fifth week arrived, Mia was now thinking it was time to return to the shop. Winn was a good baby, feeding well with pureed fruits and oatmeal, was now nursing 3 hours apart, and could spend hours in his rocking swing—made self-rocking by Hollis' bright mechanical mind. Mia was reading in the parlor, as Helena was making a supper casserole. Without a hint of distress, Helena came out of the kitchen as she said, "Mia, we have a problem!" Mia nonchalantly put her book down and turned to look at her mom. There, pointing a gun at her mom's head, was the scruffiest excuse for a man. Mia instinctively put her hand in her pocket to pick up her Bulldog, but hesitated when she heard more men coming in the front door.

The five-man leader finally spoke, "you ladies and the baby are coming with us for a short ride." Mia hesitated and added, "do you men know who my husband is and what he will do to you if you kidnap us?" "Lady, shut up, all we know is that your menfolk are rich, and we're going to get some of that money." "You may get some money, but you won't be able to spend it buried in the ground—you're all dead men!" Without further arguments, Mia gave her diaper bag and two jars of apple sauce to her mom, grabbed a well-dressed Winn, and walked to the waiting buggy. Mia contemplated shooting all five kidnappers, but decided against it when she realized that shooting five gun-toting outlaws, with a five-shot pistol, was foolish were she to miss one, she would be dead.

A while later, Palmer was talking to Gloria in the shop's business office when Ellsworth came barreling in. He had lost his wind and could barely speak. Finally, Palmer got the message, "I always come home for lunch with Helena. Today, I figured she was still with Mia, so I went there. There is no one in your house and the baby's diaper bag is gone as well. Someone has taken our wives and baby boy."

Palmer responded with instant guilt. He knew he would deal with that at a later time, now he had to find a way to get his family back. "Ellsworth, would you walk over to the Lightfoots on Waters Street and ask them to come to my house in full gear." Making it back to the house, Palmer went thru the entire house looking for a clue that Mia or Helena might have left him. Finding nothing, he went outside where Mistah and Missi were waiting. After giving them the bad news, the Lightfoots went over the tracks in the yard. "It looks like four horses being ridden, one horse trailing behind a buggy, and the tracks are all non-descriptive. Once they get to the street, we will lose them. So tracking them won't work this time. We need to find another way to get a lead." "Ok, let's go see Sheriff Belknap."

"Sheriff, Mia, Winn, and Helena have been kidnapped and we have no way to track down their kidnappers. Can you think of a way we can identify these outlaws and get a lead?" After the sheriff settled down, he said, "well, there aren't any new faces in town, so forget the mob, this is likely the work of 'no-goods' we have in town. These individuals are petty thieves, footpads, card cheats, or other nuisances. Now, a new twist, lately some of these 'no-goods' have banded together and have succeeded in pulling off two successful kidnappings of wealthy men's families. After the ransom is paid, the hostages are released, and these 'no-goods' never appear in town again. We could only assume they had been the kidnappers, but that's not enough proof to put out a reward on them."

"Assuming this is the case, where do we start?"

"We need to talk with Sam Wilson, barkeep at the Watering Trough Saloon—a regular hangout for 'no-goods.'"

"Sam, we need your help. Someone has kidnapped Helena Myers, Mia Bodine, and baby son. I'm suspecting a local gang of 'no-goods.' Any ideas?" "Well, I might be able to help. Big Dick Barber has recently put together a group of four local saddle bums. Now, they gather here every night." Sheriff Belknap added, "but if they are the kidnappers, they'll likely not meet tonight." Palmer added, "or one man, like the leader, might stay behind to see what the law does, or stay behind to collect the ransom. What does this Big Dick look like?" "Can't miss him, six feet, 300 pounds, full black face beard, wears his pearl handle colt in a cross draw, and has a red vest full of tobacco juice stains—plus he don't smell very good. Come back around 7PM, and he might be here. If it's not him, it could be one of his gang, and I know them all very well."

The Trio went to Grady's for supper, when Ralph came running in, holding a note in his hand that he had found on Palmer's front door. Ralph gave the note to Palmer who then passed it on to Mistah, Missi, Sheriff Belknap, and Ellsworth. Palmer then explained that Mia, Winn and Helena had been kidnapped and added, "this note was not on my door after the kidnapping. This proves that a kidnapper is still in town—and we're going to put our hands on him in a couple of hours."

*

After leaving everyone at the sheriff's office, the Trio arrived at the Watering Trough at 8PM. Sneaking a look over the batwing doors, Palmer spotted Big Dick drinking alone at his own table. "This is how we're going to play this. I'll go in and belly up to the bar. Have a chat with Sam and that is when Big Dick will clear out. Mistah you take the back door and Missi you take the front door. Put him down with a light tap to the forehead with your war club. I need him alive at all costs."

Palmer walks in, and has a chat with Sam. "I'm sure you spotted our suspect alone. Now he's giving you that furtive look that outlaws are famous for—looking at you, but pretending he's not." "That's Ok Sam, I'm certain he'll be bolting any minute and walk right into a determined savage, heh?" As predicted, Big Dick got up and pretended to slowly walk outside to the privy. After opening the door, he got a tap on the head as he fell to his knees. Just stunned, Mistah did another tap, and this time Big Dick laid out like a beached whale. When Palmer and Missi arrived, they all pondered how they would take this 300 pounder to a cell in the sheriff's jail. Fortunately, a homesteader was driving by, and for a dollar, he gladly gave them all a ride to the sheriff's office—after the four of them managed to unceremoniously load the whale in the wagon.

Now fully manacled to four points on the cell's steel framed cot, Big Dick's face was splattered with water till he woke up. With a full hidden audience, Palmer then took over. "Ok, you big ass, I know you had my family kidnapped, and I want to know where your 'no-goods' took them." "Hey Mister, I don't know what you're talking about. What are you going to do? Torture me like you gelded that mob man in Albuquerque." "Heck no, that was to instill fear, what I'm going to do to you is cause temporary insurmountable pain that doesn't leave any marks." "Ha, ha, like bull you are!"

Without any further words or delay, Palmer straddles his subject, forces his lower jaw open and shoves the awl deep in the nearest rotten molar. The man expressed wonder, shock, muscular response, and loud screaming all in the first second. Then he appeared to have total body convulsions, wet himself and crapped in his pants. Pulling the awl out, he noticed the Lightfoots brushing off goose bumps as the sheriff was holding on to the bars with white knuckles. Without hesitation, the awl went into another molar. This time Palmer wiggled the awl in all directions. Big Dick's body seemed to gyrate in the same direction the awl was pointing. After several minutes, Palmer pulled out the awl and said, "you know, I can continue this all night. So, let's get real. You are going to prison if you're lucky not to hang. Now if you tell me where my family is, I will tell the judge that your cooperation saved my family. You'll likely get a light prison sentence, while your buddies will either get a bullet or hang. So, what will it be—talk or open wide."

"No more..................no more. I can't stand another jab. I sent my gang to Pinos Altos. One of the guys has a house there. All I know is that it is on a street off Main Street. I don't know the street's name or number, but I did hear one of the boys say that the color is enough to make you puke. They are to release your family only when I arrive with the money, or I send them a telegram with a location to meet to divide the money."

With a good road to Pinos Altos, the Trio decided to make the 9-mile ride under moonlight. They arrived at midnight, took a hotel room and stabled their horses in the hotel's barn. After an early breakfast, the Trio designed a plan. It was like looking for a needle in several haystacks. Without some sign left by Mia or Helena, it would take a week with the local sheriff, to start checking every house off Main Street—even if they started with houses having an ugly paint color. Getting their horses, they slowly went down one side of Main Street as they counted 9 side streets. They then turned around to check the other side of the street. After going by four streets, Missi suddenly stopped and said, it's this street boss. Palmer had never doubted either of the Lightfoots, and so automatically followed Missi into McNamara Street.

Missi was slowly riding when she again suddenly stopped. "It's that ugly house six houses back. I didn't want to stop in front of the house, so I rode by." "Do you mean the house painted a bright yellow with green trim?" "Yes, the color of a newborn calf's poop." "Now, how on earth did you choose the correct street and house?" "Simple, what is a 'safety pin' doing on the ground—if not left by a mom with diapers to change, heh?" "Well, I'll be darned, for sure!"

*

The Trio knew where the kidnappers were, and now had to devise a way to separate them from the hostages, to prevent collateral fatalities during the rescue. Mistah sneaked onto the porch and looked in a window. When he returned, he said, "the ladies are in the front parlor and the outlaws are in the rear kitchen drinking liquor." "Good, this is what we're going to do. Mistah, you sneak into the barn, saddle their horses and as you get ready to leave, leave a stick of dynamite attached to a main supporting beam—light a three-minute fuse and that will give you enough time to get yourself and the horses safely away. After the explosion, Missi and I will bust thru the front door and rush the kitchen where the outlaws will likely be looking out the rear window."

Once Palmer saw Mistah leading the four horses away, he and Missi made their way quietly to the front porch. Palmer tested the front door and found it unlocked. Then, KABOOM. As expected, the outlaws made their way to the windows as Palmer and Missi appeared in the kitchen doorway. "Put your hands up, you dingbats are done. Turn around and don't go for your guns or you're dead."

As they turned around, Palmer realized that an outlaw was missing. He was about to say something to Missi when a shot ran out. Mia was standing there with a smoking Bulldog in her hand, as the outlaw was pushed back into the water closet. Mia then added, "this piece of crap was in the water closet taking a dump when he came out in his union suit, with his pants down to his ankles, but with a pistol pointed at Missi. I had no choice, for it was the time to kill or be killed."

In no time, the three living kidnappers were manacled, Mistah went back to get the outlaw's horses as they draped the dead outlaw over his horse's saddle. The living outlaws were loaded on their horses, an ankle manacled to a stirrup, and their hands manacled in the front so they could hold on to the saddle's horn. Palmer then told the outlaws, "if you try to run off, I will shoot you. If you fall off, you'll get trampled to death cause we ain't stopping for you. From now on, you're dead to me!"

After getting Mia, her mom and Winn settled in the buggy, the local sheriff showed up. "Hey, I know who you are. You run the Bodine Agency in Silver City. Tell me what happened here, and are you responsible for collapsing that barn with dynamite?" Palmer had a long talk with the sheriff. When the sheriff realized that these outlaws were kidnappers, he was more than happy to let Palmer bring them to Sheriff Belknap—especially realizing that the town council would take possession of the house for a quick sale. Palmer quickly wrote up a statement, that was signed by all parties involved, and the group headed home.

*

A week later, after a rewarding family supper put on by Ella and Helena, the Duo had some reflective time in their parlor. "You do realize that this was the third time you got kidnapped." "And I must admit, that you got to us quicker than the other two times." "Yes, well that's thanks to Missi's astute awareness of those safety pins. Irrelevant of that, you must realize that we are candidates for more kidnappings." "Why?" "Well, according to Sheriff Belknap, this is the third town kidnapping in 30 days. The victims are always family of wealthy men. And I guess we qualify with our four successful business." "Oh, well I'm planning to return to work in two days, so what do we do, we can't stop living?"

"When I dropped off the kidnappers, Sheriff Belknap said he had a solution that would make kidnapping a potentially lethal situation for these outlaws." "Really, and what might that be?" "Use our old office as the dispatching center for the 'Bodine Bodyguards.'" "Bodyguards, like someone escorting the wealthy and or their families?" "That is absolutely correct. Plus, the bank employees that pick up the merchants' daily deposits. I never realized that these men are robbed regularly by footpads. It has now gotten to the point, that the bank is planning to cancel this service since they lose more than the profits they make on the deposits. So, the merchants would likely pay for bodyguard service every day between 3:30 and 5PM."

"Hu'um, do we really have that many wealthy people in this town?" "Well, there are many private underground gold mine owners, and with the price of gold at $320 a pound, there are quite a few well to do people that are leery of these kidnappings. They're apparently bugging the sheriff for organizing some protection—which is never going to happen with three deputies."

"What would you charge for this kind of service—considering we are now paying our stitchers $5 a day?" "I think we would have two rates. For an 8-hour period or for a short event under 1 ½ hours. So the bank pickup schedule would cost $10, for two men. That's about a dollar charge for each of the 10 merchants that do business with the Community Bank. For an armed escort under 11/2 hours, the price would be $5 per bodyguard. For an 8-hour period, the charge would be $20 per bodyguard or $35 for two bodyguards."

"At those rates, the agency stands to make a profit." "Of course, if a business cannot make a profit, then it should close its doors." "How much would you pay these bodyguards—by the hour or by salary?" "There is likely to be slow days or days with unused hours. For this reason, I would place all our men on a fixed salary with the same benefits you gave your employees the other day, plus a death benefit for living dependents."

"Give me an idea of a weekly salary?" "I would start at $25 a week and work my way up according to past experience. For any man with a lawman's experience, I would start at $30 a week. Let's use the sheriff's number one deputy—Liam Burke. He has 4 years' experience, is a sound lawman, who is ready for the sheriff's position. He has been thinking he may have to leave town to get this job. He is making $70 a month with housing in the jail and two meals a day. He is now in a quandary, since he is courting a local gal and he knows he cannot support a wife and family on his wages. Leaving town is no longer an option, because his gal has a good job, and she wants to continue working. Now, this man I would offer a salary of $40 a week to be a working manager/dispatcher in charge of the office." "I didn't know Liam was courting someone!" "Uh, you don't know, do you?" "No idea, who is it?" "Josie, your designer!" Palmer Bodine, you knew, and you didn't tell me—you buggar!" "Now, you have to keep quiet till Josie makes the announcement, hey?"

"Alright, but good for Josie and Liam, that's a good match. Now how many bodyguards would you need, where would you find them, what qualification would you be looking for, and what kind of training would you give them?"

"After thinking about this for a week, I think we'll need a dozen men. According to the sheriff, there are plenty of good local men that are proficient with guns, reliable, sound and have common sense. On top of that, apparently several of those men are your stitchers' husbands. So, I would advertise in our paper. Before giving interviews, I would ask Sheriff Belknap and Elmer to weed out the bad apples. Once the interviews start, I would first need proof at the range of their gun handling skills. Once they pass that, I would look for the most important quality that a bodyguard must have—he must be ready to take a bullet to protect the person he is hired to protect, or willing to fight would be robbers of the money they guard. Once a man or woman accepts that responsibility, I would be looking for common sense, astuteness, and willingness to accept any assignment as well as working with any of the bodyguards—including women. The one thing that I will not accept is arrogance—that's a trait that does not belong in a bodyguard service."

"What about training?" "Now I haven't worked that out, but they will have a full week of training." "I'd say you've already worked out most of the kinks.

So when do you start advertising?" "As soon as you give me that nod of approval, my ad is ready for the next paper as is my new sign ready for Marc to proceed, heh?" "For sure. Here comes our fifth business."

*

Three days after the ad appeared, the publisher delivered 29 applications. Each one included age, years of education, lawman experience, firearms ability, work experience, marital status, and optional recommendations. Palmer presented the names to Elmer and Sheriff Belknap. Words like, drunk, no-good, liar, ladies' man, never on time, can't be trusted, arrogant bastard, will rob you, will skip on the job, a coward, will find a way to skip work while maintaining a salary; were all words that caused Palmer to pull out their application. In the end, he was left with 19 names. The interviews were now set at 4-5 per day.

The first interview lasted all afternoon. Liam Burke was a born leader, was proficient with all firearms especially the pump shotgun, and passed all the qualifications set by Palmer. When asked if he was interested in being the director, manager, dispatcher and a working bodyguard, Liam accepted, and was happy with the salary offered as well as the short and long-term benefits.

That night Mia related the story that Liam had sneaked in the factory's rear door and went to see Josie in her office. To everyone's shock and surprise, Liam and Josie walked, hand and hand down the work aisle to Mia's office to announce that they were getting married.

The next day the interviews started. Palmer would allow Liam to ask questions if he so chose, and at the end of the interview, Liam had a choice to give a positive or a negative nod. No nod would mean that it was Palmer's choice to make. Two interviews went well, and the men were hired. Then the third one was a classic. A man walked in, with a swagger, sat down without being asked, went into a slouch position, and crossed his leg like he was a glowing star.

"Besides your application, what would you add to this group of bodyguards?" "Well, I am well known amongst the rich. I play high stakes poker with the men, and the ladies like to have me around. I will bring in a lot of well to do customers, who will specify that I be the hired bodyguard. In return for this extra business, I want to share with the profits instead of being on a fixed salary—say a third of the profit from my assignments!"

Palmer lifted an eyebrow and never hesitated to say, "thank you for coming today, but we will not need your services." "What, you're dismissing me, what is wrong with you? Can't you see the opportunity you are throwing away—I'm the goose with the golden eggs."

"Wrong sir, you're the turkey full of crap. You're nothing but a smug smart ass who thinks he is better than anyone else. Well let me tell you, your poop smells like anyone else, you have an ass hole in the same place as other men, and I would never, ever, consider assigning you a client, as a representative of this company. Now, get the hell out before you inherit a good kick up your butt hole—which is what you deserve!"

Over the next two days, five other candidates were rejected. The reasons included: refusal to take a bullet for a client, not having any common sense, would not take assignments after 5PM, would not work with black men, and would not work with women.

By the end of the interviews, Palmer and Liam had chosen a dozen good candidates. Liam then summarized their choices: everyone had an 8th to

10th grade education, two had one year of a business college, two had lawman experience, one was a bounty hunter, all had a good general work records, half the men were married, two were unmarried women, three men were black, and all applicants were generally proficient with firearms, although many needed practice.

The next week Liam worked with Marc Weber to modify the original Bodine Agency office. The walls were gutted and rearranged. The center of activity was a large gathering area for a dozen agents to enjoy pastries and coffee while waiting for their assignments. Liam had his own office, and a separate office was reserved for the two-business college trained guards. A maintained ice box was added to keep the bodyguard's cold lunches. A large map of the city and its surrounding roads was attached to a wall—as every agent had a different color tac that showed where his assignment was for the day.

Like most businesses on Main Street, a barn was common behind the stores and offices. Marc had expanded the horse stalls to eight and had added a lean-to for the four two-seat buckboards that were kept for transporting guarded families with kids and supplies. Any down time, which was a daily occurrence, meant that the agents went to the barn to do daily chores.

While these renovations were taking place, Palmer was busy designing a training program. Once the five-day content was prepared, he had the printer prepare a manual and ordered three dozen copies for future use.

Training week started. The first day's subject started with 'know your surroundings,' as everyone met in the office's gathering room. Palmer started, "don't wait for a problem to hit you in the face, learn to anticipate its likely occurrence. As an example, you are escorting a client in town as you spot a man standing a 3 o'clock, one at 9 o'clock, and one at 12 o'clock. The likelihood is this is a kidnapping in the making—in broad daylight no less. The first thing you do is to protect your client by moving him or her into the nearest building. If you were right, guns will be coming out. Always deal with the outlaw who could shoot you in the back. Then deal with the others facing you."

"This brings up the basic mantra used by lawmen, bounty hunters and bodyguards—when an opponent goes for his gun, it's time to kill or be killed. If you live by that rule, you will be ready to protect your client."

After presenting several scenarios, Palmer was faced with the same question, "how can you anticipate a person's or persons' actions?" "It's a matter of learning how to read a person's demeanor. Some of this may be natural, but a lot is learned. As examples: is a person's look natural or is a furtive look, does one's greeting fit the situation or is it excessive, does a person's location fit or is he out of place. Years ago I learned that if you stare at someone, eventually that person will respond. In time, you'll be able to pick out the fakers, and those who mean you harm."

After another hour of discussion, the trainees went to the local town range. Palmer was expecting each operative to achieve three techniques:

1. To rely on their pump shotgun as their 'go to gun,' be able to 'slam fire' their pump shotgun, and hit a 5-gallon bucket at 15 yards—without aiming and with #3 or 00 Buckshot.

2. To go to their handgun as their backup firearm. While holding the empty pump shotgun with the weak hand, quickly draw the pistol, cock it and hit a 5-gallon bucket at +-7 yards. Note: quickly drawing does not

mean the fast draw of gunfighters—but it guarantees hitting the target.

3. To use a lever action rifle as a speed firearm. By cycling the lever as quick as possible, the shooter should be able to hit 50-yard separated 5-gallon buckets with accuracy.

That first day at the range, Palmer demonstrated all three firearms. The class was then informed that they would practice each firearm for a half hour each day—more if they wished since ammo was free.

That evening, in their parlor, Palmer started, "how was your first day back at work, now with a baby?" "Winn is such a good baby. He spends hours in his self-propelled swing. He naps well and only cries when he's hungry. I asked Agnes to make a backpack with holes for his arms and legs. That way we can now walk from home to work with Winn on our backs."

"As far as work goes, Alice was glad to return to her old duties. Gloria had a thousand forms and communications to attend to. I spent a lot of time with Ralph and Ella going over the surplus inventory. We have two thousand pieces in surplus with an even spread of pieces. Everything is selling well, and the surplus has been kept as low as 1,000 pieces and as high as 3,000 pieces. Wards is ordering +-2,000 pieces regularly every two weeks and it's always a mixed order. So for the immediate future, nothing will change since Waldo often asks for an extra 1,000 pieces when his inventory gets too low."

"Have you detected any personnel problems, after all, you have a hundred women in the same building. Those kinds of problems would not have surfaced during your absence." "No, but I agree with you. I think I'm going to put out a question and suggestion box for anonymous comments. Now what about you. How is the training session going and what's new at the pit?"

"First day was a complete success. Every man was asking appropriate questions and I could detect a sense of sincerity. More info as the week progresses. As far as the pit, there is a new issue. The hammermill was sold to a large conglomerate and the manager has raised the cost for all three areas. Since we don't use the rock crusher, we have to pay a surcharge for the hammermill and the grinder. Plus, we take second fiddle to full use customers, and again our boxcars are piling up in the holding area. We're going to have to do something about this, but I'm waiting to find out what Harvey has discovered."

As usual, the next day started with classroom work. "For your second day, the subject today is, 'maintain a secure zone.' Any man or men who come within an arm's length of your client is a suspect. The classic example is meeting a man on the boardwalk. He may smile, doff his hat to the lady, say hello, or say nothing. But as soon as he passes you by, turn around and watch him walk away. Don't be surprised to see him do an about face and try to 'buffalo' you with his pistol or shoot you. The same is true in meeting a man or men on horses—that has happened to me, and thanks to a horse smarter than me, I survived. Once this initial potential harm is resolved, stay alert, as his associates may try to finish what the first man did not accomplish."

Several questions were floated, but the one that impressed Palmer was, "do we shoot a man for brandishing a firearm?" "If you meet a man and he pulls out his pistol, he's not doing this to show you the nice metal engraving. Smarten up, you will be wearing a security uniform, and this type of activity will certainly mean your death if you don't react."

"Uh, what uniform?" "Ok, after class, we'll skip shooting practice. The first thing you do is to go to Mia's factory. There, the three supers will measure your leg length, waist, chest size, neck size and sleeve length. Afterwards you will leave with four sets of denim to include jeans, casual shirts, and vests. Afterwards, stop at Elmer's store and get your new black hat. Your next stop is Waterman's gun shop where Winston will exchange your pump shotgun's barrel and magazine tube for the short version, and change the shoulder stock to a pistol grip. Finally, stop at Mahoney's Leather Goods. Stan will fit you with a black holster rig to include a belt, a shotgun holster, and a multi position pistol holster. Oh, and before I forget, pin this on your vest or shirt. The local tinsmith has created this design to include Bodine on the left side, Bodyguard on the right, and BB in the center with a number from 2 to 14—for you are the first team to start, and I'll wear #1 and Liam will wear #2."

Liam spoke, "wow that is a very nice touch and it offers some degree of respectability." "Actually we want you all to appear recognizable and presentable. So kindly show the uniform and agency some respect; and so please bathe, shave, get timely haircuts, and change your uniforms regularly. Tomorrow, wear your new look, and after the classes, you'll be able to practice shooting a pump shotgun with a pistol grip."

That evening, Harvey showed up at the Bodine's home. My research was quite enlightening. The smelter staff is not happy with the hanky-panky the hammermill is pulling off. They have slowed down their production and so the smelter is short of work. When I suggested that they sell us a lot adjacent to the smelter so we can build a hammer and grinding mill, they immediately agreed to the sale. The 5-acre lot will cost $2,000. If you agree with it, I'll put a deposit and see Henry for a quote on the hammer and grinder—but powered by an air compressor instead of a water wheel. If available, I will then see Marc Weber for a building estimate. Then I will return with the estimates for you to scrutinize and make a final decision." "Sounds good, so please proceed, but see if Hollis is available to put this plant together." "Oops, good point. It's not wise to have all the parts, but no one to put them together, heh?" "For sure!"

The third day at class covered the topic, "Politely say no, but insist." "You have the responsibility to direct a client's activities to keep them safe. If they force the issue, then do your best to still protect them. When you report this client's behavior, Liam will likely warn the client or summarily fire them. Bottom line, you may be a hired gun to them, but that doesn't mean they have the right to increase your risks. If a client needs an event that is particularly dangerous, schedule it the next day, when two or more bodyguards can be assigned."

"And that reminds me, as a hired gun, you are an employee. As a rooster doesn't play around in the hen house, then do not get emotionally or sexually involved with a client of the opposite sex. If this is a potential conflict, then Liam will reassign you." After a few questions, Palmer invited the group to the range for an entire afternoon of getting familiar with the Winchester 1897 pump shotgun that was altered to function like a long pistol.

The fourth day of class included three short topics. The first was, "stay close to your client." "It's obvious that you cannot guard someone if they are not in visual range. But there are times when you need to give your client some privacy. Such as the obvious lady's need to use the privy. But also businessmen and lawyers need to speak to customers in private. Just stay out of the office but in the same building." Without any questions, Palmer moved on.

"The second topic is, 'Bounty Rewards.' In the event of a gunfight, some of the attackers will be professional criminals with a bounty on their heads. If that happens, the bounty rewards will go into a general fund. The shooter gets two shares, the agency gets two shares, and every other man gets one share—so the rewards are divided by 16 to establish the value of one share." There were signs of unexpected, pleasant surprise.

"The last topic, and the most important, is 'I feared for my life and the life of my client.' Let me explain, if you are unfortunate to have to kill an attacker, when the law arrives, say that line before you say anything else. Then you will have to give more details, but manage to repeat that line again and again. The lawman needs to feel that this was a 'self- defense' shooting from a trained security man." To Palmer's surprise, there were no questions—again!"

"That's it for today, have a nice shoot. Tomorrow, our last day, we will follow a different format. I want every man to come to class with a question that is of importance to you—and come with a second choice in case your question is asked before we get to your turn. When you arrive, you'll pick a number out of a hat to give each man a calling order. Don't miss your chance in setting your mind at ease. If there is time, I'll entertain other questions till everyone is satisfied. Take the time, and discuss it with your family. Your significant others may see an issue that you missed. Good luck, and see you in the morning."

***

CHAPTER 13

Tying Loose Ends

The next morning, after a prolonged coffee/ bear paw and social hour, Palmer called the class to order. After pulling #6 out of the hat, the first question surprised Palmer. "I understand the medical insurance, short-and long-term disability, and the retirement benefit. But I'm not clear on the death benefit. Would you review that before my question?"

"Sure. If any of you die in the line of duty, your dependents will receive a year of your salary. Now dependents include a wife, children or parents who depend on your income." "So there is no further support after that money is gone!" "Officially, per your signed employment agreement, that is correct. But I will assure you that I will never leave your dependents in a lurch, and they will never want or miss out on life. If any of you need further assurance, see Liam privately, and he will explain a special fund to you."

"I still have trouble reading people's faces, posture, or body language. Are there profiles that fit would be attackers?" "No, you can't say that a well-dressed man is safe, that a woman won't pull a gun on you, that a scruffy individual can be ignored, that someone acting drunk is of no significance, and so on. You have to teach yourselves these living skills. If you work at it, in due time, you will learn to read people. My only advice, until you can trust your instincts, 'don't trust anyone.'"

"As bodyguards, do we have to perform jobs or errands for our clients?" "Absolutely not. I realize that some clients may think that they hired you for the day, and that should include free side labor. You are not tellers, merchant's helpers, errand boys or shelf stockers. You are hired guns and you should politely remind the clients of that fact. If they insist, don't argue, but inform them that you would not return the next day. Those clients don't really want a bodyguard."

"If a shoot goes bad and we are charged, who pays the legal fees and are we temporarily laid off?" "The agency pays all legal fees whether you are in the right or wrong. You won't have client contact, but your salaries will continue until the matter is settled—presumably by a judge's ruling."

"If a client needs to use the privy, do we let them go or what?" With natures call, you have no choice. Let them go, but stay within visual range. If you have to use the privy, leave your client in a safe place where there are other persons present."

"I'm not clear what makes a shooting unquestionably justified." "Remember, when an aggressor has a gun in hand, it's time to kill or be killed. It helps to have witnesses who profess that it was a self-defense action. But that will not always be the case. The grey zone is when you shoot an attacker with his pistol coming out of the holster, and then drops the pistol back in the holster before collapsing. Without witnesses present, don't forget to use the self-defense line when the law arrives. I have never waited for a gun pointing at me before firing my weapon."

"What do you do when you are facing too many attackers." "That's probably the most difficult question to answer. First, are the attackers clearly gunfighters or are they the run of the mill cowboy. Secondly, how good are you with your pump shotgun—which holds four OO Buck rounds. Third, is there some safe cover for your client. Fourth, how secure are you that you can handle the threat. As you can see, I can add many more variables. The point is, that you have to make a quick decision and stick to it. Other than fighting it out, at times it can be wiser to back off and be able to fight another day. I will admit, that saving your client and yourself is the prime directive."

"Do you allow a client to carry a firearm?" "Yes, as long as the client recognizes that he or she is not obliged to participate in their defense. As far as it goes, never count on a client's help. If it is there, so much better for you. Always offer an escape to the client, and if they decide to stay, then you're free of liability"

"If we identify potential attackers, do we confront them, and go on the offense?" "No, you are always in a protective and defensive mode. To go on the offense is asking for a charge against you. Don't do it!"

"What do we do if a client gets shot?" "First, put down the attackers. Then get the client to the hospital. If the client can't walk, commandeer a passing wagon and get to the hospital. Now, unless I lost count, we are down to the 12th question."

"Do we get the $100 bonus for signing on like all your other employees?" "Well that was for moving into town and for a wardrobe upgrade. Since you are all locals, you won't be moving. Incidentally, did you get charged for your wardrobe, new hat, tin badge, modified pump shotgun and your new gun-belt and holsters? Well, those things came up to $215 per person, heh?"

"With no further questions, Palmer closed the discussion. "You are all aware that we have been advertising a private bodyguard service in the daily newspaper. Well we have a dozen clients signed up for the service. You have the rest of the day off, but expect an assignment come morning."

*

That evening, Harvey stopped over on his way home. "I've been busy working with Henry, Hollis, and Marc. All three men have solid proposals with firm costs. I have scheduled a tentative meeting at Henry's with Hollis and Marc, if you are both available tomorrow at 9AM?" Mia nodded as Palmer said, "we'll be there? Is there anything we should know ahead of time?" "Well, yesterday the smelter manager notified me that the competing conglomerate group had offered $2,000 over our deposit. The manager did not like that kind of underhanded activity, and suggested that a $2,000 bank draft would secure the 5-acre lot. So, I made him the draft, registered the transaction, and got this deed in your name. That's the first time I spend your money so freely, and if you decide against the proposals tomorrow, I will buy the lot back with my own funds."

Mia started laughing as Palmer pretended to look perturbed. After extending the dismay, Palmer finally said, "as usual, you done good, Harvey. See you tomorrow." Afterwards, the Duo worked on Palmer's notes throughout the past five days of classes. Questions and comments were added to each daily topic, including the dozens of questions from the last day. Palmer was planning to have them published and added to the surplus of manuals for future use.

Arriving at Henry's office, the Duo walked into a catered breakfast of hot bacon/egg sandwiches, with coffee and bearpaw pastries. Turning into a social event, the actual meeting didn't begin till 10:30. Henry started, "Hollis has been working on this project for days, and so he should be the one to present the proposal. Afterwards, I will present the costs involved, as Marc would present the building costs."

Hollis took over, "I have taken the tour at the hammer mill next to the smelter as well as reviewing several other standard designs. I know I can make a mill more efficient than the existing one. Your competitor's mill can process 75 tons of crusher-run rocks using 16 men in an 8-hour shifts—and 150 tons in their two shifts per day. Their production slows down if they have to do the actual rock crushing. What I'm about to propose can easily handle your daily production of a full boxcar weighing +-75 ton—in one 8-hour shift with eight men plus a foreman." "That sounds great, so break it down for us." "Be glad to:

1. A power plant. In a separate shed, we have a natural gas-powered boiler, conversion equipment to convert steam pressure to an air compressor with a huge air pressurized storage tank. Piping, valves and gauges included to bring compressed air to the mill. ($3,000)

2. The hammer. The heart of this unit is the hammer plate. This is a 2X2 foot hardened steel plate that is 1.5 inches thick. It comes

with a lifting air cylinder, a ½ inch reinforced grate, gauges and valves, a rake, a mixing module, a hopper, a protective shroud, and a conveyor belt from the boxcar. Now to do 75 tons a day, you need two of these. (3,000)

Mia jumped in. "Palmer has seen this thing in operation, but I haven't. Can you explain how this all works?" "Sure, the operator runs all the levers. First, he fills the hopper by activating the conveyor belt. Then he lifts the hammer, fills the grate with stones from the hopper, passes the rake to spread the load, pulls the hammer lever and the hammer falls. Then he activates the spreader that moves the residual rocks. Then the process restarts as the ½ inch stones are conveyed to the roller-grinder." "How safe is this for the operator?" "Very, the shroud protects him from flying debris, plus he has to stand at least 16 inches from the hammer in order to pull the levers. In addition he wears a leather apron, a helmet, and eye goggles." "How heavy is this hammer. "The plate itself weighs 300 pounds. Plus we add six 40-pound concrete blocks on top for the extra weight. If the rock is too hard, we can go to 15 blocks if necessary, but sedentary rocks should get pulverized with a 500+ pound hammer falling from 30 inches." "Thanks, and then what is next?"

3. The roller-grinder. This is a concrete 6-foot long roller with a diameter of 18 inches that weighs 1,800 pounds. The concrete is protected from wear with a hardened steel sleeve. It arrives from the factory in six 300-pound rolls on a spindle that can be managed by four men. The base that will hold this roller is built in place with steel and concrete. The grate only allows sand size particles to fall through to the conveyor heading to the smelter. So the parts include, gear work, the roller, a constructed base, a continuous mixer that follows the roller, and a conveyor to the smelter. Again to handle two hammers, you'll need two rollers." (3,000)

Marc then took over. "Hollis has decided that we need a building that is 50X150 feet to house a boxcar, two hammers, two rollers, two conveyor belts, a water closet, a breakroom, insulated walls for sound control, a full concrete floor, reinforced staging for the hammer and roller, a power plant shed, a 10-horse barn, a septic system, and a business office. Now, I have broken down all these items with very exact costs and the total amount of materials plus labor and my standard business cost comes to $5,000. With such a project, I add $1,000 line of credit, for miscellaneous expenses and overruns. The one guarantee I will provide is that with a $6,000 deposit, there will not be any late charges whatsoever and a credit is possible. That's how sure I am of my figures."

Henry then added, "now, you need someone to install all these parts to make a working plant. I suspect you'll want Hollis to get this functional. You may need to add several men to help him out. But that's up to you." "So, you mean for $9,000 we can get all the parts from you?" "Yes, and my prices are firm without late charges."

"And Marc, how long will it take you to get this building up and build reinforced bases for the hammers and rollers?" "Two weeks since we also need to bring water and natural gas to the plant, and install a septic system."

Henry saw the Duo was thinking about this, so he added. "Out of curiosity, how much are you paying to have 75 tons of crusher-run hammered and rolled to sand size particles?" "$1,000 per boxcar plus their insulting $200 surcharge—and with frequent waits with boxcars parked outside. I know what you're saying, we can get the 75 tons processed for a hundred dollars. It's a done deal. Let's sign the contracts and we'll give each of you a bank draft."

As they were leaving, Mia was delaying Hollis, as Palmer had stayed behind to talk privately to Henry. Five minutes later, Palmer came out and invited Hollis to a free lunch at Gradys.

Over coffee, Palmer started talking. "I know we went over this before, and you didn't feel we had enough work to keep you busy. Now, it seems we do. First of all, Henry hired you twice to repair the steam shovel's boiler and once to help replace worn gears. Emmett called you twice to repair broken parts in the small locomotive. I know, that you were called three times by Kip with issues regarding the power plant and air compressor. Mia also tells me that you are behind in the monthly sewing machine maintenance as well as a power cutter that broke down with no repair man available. Also, our service contract on the 100 sewing machine is due soon and that's up to $50 a month. Harvey also tells me that he has to call upon you to repair the steam plants that run the drills. So to make a long story short, I believe we have enough work. How about coming to work for us exclusively--with one exception.

"You mean on salary?" "Yes." "That appeals to me, what are you offering?" "That depends on what was your highest weekly pay since you helped build the factory, and what are you making now with benefits?" "My highest week was when I had overtime building your factory and that was $62. Now I average $30 per six-day week without a single benefit."

"Fair enough, here is my offer. $150 a month with four free days each month for you to work for Henry for extra income. If he doesn't need you this month, the days are not lost since unused days accumulate for next month. That is the exception I originally noted. When you work for Henry, it is truly extra money, since your salary with us is fully maintained when you're working for Henry."

"All our employees have benefits to include three paid holidays, one paid weeks' vacation in July, medical insurance for the family and short-term disability benefits. After 5 years, we now include permanent long-term disability. After 15 years, we include retirement benefits. To sweeten the offer I am prepared to add..................STOP. You are more than generous. I would be honored to work for you, way down deep I knew that from the days when you cut pipes for me—for I knew then that you two were top notch stock."

Palmer extended his hand and added, "now that you work for us, let me assure you, that if anything happens to you, your wife will never have any financial woes. We will take care of her and or see to it that she is taken cared for. If you need any clarification on this unwritten assurance, talk to Harvey and he will explain the BF."

"Marc said they would start by laying a concrete floor in the morning. If you remember the factory, I think you'd better be on the premises right from the start, heh?" "Without a doubt since I need high grade concrete under the hammer and roller, and supplemented with steel rebars. See you at the job site—again."

*

One week later, the mill's shell was up, and a selected team was doing partitions and work for Hollis. Hollis had chosen three of the future workers to help him set the plant up. The other carpenters were building a barn and or a septic system.

The Duo was home in their parlor when Palmer asked what was new at the factory. "Well that suggestion box has been a useful addition which is revealing many simple and complicated alternative ways to do things. I have implemented several suggestions, but the real eye opener was finding something that I and the A-team had missed. The two expediters would end up running and work up a sweat. I watched them and knew that something had to be done. Concurrently, I started an elected category called, 'employee of the month.' To no surprise, the expediters, Wally and Nigel, won with 85% of the votes. So tomorrow they will be properly recognized." Afterwards, the Duo prepared the scheduled six-month interim profit-sharing meeting.

At 3PM, Mia rang the closing bell, and everyone was herded into the breakroom. Mia ran the meeting. "Again, we have had a profitable six months and it pleases me to share the profits for the second time this year. Palmer will pass your envelopes, but don't open them till he is done. Ok, open them and enjoy." The Duo heard—another $100, wow, unbelievable, such a grand business, we are so fortunate ………and so on. Mia then thanked everyone for their continuing dedication.

"Today is also the day we recognize one of our workers with an exceptional work history. Today it is a tie, Wally and Nigel, please stand. You have been chosen by your co-workers as the employees of the month. I have two prizes for you. First is an extra gift of $100 and secondly are the two men standing behind me—these are your permanent helpers." The place erupted in a roar and unrelenting applause. Wally and Nigel were overwhelmed and could barely say Thank You.

Ten days later, the stamping mill was finished, and Hollis supervised the opening day. Fortunately, all ten employees were put thru a training session ahead of time, which allowed for a smooth opening day. The first day lasted 9 hours but still managed to process a full 75-ton boxcar. After a week of operation, Palmer got a visit from a team of Easterners who came to see him in his office at the pit mine.

The team's leader said, "Mister Bodine, there is no reason for us to compete against each other. So, we wish to buy your plant and will offer you twice what you paid to build it. In addition, we'll sign a three-year contract that freezes your processing fees per 75-ton boxcar."

"Well, let's clear the air. I am not competing against you; I am processing only my own ore. I decided to do this because you were shafting me with your fees and surcharges. Now, as long as you are fair with your customers, things will stay the same and I will not try to move your customers to my plant. However, if the other miners start complaining how you're price gouging them, then I will immediately add a second shift, and start offering specials that will put you out of business. The day that Boston moguls think they can bleed us is gone. Now get the hell out of here before I load you up in a steam shovel and dump you in my ore boxcar."

*

Over the next weeks and months, things were rolling along. Mia had her first bona fide permanent disability—which was in a worker with one year short of being vested but plague with crippling arthritis. It was a crucial time, as all her employees were wondering what Mia would do—stand by her employee or the rules regarding long-term disability which required 5 years of employment to be vested. Mia stood by her employee and placed her on life-long full salary with permanent medical insurance.

With fall arriving, Josie had designed some striking fall jackets that extended to the belt line but above the pistol. Waldo would let the retailers push the jackets, while Wards added a flyer advertising the new jackets, and placed a copy inside the box of products returning to customers. By the time winter came, Josie had insulated winter jackets ready for production. Three types were available—a boot length long duster type insulated coat with a slit in the back for horse riding, an insulated town coat that extended below the holster, and one that fit just above the pistol.

Finally, the Duo had their second "where do we go from here meeting." Mia pushed Palmer to go first. "As far as the gold mine, nothing will change as long as the gold vein holds out, but what I hear is that these underground gold veins are beginning to play out as the population drops in town with many mine closings. As far as the pit mine goes, well Henry will retire soon, and he's interested in selling the steam shovel. We'll do that and I can see the day when we'll have a second shovel in operation. The deeper we go, the higher the copper yield, and now with the copper price up to $4, we stand to increase our profits."

"So you think the future is with copper mining?" "Without a doubt, pipes and electrical wires will drive up the value and demand for copper. The 1900's are just around the corner and we'll be operational till our son takes over the next generation."

"What about this bodyguard outfit?" "I'm certain that it will be a success by the current use. There is a demand for them while this town stays bustling. Today, it has twice the population of Deming, but the future will bring businesses to Deming on the main railway route as Silver City starts to decline with the times. For our generation, I believe our businesses will survive the expected evolution of communities."

Mia added, "with what you are saying, if people start moving out of town for work, it seems wise that we hire as many pit mine workers and bodyguards that are our stitchers' husbands, heh?" "Yes, that is an excellent idea."

"Now, what is in the future for your factory?" "I am not certain if we are on a plateau, awaiting the next plateau, or whether we are at an apogee and the next move is downhill. For now we are keeping the status quo. I may soon have to take some extended time off, but I assure you that my

A-Team can run that place. I will however have a weekly meeting with my A-Team to stay current and make crucial decisions."

"What's going on, are we going on an extended vacation?" "No, just raising our family, for you see, I am pregnant. With a toddler and a newborn baby, it will not be easy to try to work at the shop. I guess I need an artistic and business-wise daughter to follow my footsteps, heh?" "For sure! Thanks, Mia, a baby girl would be nice, but we'll take any healthy one anytime."

"Well dear, you said something some time ago that finally registered in my head. You said, 'WE ARE SO BLESSED.' I would like to add, 'TO HAVE A LOVING AND HEALTHY FAMILY, AND BE ABLE TO LIVE THE AMERICAN DREAM.'"

The End

***

Printed in the United States
By Bookmasters